I0588194

KEEPER

FIRST ORDINANCE, BOOK TWO

CONNIE SUTTLE

Copyright © 2014, 2018, by Connie Suttle
All Rights Reserved

Print Second Edition (2018)
Print ISBN: 1-63478-072-8
Print ISBN-13: 978-1-63478-072-8
eBook ISBN: 1-93975-932-3
eBook ISBN-13: 978-1-93975-932-0

This book is a work of fiction. Names, characters and incidents portrayed within its pages are purely fictitious and a product of the author's imagination. Any resemblance to actual persons, living or dead, is purely coincidental.

This book, whole or in part, MAY NOT be copied or reproduced by electronic or mechanical means (including photocopying or the implementation of any type of storage or retrieval system) without the express written permission of the author, except where permitted by law.

Published by:
SubtleDemon Publishing, LLC
PO Box 95696
Oklahoma City, OK 73143

Cover art by Renee Barratt @ The Cover Counts

To Walter, Joe, Larry, Lee, Dianne, Sarah and Mark.
Thank you.

ACKNOWLEDGMENTS

As always, this book is the result of collaboration. If it weren't for the support of my editor, my cover artist and my beta readers, it would be less than it is. All mistakes, as usual, are mine and no other's.

About the Author:
Connie Suttle lives in Oklahoma with her husband and a conglomerate of cats. They have finally banded together to make their demands, which has proven disconcerting to all humans involved.

You may find Connie in the following ways:
Facebook: Connie Suttle Author
Twitter: @subtledemon
Website and Blog: subtledemon.com

ALSO BY CONNIE SUTTLE

Blood Destiny Series:

Blood Wager

Blood Passage

Blood Sense

Blood Domination

Blood Royal

Blood Queen

Blood Rebellion

Blood War

Blood Redemption

Blood Reunion

Blood Destiny Series Boxed Set (Books 1-10)

Blood Recall

Blood Alliance*

Legend of the Ir'Indicti Series:

Bumble

Shadowed

Target

Vendetta

Destroyer

Legend of the Ir'Inditi Boxed Set

High Demon Series:

Demon Lost

Demon Revealed

Demon's King

Demon's Quest

Demon's Revenge

Demon's Dream

God Wars Series:

Blood Double

Blood Trouble

Blood Revolution

Blood Love

Blood Finale

Saa Thalarr Series:

Hope and Vengeance

Wyvern and Company

Observe and Protect*

First Ordinance Series:

Finder

Keeper

BlackWing

SpellBreaker

WhiteWing

~

R-D Series:

Cloud Dust

Cloud Invasion

Cloud Rebel

~

Latter Day Demons Series:

Hot Demon in the City

A Demon's Work is Never Done

A Demon's Due

~

Seattle Elementals Series:

Your Money's Worth

Worth Your While*

~

BlackWing Pirates Series

MindSighted

MindMage

MindRogue

MindMaster*

~

Black Rose Sorceress Series

The Rose Mark

Rose and Thorn

Black Rose Queen

Queen of Thorns and Roses

Future Wars Series

Buffer Zone

Black Zone*

Other Titles from SubtleDemon Publishing:

Malefactor

Transgressor

Underhanded*

by Joe Scholes

*Forthcoming

CHAPTER 1

Avii Castle
Quin

Jurris was pale, weak and alive.

The Kondari had abandoned their attempt to destroy Avii Castle.

For now.

I knew High President Charkisul, his son, Berel, and Hadris Jem were prisoners of a new Kondari regime, but there wasn't anything I could do about it.

Master Cook Nina placed a cup of hot tea in my hands as I sat on the floor away from Jurris' bed, shivering from shock.

Justis sat at his brother's bedside, talking quietly with the King. Ordin and Gurnil hovered nearby, as did two of the King's personal guards.

"Can you stand?" Nina asked softly. "Dena is waiting outside the King's chambers, hoping you will join her."

"I'll come," I said, embarrassed that my voice quavered when I spoke. I was grateful that Dena waited for me; I needed her support to get back to the Library.

Amlis, Omina and the others waited there; Omina and Fen needed healing. I worried that my strength would not be enough to save either.

~

Amlis studied his surroundings—row upon row, shelf upon shelf, of books stood about him. Two yellow-winged servants had brought blankets, hot drinks and food, but his mother refused anything except the blanket.

She'd lost so much blood already; her body trembled with shock and he worried that she'd die before any healing was offered by their winged hosts. Sofi tended the Queen as well as she could while Yissy, standing close by, looked on in silent curiosity.

Fen accepted a cup of hot tea, working around the wound in his left shoulder. "I never thought to be here and still living," Rodrik muttered as he sipped the tea he'd been given. Beatris, who'd hidden in the belly of the ship during the trip, shivered beside him before wrapping the blanket tighter about her body.

Amlis snorted a reply. His mind still played about Finder's image—she had wings and helped rescue him and the others from the sea. It puzzled him, too, as to who'd attacked their vessel, with devastating weapons he had difficulty comprehending.

"It was the Kondari," Finder walked in with assistance from another—a yellow-winged woman who cast worried looks at Amlis and his companions. "Normally they wouldn't have done that, but there was a coup."

"Finder, will you heal the Queen?" Yissy's voice was high and innocent.

"If I don't faint, first," she replied.

~

Quin

Omina's wound was the worst and if she weren't tended soon, it would be too late. Already, she'd lost much blood.

"I will assist," Daragar appeared, causing Sofi to utter a half-shriek of terror. Yissy hid behind Sofi's skirts at the sight of the tall, blue-skinned Larentii; Rodrik's hand went immediately to where his sword would be, had he been wearing it.

"You should never offer violence or offense to a Larentii," I held up a hand to stop Rodrik from stepping forward. "You have no idea what you see before you."

"I have never seen such," Amlis gripped Rodrik's arm to pull him back.

"You have seen such now, young Prince," Daragar said. "Allow me to help Quin, if you wish your mother to live."

"Quin?"

"A better name than Finder," Dena huffed, offended on my behalf.

"Please, no bickering, save it for later," I said and walked unsteadily toward Omina. That's when I discovered how Daragar intended to help. He didn't plan to do any healing; he only intended to give me strength.

I imagine it was a highly unusual sight that met Ordin and Gurnil as they walked into the Library. I healed Omina's wound—a Larentii holding onto me as I held my hands on Omina's side, all of us bathed in golden light as the wound sealed and infection disappeared.

Fen's wounds were nothing compared to hers.

"Thank you." I wrapped my arms around Daragar's neck before he left me that night. He smiled at me, his bright-blue eyes shining brighter before he nodded and disappeared.

"You're confined to the Library for the moment, but you may wander the terrace outside," Gurnil informed our guests the following morning. He was right—Justis had posted two guards outside the Library doors, changing them every four hours or so.

Breakfast had been brought and Dena, thinking to provide support for me, stayed and ate with us.

Justis had also confiscated any weapons left with Rodrik, Amlis and the others, including small eating knives—they had nothing left except hands or fists with which to harm anyone. Amlis didn't like it, I could tell, but this wasn't his castle or his kingdom.

I wanted to ask Justis whether any communication had come from Kondar, but held back—I was afraid to know how things stood there.

High spots of color appeared in Omina's cheeks whenever she met my gaze, as brief as those moments were. Rodrik, too, failed to look at me for any length of time. After all, Justis, Commander of the King's guards and brother to the King, had touched my shoulder moments earlier and nodded to me before leaving the Library.

They thought me more important than I actually was. Justis was merely conveying his thanks to me for saving his brother's life; I would hold no sway over the King when Jurris demanded to see our guests.

I hoped he wouldn't command their deaths—these had no connection to Camryn's and Elabeth's assassinations, after all.

Wolter, though, gazed at me in wonder while he ate what yellow-winged servants placed in front of him. Deeds, sitting beside Wolter, did the same.

"I wasn't aware that there were White Wings," Omina said finally, her eyes remaining on her plate.

"There aren't," Gurnil said. "We have no idea where these white feathers originated, unless it is from the cutting away of Quin's nubs whenever they formed." His words were curt and accusing as he flung them across the table at Omina.

I recalled that Ordin had assisted in Amlis' birth—had Gurnil known Omina as well? My gift told me they'd met before, and that Gurnil found Omina somewhat high-handed. I didn't disagree with his opinion.

"The court physician demanded it," Wolter admitted, lowering his head. "The only recourse I had was going to the King, and I had no desire to place Finder's life in jeopardy by doing such a foolish thing. Tamblin would have killed her outright."

"He is no king. I ask that you remember that within these walls," Gurnil snapped.

"I agree," Amlis nodded. "He is no king."

"You are the youngest Prince?" Gurnil turned toward Amlis.

"Yes. I ask that you treat my mother with kindness—she is still recovering," he said.

"I will do so, if you will call Quin by her proper name," Gurnil responded.

"I wasn't aware that she had another name," Amlis said. "I will address her as Quin, as she has saved my mother's life, as well as the others, here."

"Does that include yours?" Gurnil asked.

"Yes. Several times. She was beaten for dumping a plate of poisoned food before I could eat it," he shrugged. "I owe her for that—and many other things."

"I am sorry," Orik began. "Very sorry." His apology was aimed at me.

"That is in the past," I shook my head at him, letting him know that he needn't tell of his part in my delivery to the Avii. "I mourn for Master Farin," I said. "We will all miss him, I think." He'd advised Omina for years uncounted, and acted on her behalf many times. He was more than a court physician and everyone at the table knew it.

"Finder—Quin—when did you find your voice?" Sofi asked.

"I have had it many years," I said with a sigh. "When it came, I was too afraid to speak."

"You knew too much," Wolter nodded.

"Too much," I agreed.

"I find this difficult to understand," Amlis rose from the library table that served as our temporary breakfast table. Gurnil and I watched as the Prince strode toward the doors leading to the terrace outside.

"Master Gurnil, there are many things to consider," I turned to him. "The coup in Kondar being chief among them, along with Tamblin's desire to sail away from Fyris and attack it."

"Will he carry the ring with him?" Gurnil rose swiftly and blinked at me in confusion.

"He never takes it off," Omina answered for me. "Why is that important?"

"Because the ring keeps Fyris hidden from Kondar and any other country," Gurnil snapped. "Quin, who has taken over Kondar? Where is the High President? We must think on this and quickly."

"We need Justis, and a willing ear from his brother," I sighed, knowing neither would be easy.

~

Kondar

Dorthil Crasz had ordered the commander of the botched attack on Avii Castle killed. When his fellow officers refused to deliver the death, Dorthil ordered all imprisoned. He had no interest in excuses and lies—when they claimed the glass castle took no harm from their best weapons, Dorthil knew they were lying.

The voice the pilot claimed to hear, telling him not to fire?

That had to be an outright lie or a hallucination. Dorthil snorted at the thought of it. Word was spreading throughout Kondar that the High President had deserted his office, leaving Dorthil in charge. News agencies were couching the reports in disbelief.

Some were calling for direct word from the High President. Dorthil dispatched troops to shut down news agencies.

They'd learn soon enough who was in charge.

~

Le-Ath Veronis

Kooper Griff, Director of the ASD, dropped a file on Renée Coffin's desk. She'd only worked for Queen Lissa as an assistant for a few months, but filled a much-needed gap in the growing necessity for technical assistance and public relations. She worked well with Lissa's other assistants, Grant and Heathe, which was also a plus in the Queen's eyes.

"What is this?" Renée tapped the file while studying Kooper. She could scent the shapeshifter in him and knew, through Lissa, that he was a deadly lion snake when he turned. Ildevar Wyyld, Founder of the Reth Alliance, couldn't have picked a better ASD Director, in Renée's opinion.

"Information for the Queen when she gets back. I don't feel comfortable putting this on a comp-vid. That's why it's on paper," Kooper sighed.

"That's not good," Renée shook her head. "I'll put this in her file—the one she looks at first."

"Good. Where is she, by the way? I wasn't informed that she'd left."

"Ildevar Wyyld asked for a meeting. She went to Wyyld II last night," Renée said. "An emergency of some sort."

"I wonder if the two events are connected," Kooper muttered before turning to leave.

"I'll make sure she reads this right away," Renée called after Kooper. He raised a hand, letting her know he'd heard.

"Rainy, your sire is here," Heathe's voice sounded on Renée's comp-vid. Heathe used the nickname he and Grant had given her. Renée was four-and-a-half years a vampire and Montrose, her sire, had come to check on her. He did so twice a week, although Lissa informed him four months earlier that Renée was capable of working on her own.

Renée didn't mind; a few vampire lessons notwithstanding, she liked her vampire sire.

Very much.

~

Kondar

"Dorthil should have thought twice before tossing me in here with you," Firth Quel murmured as he worked on the locking device holding them inside the abandoned underground bunker. "I designed these locks myself."

"Dorthil has never bothered with research, you know that," Edden Charkisul agreed. "At least he failed to install vid-cams here. That

7

proves he moved hastily. He doesn't have enough of the troops to back him. He may have a riot on his hands already."

"The populace is unarmed," Melis Norwal, Edden's Chief of Security, pointed out. "What will they do when Dorthil attempts to shut down the news agencies with armed troops?"

"I'm hoping that the troops will side with their friends and family, some of whom may work for those news agencies," Edden huffed. "We have to get out of here, and we have to stay alive. Dorthil may find at least three of the five Presidents standing against him. Especially when he starts shutting down their sources of information."

"Where do you wish to go? We must stay hidden until it is safe," Melis reminded the High President.

"I wish we could fly to the Avii. It is my hope they'd take us in. I can call troops from there—we still have a fleet between there and Yokaru."

"Then we need an airchopper or a ship," Melis nodded agreement.

"Or allies with those things," Hadris Jem observed.

"Hush, I hear something," Firth whispered.

"May the gods be merciful," Edden breathed and pulled Berel behind his back to protect the boy.

Wyyld II

"They died of radiation poisoning?" Queen Lissa examined the images Ildevar provided.

"When there was no source of such on their planet to begin with. I've had forensic specialists working on these bodies the moment radiation poisoning was verified in the autopsies."

"Did they find anything?" Lissa, Vampire Queen of Le-Ath Veronis, asked.

"Something frightening," Ildevar sighed. "I believe it may have been left behind by one of the Hidden."

"They're all dead," Lissa began.

8

"Their works may not be dead," Ildevar responded. "This, if my fears are correct, could destroy everything."

"I need to speak with my sister," Lissa muttered angrily.

"I wouldn't mind being included in that conversation. Kaldill, too, has expressed interest." Ildevar named the King of the Elves, who resided in a hidden section of Wyyld II.

"Fine. If I can find her, I'll let you know."

"Finding the Mighty can be difficult, even in the best of times," Ildevar agreed. "If I find her first, I will send a message."

Kondar

"Stay calm," Edden breathed as the door swung inward. Jhak stepped inside the bunker, a weapon slung over his shoulder. Three others with weapons walked in behind him.

Berel gripped his father's arm. *Would they perish at the hands of a trusted guard?*

"We've come to get you out of here," Jhak said softly. "You have to come now—there is rioting in the streets. The people now believe you dead and Dorthil has commanded the troops following him to fire on anyone who attempts to oppose his takeover."

"But you," Edden hissed accusingly.

"I know. They threatened my family. They're outside—in the airchopper. We can make it to Aviaa if we leave now."

"If Dorthil's troops don't shoot us from the sky, first," Melis muttered and held out his hand to take Jhak's weapon. "Follow me, High President. We'll get you safely away."

Fyris

Vhrist

"I hear my wife sailed away last night. Tell me she sailed for Lironis," Tamblin demanded.

Rath refused to cower before the King. "That was her plan, my King," Rath lied. "If she does not arrive in Lironis in three days, I suspect treason."

"I suspect treason already," Tamblin snapped. "My son went with her, did he not?"

"She did not wish to travel without him. She trusts none of the guards—not after that filth," Rath jerked his head toward Yevil, "attempted to murder her." Yevil, released from prison, stood at the King's right hand. Tamblin held up a hand to keep Yevil from speaking.

"Remember you are in the presence of the King," Tamblin thundered. "Yevil is my trusted advisor."

"And the one who arranged to kill your firstborn," Rath hissed. "Everyone knows it—except you. Timblor died for nothing, because Yevil wanted it thus. He desires all our deaths—do you not realize that?"

"What could he gain from such a desire?" Tamblin's voice became cold. "He is a citizen of Fyris, just as you are."

"Yet murders happen in Fyris every day—for no good reason," Rath replied.

"I weary of this conversation," Tamblin waved a hand. "I will imprison you for a moon-turn—long enough for Omina to reach Lironis and send word of her arrival back to me. If Amlis does not return with that message, I will declare him an enemy to the crown. If my son fails to return, I will see you die and launch my ships on the same day."

"As you will it, my King," Rath offered an insincere bow. Two guards came forward and escorted him from the King's presence.

～

Avii Castle
Quin

"At least you're looking me in the eye, now," Amlis said as I approached him.

"You have no standing, here," I said evenly. "Neither do I, as far as the King is concerned. If you harm me, however, you will be most sorry, I assure you."

The Orb floated behind me, which troubled Amlis, I could tell. Rodrik stood not far away, wishing for the sword he always carried. Justis had it, now.

Both men stood on the terrace outside the Library—the others were bathing or sleeping in the rooms they'd been assigned. "What is that thing?" Rodrik whispered. He'd never seen such—the Orb floated on its own—with a will of its own.

"They call it the Orb, but it lives in some way, I think," I shrugged. "It is the reason I survived my first few moments here."

"They wanted to kill you, didn't they?" Amlis asked.

"They tried twice. The Orb threw them back both times. In the past, it gave counsel to their King and Queen—the ones your father murdered—with Yevil's help and the weapon he carried."

"Why do we have no writings on it?" Amlis went on, watching the Orb closely.

"Would you believe such?" I shrugged.

"Unlikely—without seeing the truth of it. Just as seeing the blue giant last night convinced me."

"He doesn't live on Siriaa," I said. "I do not know where his home is —we've never discussed it."

"What do you mean?" Rodrik exploded. "Siriaa is all there is."

"I've heard tales of many worlds outside our own," Gurnil responded as he walked up beside me. "I have no proof—except the Larentii, of course. Daragar is not the first of that race to visit us. They only come to Aviaa, too, which I find puzzling. Quin, the King wishes to see you this morning. These others he will deal with later."

"I should change," I sighed, brushing a hand over the yellow top and trousers I wore.

"Wear green," Gurnil urged. "Justis will arrive shortly to escort you."

I knew Gurnil—and Ordin—had the idea that dressing me in green might convince the King to place me in the Healer's Guild. It was a good plan, except I had no green wings. Jurris was consistent in his prejudices—I understood that easily enough.

I had no idea why Jurris wanted to see me, except to absently pat my head and send me back to cleaning Justis' quarters. Surprisingly enough, the Orb followed as I dressed and waited for Justis to collect me.

$\sim$

"What will they do with us?" Rodrik whispered after Gurnil and Quin disappeared inside the Library.

"I doubt they'll kill us," Amlis snorted. "They could have done that before—when Camryn and Elabeth died."

"That doesn't keep them from tossing us into an airless dungeon," Rodrik pointed out. "Or from keeping us there until we die."

"How is Beatris taking this?" Amlis asked.

"She's sleeping," Rodrik mumbled. "I won't disturb her with this worry, yet."

"Mother, too," Amlis agreed. "Although I can barely see the faintest of scars after Quin healed her, she is tired—likely from blood loss."

"Fen, too. I wish we'd known these things while Finder—Quin— was still in Lironis."

"Would we have been any better than we were?" Amlis asked.

"I know not," Rodrik shook his head. "We'd be dead without her intervention—several times over. You heard her—she said she has no standing here; we share the same circumstances."

"We are exiles, Rod. My father will make sure of that," Amlis replied.

"We are homeless," Wolter nodded as he and Deeds approached. "That makes you no less a Prince," he lowered his head briefly to Amlis. "I worry greatly for those we left behind."

$\sim$

Quin

"Do you wish to fly to my brother's terrace?" Justis asked. He'd knocked on my door after having a brief conversation with Gurnil in Gurnil's study.

"If that is what you want," I agreed. "I have only flown once—when the Orb instructed me to do so last night."

"The Orb did much instructing last evening," Justis agreed. He wanted to smile; he didn't. I knew then that the Orb had directed him to deliver Halthea's death. He had no idea what his brother might do as a result, which left both of us in confusion.

So many questions bubbled up—questions I refused to ask. Why had the Orb spoken to Justis and not Jurris? It could easily have warned Jurris away from Halthea's attack. Gurnil and Ordin had also received messages.

Perhaps only the Orb had those answers and I dared not ask it. "Come then, we will test your wings a second time," Justis nodded to me. "Gurnil and Ordin will also come."

That's when I knew the King's Council had been summoned. I would have to face all of them.

I think I would have been lost in the pleasure of flight if I hadn't been summoned by the King of the Avii. Instead, the short flight was plagued by my fears as to what the King planned to do with me.

Justis had told him only that morning that Halthea was his half-sister. It was a secret perhaps Jurris shouldn't have heard. Justis had his reasons, but as I knew it, too, that placed me in danger. I wished then that I'd never bothered to speak in the first place. None ever worried that I'd spill secrets, then.

Kondar

"What is this?" Edden stared through the airchopper's window.

"Your escort, High President," Jhak replied.

At least fifty airchoppers surrounded them and now flew in a protective formation. "We need this much of an escort? I believed we'd be escaping in secret. Or at least I hoped as much," Melis grumbled. "What if we're attacked?"

"I'm getting information now," one of the pilots tapped his headset and turned to reassure Edden. "The military is now refusing to obey Dorthil's orders. Two newsvid facilities were destroyed and employees died while transmitting information. The moment the people realized Dorthil intended to kill them, they took to the streets. Word is that Dorthil is now fleeing toward Sector Two, which offered asylum. Welcome back, High President."

"Where are we going, then?" Edden asked.

"To the Council," the pilot replied. "It seems they've already sent for the fleet outside Yokaru; it will arrive in three days."

"Will you relay a message, then?" Edden asked.

"Of course, High President."

"Ask that three ships remain outside Avii Castle. I know ours attacked them last night. I need to repair that damage if I can. Tell them to send messages that the coup is over and there will be no further attacks."

"Yes, High President."

"Father, may I go? I wish to see Quin," Berel asked.

"I believe I can send someone with him," Melis offered. "Jhak, perhaps?"

"Yes," Edden nodded. "Jhak and two others will travel with Berel to Avii Castle, to make amends."

Shaaliveer

"Father," Morid set a comp-vid at Marid's elbow. "There's another communication from Cayetes."

"I have nothing further to discuss. He was told how to handle the containment spheres. He was also warned that what they contained was dangerous. He ignored those instructions and deserves anything he gets." Marid shoved his journal into a drawer at his son's sudden appearance in his study.

"You may be placing yourself in danger from two sources. You run the risk of being crushed between them," Morid pointed out.

"You think those buffoons will be able to reach me? I have a plan. That fool on Siriaa didn't know we'd already collected much of what we needed; I only wanted him as a backup. With a brainless politician in control of the planet, and with me in charge of him, we can effectively shut out any interference by the Alliance. Eventually, even Cayetes may come to us when we offer asylum—for the right price, you understand."

"Father, that's insane. Surely you realize that. These criminals, if you offer them a place, will begin to fight for control. You'll lose, as will the inhabitants of that planet. Look at Vogeffa I. Non-Alliance and ruled by a corrupt government, it did the same thing you propose; offering space to known criminals and crime syndicates, for a fee. Cayetes moved in and took the others out. He has all their holdings, now, and the government is only a puppet covering his hand."

"Their government wasn't run by a talented family of wizards," Marid snapped. "We will hold them in check."

"I have no desire to hold criminals in check with my talents, Father." Morid stalked from his father's study.

"You'll do it if I tell you," Marid huffed.

"Fly faster, you fools," Dorthil snapped. The aircraft he traveled in belonged to the High President. It, and the title, should be his. Who knew that killing a few foolish journalists would arouse such anger in the population? He'd done the people a favor—journalists always spoke ill of everything.

Even his allies on the Council turned quickly against him—

although three of them would no longer have a Sector to call home if he had any say in the matter.

"None have been sent against us as yet," the pilot responded.

"All the better," Dorthil snapped.

~

"Son, tell them they have nothing to fear from us—the coward has run away," Edden dropped a hand on Berel's shoulder before entering the Council chambers. "Never forget that Kondar is still in danger from the poison. Find out anything you can—if you can—while you're there. I've instructed Jhak to bring you back in three days."

"I will, Father," Berel nodded.

~

Avii Castle

Quin

The soft rumble of muted conversation greeted us as we walked into the King's presence; I was surrounded by Justis, Gurnil and Ordin. Ordin had beamed at my appearance moments earlier and nodded his approval at my green clothing.

One cannot expect sudden acceptance, however, from those who'd previously despised you. I knew this was so and had I used my gift, could have seen it in the faces we passed on our way to the King's throne.

Jurris, a cup of juice at his elbow, watched as we approached. The Orb, floating above our heads, silenced more than a few in the crowd. Jurris still wasn't strong—he'd nearly died the night before.

I—and those around me—knew it, but few on the Council did. They only knew that Halthea had attacked the King and died at Justis' hand as a result. None faulted Justis; Halthea wasn't liked by any of them. I wondered whether Jurris realized that.

"I have made a decision," Jurris announced once we'd come to a stop before him. "In three days, those from Fyris must return there—they have no place with us."

Shocked, I could only stare at the King while he held up a hand to quell the immediate murmurs among the Council. "I know what the Ordinance says. That is why I will do now what should have been done eighteen turns past. I will send my brother and some of his troops with the Prince, who will wrest the throne from his murderous father. I have decreed it; thus shall it be."

Jurris' hand dropped, indicating the finality of his words.

CHAPTER 2

*A*vii Castle
    Quin

"You are to go with me," Justis informed me later, as Gurnil, Ordin and I sat inside Justis' quarters, still stunned by Jurris' decisions.

"I wish to go as well, to record the events," Gurnil snapped.

"I doubt Jurris will stop you," Justis ruffled his wings in an agitated fashion. "I have no real desire to stand upon the stones where Elabeth died, but that is greatly outweighed by my intention to avenge her death."

"The poison is seeping into everything there," I said, standing abruptly and voicing my concern. "We may all perish. What does the King hope to accomplish from all this?"

"Quin, perhaps it will keep that filth who wears Tandelis' ring from leaving Fyris and revealing it to all," Gurnil offered quietly.

"Master Gurnil, perhaps that is where we err," I sighed. "Have you ever thought that Kondar or Yokaru might help us with the conundrum of the poison? Perhaps their technology can at least define it before it kills us all."

"The First Ordinance commands that we keep Fyris hidden from all others," Ordin began.

"I believe that became moot the moment Queen Elabeth died," Justis interjected. "Her saving of Fyris is also in the First Ordinance."

At that moment, I had a terrible desire to race into Jurris' quarters and seize what he kept hidden from all. I was desperate to read what was written in that book.

"You think the First Ordinance is no longer a command from Liron himself, then?" Gurnil asked.

"Nobody has seen Liron in a very long time," Justis replied. "Surely he would have come when Elabeth and Camryn fell."

"You're saying he's never coming again, is that it?"

"I am saying that," Justis said, rising from his seat and gazing out the clear glass window of his suite. I realized he gazed toward Fyris. And Liron? A god that never appeared to exact vengeance against those who cursed his name daily?

I doubted very much whether he was likely to appear again, as Justis said.

"Then I shall come. Perhaps physicians from Kondar," Ordin began.

"You forget the coup," Justis pointed out.

"The coup has been overturned."

Berel stood in Justis' doorway, accompanied by three Kondari soldiers and five black-wing guards. As he spoke in Kondari, I relayed Berel's message to the others present while I trembled with relief.

"I am grateful; I worried for your safety," I said as Berel consumed a dessert in Master Nina's kitchen.

"I was terrified," he said, his eyes meeting mine. Justis, Gurnil, Ordin and the guards—Avii and Kondari—sat and listened to Berel's tale of the coup while I translated. "Father is sending three ships from the fleet to guard Avii Castle," he added. "He extends his apologies for the attack."

"It availed him naught," Justis pointed out. "The castle is impervious to attack, although three outside the walls died in the assault."

"I am sorry for that—more than I can say," Berel admitted, his shoulders drooping.

"It was not your fault or your command that resulted in those deaths," Ordin said. "Do not take responsibility for another's crimes."

"I am my father's representative here," Berel said. "He will be saddened by this news, just as I am."

"I will convey your condolences," I offered. "To those closest to the ones lost."

"We must find a ship," Gurnil stood and stretched. "If we are to leave in three days." He turned to walk toward the nearest terrace; he intended to fly to the Library.

"You're leaving?" Berel blinked at me.

Justis opened his mouth to make excuses to the High President's son. I held up a hand. "Commander Justis, I have never read the Ordinance and do not feel bound by it. It is time they knew—they already know of the poison, and unless I miss my guess, they know of the wood ships that come occasionally from Fyris' shores."

If I'd fired Yevil's ancient weapon inside Nina's kitchen, it might have caused less of a stir. Regardless, I found myself sitting in the Library minutes later, Berel listening raptly as I told him what I knew of Fyris and why it was hidden.

"Father, they don't know the origin of the poison any better than we do," Berel explained. He sat on the Library terrace, his tab-vid in his hand while he spoke with the High President.

"The King says the people who came last night from that hidden land have to leave in three days. Quin, Commander Justis and several others are going with them, but first they need a ship. None of the fishing vessels the Avii have are large enough to carry that many people. The Chief Librarian thinks they should take several small boats, instead. I find that dangerous—those boats are too small to make a long journey."

"You think to find the source of this poison, don't you?" Edden said.

"Yes. This may be our chance. I heard, too, that the Avii think a magic spell hides this country from the rest of us. I can't believe that is true. It has to be some sort of shield we haven't dreamed of yet."

"That would be my thought as well," Edden agreed. "Offer them the three ships I'm sending. I'll make sure our best science teams are on board. I hope we can unravel this mystery before it kills us."

"Commander Justis says that one of the residents or one of the Avii must be aboard the ships to get through what he referred to as the straits. I don't know what that means, but we'll have to carry some on each ship to pacify their beliefs."

"Make sure Quin is with you on the flagship, then," Edden said. "Stay close to her. She will ensure that you do not fall ill again."

"I intend to do so, Father," Berel said. "I believe Commander Justis is thinking the same thing."

"What happened to their Princess?" Edden thought to ask.

"More of their magical thinking," Berel explained. "There is this thing—they call it the Orb, I think, and they attribute magical properties to it. It is reported to have changed Princess Halthea's wing colors to a servant's yellow, and when she attacked the King because of that, she was killed for making an attempt on his life."

"This is almost too much to think about," Edden breathed. "Son, I must go—Dorthil is stirring up trouble in Sector Two. We must see to this new threat. Keep me advised whenever possible."

"I will."

"The High President is offering three ships?" Jurris studied Justis curiously. "I care not that he knows about Fyris," the King waved a hand in dismissal. "Perhaps the burden of the Ordinance can be lifted from Avii shoulders and placed upon the Kondari, instead."

"You know that is not what the commands are," Justis said.

"Whose fault is it that the poison spreads?" Jurris snapped.

"Tamblin's, and if Quin is correct, his right hand, Yevil Orklis."

"Yevil? I have not heard of him before. I care not. Let them send ships if they want. It matters not to me."

"You are tired, my King. Shall I send for your dinner so you might sleep after?"

"Yes."

⁓

Quin

"I want to come with you." Dena's arms were crossed stubbornly over her chest.

"I would say yes, but Master Gurnil must approve," I pointed out. "If you want to walk into that quagmire of intrigue, mistreatment and poison, you're more than welcome to it."

"I'll go ask him now," she declared and almost ran from my bedroom.

Squaring my shoulders, I surveyed the piles of clothing on my bed. Gurnil said to pack as much as possible, as he had no idea how long we might stay in Fyris.

The plan, of course, was to travel to Lironis. Omina hoped to rally the people behind Amlis and herself, forcing Tamblin to come running back in an effort to reclaim his throne.

Any way you looked upon this ill-conceived plan, it involved death and civil war. To me, that could not be a good thing, as the poison would only spread farther while people fought and died for a land already in its death throes.

"He asked me to come." Dena was back, clapping her hands in excitement. I wanted to tell her what she would find upon the shores of Fyris. I couldn't—this could be the last happiness she experienced for a very long time.

⁓

"Ardis?" Justis called.

Ardis, formerly a captain under Justis' command, woke from a light sleep. That's all he could do, now—eat the meals brought to him and sleep in between. His days were winding down, too; he no longer counted them. He'd be shoved through the gate for listening to a vindictive, Red-Wing Princess.

"I'm sure you know Halthea is dead," Justis began as he unlocked the door to Ardis' cell. "My brother, who was saved from death after Halthea tried to kill him, has granted the request of the one who healed him of what should have been fatal injuries."

"What?" Ardis stood, confusion crossing his features. "Then tell Master Ordin I will be forever grateful," he added after a moment.

"You do not owe Ordin thanks. You owe Quin," Justis snapped. "I wouldn't have carried this request to the King had it come from Ordin, because he would not have made it. You nearly killed Gurnil, you thoughtless oaf."

"I did not intend to hit him so hard. He rushed toward me, intending harm."

"What were you intending toward Quin?" Justis hissed. "I fail to find reason in her request to spare your life. Nevertheless, the King has seen fit to let you go, if you agree to stand beside me when I travel to Fyris in three days. We may be fighting Tamblin before this is over, and you may as well pay Quin back by acting as a proper guard."

"Fyris?" Hope lit Ardis' eyes for the first time in years. "I would be grateful for the chance to kill that bastard."

"I am ahead in that line," Justis said. "You will be without rank—you lost your captain's privileges when you followed Halthea to the Library instead of coming to me, first."

"It will not happen again, I swear it," Ardis slapped a fist on his chest.

"Not for Halthea, anyway," Justis huffed. "Come. There is much to do."

Shaaliveer

"How much do we have left?" Marid asked.

"Father, we have hundreds of spelled spheres filled with it," Morid replied. "More than enough to destroy millions." Morid was glad that Marid had temporarily backed away from his scheme of ruling Siriaa. The fact that Cayetes stopped sending threatening communications helped a great deal.

"Millions is exactly what I intend to make off it, too," Marid smiled. "Our first endeavors have gone well, don't you think?"

"People are dead because of it," Morid pointed out. "I never thought you to involve yourself so readily in murder. Cayetes is sick from it, too. I'm just glad he isn't still trying to get back at us for mishandling the poison."

"Cayetes knows better than to come against an entire family of powerful wizards. Besides, do you think your protection spells do not cause deaths?" Marid snapped. "Think again."

"If someone attacks one equipped with protection spells, then they get what they deserve. These were unsuspecting and potentially innocent."

"Faugh. You think too much," Marid waved a hand. "Get your equipment packed. We leave Shaaliveer in three days."

~

Grey House

"Grandfather, I have news," Nissa said as she slid onto the chair before Glendes Grey's desk. All her life, her grandfather had never changed his private study. The spelled desk with clawed feet stood upon a priceless Serendaan carpet, also spelled against signs of wear.

Glendes, too, looked no different than he ever had. The Greys were nearly immortal, after all.

"What news?" Glendes looked up from his comp-vid—Grey House had just reported a profitable year and paid taxes to the Reth Alliance.

"I heard the Belancours are moving away from Shaaliveer."

"Marid, that old dinosaur, is finally leaving? The local government is likely cheering him on."

"I heard it from Mom," Nissa reported. "She says there are other things going on, too. She wants all of us to be wary."

"Queen Lissa said that?" Glendes' interest increased immediately. "Did she tell your father as well?"

"Daddy knows," Nissa nodded. "We had lunch with her yesterday."

"Why should we be wary?" Glendes asked.

"She says there's a poison out there that appears to be radiation poisoning connected to nuclear waste, only she says she's never seen anything like it before," Nissa said. "It's showing up in dead bodies, on planets that have nothing nuclear about them. There's a rumor, too, that the Hidden may have been involved in this before they died."

"So there's an unknown poison and the Belancours are moving. Anything else?"

"No, only that the Belancours suddenly seem to have plenty of money, and six months ago, I'd have said they were nearly bankrupt."

"I'll have someone investigate that. I don't know what to do about the poison, except limit visitors to Grey Planet."

"That's what I was going to suggest, Grampa," Nissa sighed.

~

Avii Castle

Quin

Dena and Berel had become friends quickly, and both were overjoyed to be going to Fyris. Amlis was happy enough to be returning, although Rodrik looked grim and Beatris unhappy.

Omina was determined, however, once she learned that three huge ships the size of small cities would be carrying her back to Fyris. I went in search of Wolter. I could find him and any other, after all.

Wolter, Sofi, Deeds, Orik, Yissy and Fen stood against the balustrade of the Library terrace, watching the sea. There, the water was clean and blue—no litter or slop from fishing boats had been callously dropped into it. It smelled of sunlight and salt instead of fish guts and garbage, as the harbor in Vhrist did.

"Which way will the boats come?" Yissy turned to me, her voice high-pitched and happy.

"From that way, where Yokaru lies," I answered, pointing westward. "They should be here before the morning sun."

"Do they travel fast?" Orik asked.

"I assume they do. The airchoppers the Kondari build are quite fast indeed. I can only imagine that their ships are also fast."

"They travel by air?" Deeds asked.

"They do, only machines must serve as their wings."

"Have you flown in one of those machines?" Wolter asked.

"Yes. I have been to Kondar," I nodded. "Twice."

"What about the other—what did you call it?" Wolter asked.

"No. I have only read about Yokaru."

"So those notes were indeed yours," Wolter shook his head.

"They are," I agreed. He'd found my old hiding place, beneath my bed. I no longer feared for my life if those were discovered, however. I feared for my life for other reasons instead.

"Marisa is dead," Deeds informed me.

"I know." I came to stand next to Wolter at the balustrade. "I do not mourn her."

"Neither does anyone else," Orik cackled.

"Who is running the castle in Tamblin's absence?" I asked.

"Old Varnell," Wolter replied. "Too old to take to the road. Too old to put up much of a fight, either, once we get back."

He'd named the eldest of Tamblin's inner circle. I'd seldom seen him, actually, and had no idea what he might do when Omina and Amlis appeared to claim the throne and dispense with his authority.

"How many guards?" Orik asked.

"Probably two dozen at most. Tamblin thinks the people are meeker than sheep. While most of the nobles and their sons have gone to Vhrist with the King, there are enough left to create difficulties for Varnell."

"Or to stand with him," Deeds muttered. "Those who think to gain Tamblin's favor by siding with Varnell."

"It will be our job to convince them otherwise," Rodrik joined us, with Amlis and Omina not far behind.

"Prince Amlis, the ships will come from there," Yissy piped while pointing to the west.

"Will they, now?" Amlis smiled at her.

"Finder said so."

"Yissy, her name is Quin," Sofi corrected.

"She may call me Finder if she wants," I shrugged. "Yissy and I know one another, after all." I smiled at the small girl.

"I have never been here. It really is glass, as Tandelis always said," Omina observed while gripping the smooth edges of the protective railing. Three Avii flew swiftly past, causing Yissy to squeal in delight. These were Brown Wings, likely curious about the ones from Fyris. I imagined that word had spread quickly of their presence.

I hoped they weren't in danger as a result. I shouldn't have worried; Justis and three Black Wings arrived in moments. I recognized one of them easily enough—he'd tried to kill me twice and then plucked at least one primary feather from my wings.

"Jurris granted you this," Justis nodded toward Ardis, a former captain in his guard.

"Then I thank the King," I said, nodding respectfully to Justis.

"Ardis will travel with us as an extra guard with no rank. He will have to earn his way back to my trust," Justis informed me.

"I hope that happens," I said, nodding to him and to Ardis beyond. What occurred next surprised me greatly.

Ardis dropped to his knees. "Thank you, Lady," he breathed, his head bowed.

～

Wyyld II

"It took many centuries to make Gaelar N'Seith as we knew it," Kaldill

Schaff, King of the Elves, said as he touched the leaves of the gishi tree growing outside his window. "We were never successful in our attempts to grow gishi fruit before. This soil seems suitable, don't you think?"

"I'll wait to taste the fruit," Lendill Schaff, Prince-Heir and Kaldill's only remaining son, replied.

"Cynic," Kaldill laughed.

"I miss the old place," Lendill sighed.

"As do I. One cannot be choosy when one's planet is reduced to rubble by rogue gods and a ranos cannon," Kaldill responded philosophically.

"They were aiming for Ildevar. They had no idea that the elves and Gaelar N'Seith would fall as well. You hid us from everyone too successfully." Lendill's voice held regret.

"We would have been overrun long ago, had that information been available to many."

"My King, someone is here to see you," a servant arrived and bowed to Kaldill.

"I had no idea I should expect guests," Kaldill replied.

"I'm glad you're not cursing," Lendill smiled.

"I can, if you wish to hear it."

"No, thank you. Who is it, Hillen?"

"A Larentii, my Prince. He says he has questions for the King."

"Why did you keep a Larentii waiting?" Kaldill lifted an eyebrow.

"I did not wish to interrupt your time with the Prince."

"I see the Prince every day. I only see the Larentii once in a while," Kaldill waved an arm. "Send him in. Immediately."

"Daragar," Kaldill crowed as the Larentii appeared before him. "I haven't seen you in years."

"I have questions and important information," Daragar replied. "Shall we find a private place to converse?"

～

Avii Castle
Quin

The ships arrived before sunrise, their gray hulls blending with the water so early in the morning. Berel and I watched them approach, thankful the air was warm enough as we stood on the terrace outside the Library.

The others—all of them—were still sleeping. Jurris informed them of what they'd already guessed the day before; they'd return to Fyris with three Kondari ships, their crew and a few Avii.

It was my hope that Omina wouldn't become an insufferable monarch—I'd not appreciated her haughty attitude in Vhrist. I also hoped she'd realize that the crew on the ships would answer ultimately to Berel, who would represent the High President while in Fyris.

"Will you have your guards about you in Fyris?" I turned to Berel.

"I hadn't thought about that yet. Do you think I need them?"

"Yes," I nodded. "No life will be safe in Fyris when Tamblin learns of your arrival."

"Then I will arrange for Jhak and the others to be with me," Berel shrugged. "Do you believe the communication devices will work from there? I wish to remain in contact with my father and Melis, his Chief of Security."

"I don't know—they have nothing of the sort there," I shook my head. "They are backward in comparison to Kondari standards. They ride horses and drive wagons made of wood. They have no refrigeration. When the day is hot, their only option is to open a window."

"You think they failed to evolve—to make the steps toward technology?"

"They have little there. Fyris doesn't have deep mines of copper, iron or other metals. What little they find is either made into pots, handmade tools or weapons. Before I became aware, they traded with the Avii; they make no glass in Fyris, either."

"What can you tell me about Tandelis?"

"Nothing. He was dead before I can remember. All records of his rule in Fyris were systematically removed from books, carvings and any other archive. Gurnil will have to supply information—he is the Chief Librarian, after all."

"We have little time," Berel sighed. "Tomorrow we leave and I have preparations to make, as well as vid-meetings with Melis and Father."

"Ask for books, then. I can read them to you if you wish."

"That would be wonderful," he nodded his acceptance.

Le-Ath Veronis

"A message from Kaldill Schaff," Renée handed the envelope to Queen Lissa.

"Why didn't he send mindspeech?" Lissa asked, examining the envelope before extending a vampiric claw and slitting it open.

"I don't know," Renée shrugged.

Lissa pulled the single note card from the envelope and stood abruptly. "I have to go," she snapped and disappeared.

Renée knew the disappearing feat was called folding space. The Queen could do it, as could several others of her acquaintance. It still unnerved her, however, whenever she witnessed it.

Shaking her head, Renée lifted the card to read. It contained three words—*Marid, Poison, Revenge.*

Shaaliveer

"Hurry," Marid shouted. "I've sent the spheres where we can find them later. We can't be caught with the evidence!"

Morid stared at the images, placed side-by-side, on Marid's comp-vid. One was a bulletin placed by the ASD, naming Marid as a suspect in the poisoning of many people. The other—that was the one that frightened Morid the most.

It was an offer of a reward—ten million Alliance credits for Marid's head, Twenty million if he were delivered alive to Vardil Cayetes.

~

Le-Ath Veronis

"Kooper, arrest Marid of Belancour. Immediately if not sooner," Lissa hissed as she stood beside his desk at ASD Headquarters. The Alliance Security Detail hadn't thought to watch Marid in a while—he'd been sinking quietly into ruin with botched spells and poor standards.

Shaaliveer had been removed many times from the lists of candidates for Reth Alliance membership because of the Belancour Clan.

"I'll have to get Shaaliveer's permission," Kooper began. Arresting a citizen of a governed, non-Alliance world required permission of the government and local support.

"I have it," Lissa tossed a comp-vid onto Kooper's desk. "They can't wait to get rid of him."

~

Wyyld II

"How do I look?" Kaldill turned before the mirror. He hadn't worn tight-fitting clothing in a very long time—he preferred loose robes, richly embroidered with spelled silks to keep their colors fresh.

"Like you work for the ASD," Lendill grumbled at his father's appearance.

"Perhaps trousers of a different color, then?" Kaldill lifted a dark-blond eyebrow at his son. With an absent wave of a hand, light-brown became black.

"I'd change the shirt, too," Lendill said. "You look good in black, Pap. You always have."

"You haven't called me Pap in at least a century," Kaldill beamed.

"Look, I know you can take care of yourself, but this bothers me. What if it turns out to be something we have no power against? We don't know who devised this mess to begin with."

"That's what I intend to find out. Daragar has agreed to go with me

31

as backup if needed. The Larentii Council immediately gave permission when I asked for his assistance. They even offered to send more Larentii if I wanted them."

"They're worried about this, too?"

"Decidedly so." Kaldill brushed shoulder-length blond hair behind a pointed ear and shook his head at the image he presented—at Lendill's advice, he'd employed power to change the color of his shirt to black.

"I've spoken with Kooper already—he's on his way to arrest Marid of Belancour." Lendill shook his head. "That old goat may have killed more than we know."

"Tell Kooper to approach cautiously—we have no idea how unstable the old goat, as you call him, may be."

"You think he can cause more trouble?"

"That is my deepest worry, my son."

"How long do you plan to be gone?" Lendill asked.

"I intend to see whether the lands of this planet can be rescued from the blight," Kaldill shrugged at his image in the mirror.

"Building the gardens of Gaelar N'Seith on a barren planet may be a simple task compared to this, Pap."

"Nevertheless, I will see what may be done."

"Good luck, then. Let me know how things go."

"I'll need the luck just to keep some of them from shooting at us," Kaldill huffed. "They have weapons—at least some of them do. It surprises me that they haven't been noticed by the Alliance yet."

"No space travel?" Lendill asked.

"They have the capability; they just haven't turned their attention to it, yet."

"Send images, then. I'll transmit everything to Kooper."

"Ask him to relay all information to Queen Lissa. I believe the Three may be interested in this before long."

"Kooper says that Ildevar and Lissa are both looking for Breanne. What about Ashe? Is he where we can find him? Charles, too?"

"I don't know the whereabouts of any of them. Hank is also on the list of those we can't find. If you have suggestions on how to get their attention, I'd appreciate it."

Kaldill found it humorous that Love, Strength and Wisdom held such mundane names as Breanne, Ashe and Charles, but perhaps they, too, looked upon his name as something strange.

"It's neither here nor there—we have to do what we can to keep this from spreading," Lendill's voice expressed discomfort. "I never thought to feel the fear of the planet beneath my feet, but I feel it now."

"You are growing as a Prince," Kaldill grinned and patted Lendill's shoulder. "It pleases me greatly."

∿

Avii Castle

Quin

"I can fly there with Dena," I said when Berel asked whether I wanted to go with him in the smaller boats the ship had sent to the receiving crevice.

"Father asked that I stay with you," Berel shook his head. "Will you travel with me, instead?" I knew then that the High President still worried for his son's health.

"I'll go with you, then—I think Dena is curious about the boats anyway."

Our luggage had already been sent—mine was stowed in a cabin next to Berel's if his guard, Jhak, spoke the truth. He'd traveled with the luggage, to ensure that it remained safe while two other Kondari guards stayed behind with Berel.

Jhak had returned, however, and now it was time for the passengers to board the ships and sail for Fyris.

Gurnil had spoken with ship's captains regarding the distance between Avii Castle and Lironis, calculating the time, once the boats went through the strait. I'd been unconscious before when I was brought through it and wondered if I'd feel it now.

"Quin, we have guests," Gurnil interrupted my conversation with Berel on the Library terrace.

I turned and blinked in surprise.

Daragar had come, and with him, a man I didn't know. If Berel hadn't caught me, I might have fallen to the ground—that's how breathless I became at his appearance.

His name was Kaldill Schaff. Daragar introduced him as King of the Elves.

He was so much more than that. Holding my breath when he took my hand with a brilliant smile, I resolved to keep his secrets.

CHAPTER 3

Avii Castle
Quin

Who needs boats when a Larentii can take you anywhere he pleases? Daragar did so, transporting all of us to our designated ships.

"We have a Larentii traveling with us," Gurnil breathed to Ordin as cabins were assigned to Daragar and Kaldill. As pleased as I was that Daragar chose to go with us to Fyris, I was just as pleased that Kaldill had come.

Power shone about him whenever I looked, and I wondered that none of the others could see it.

The ship itself was very large and run efficiently by many Kondari men and women. For a moment, it took me by surprise that women would be soldiers, before determining that it was silly to think that. Justis had black-winged women in his guard, and they were more than effective at their work.

Plus, I'd been a soldier of sorts at Amlis' side and had saved his life, albeit in unconventional ways. The Kondari and Avii had moved past that archaic way of thinking and I was glad.

"We will meet for dinner—those of us aboard this ship," Berel

35

handed a tab-vid to me. A schedule had been inserted, which I could read easily.

Orik, Sofi and Yissy were on another ship with two black-winged guards, while Wolter, Fen and Deeds, accompanied by two more Black Wings, rode the third. Omina, Amlis, Rodrik and Beatris rode with Berel and the rest of us on the flagship. Justis and Ardis were our black-winged guards, which pleased Dena greatly.

"It surprises me that this journey may only take a day," Berel took a seat next to mine in the meeting room. Windows surrounded us—the room had been designed for meetings between captain and staff, and was comfortably furnished with padded chairs and a heavy table.

I watched the deep waters pass swiftly below us and nodded at Berel's statement. I had the feeling that had Daragar and Kaldill chosen to do so, they could have moved ships as easily as people and we might have arrived already.

Perhaps they were looking forward to the trip just as much as Dena and Gurnil were. Gurnil sat at one end of the table, watching the sea and writing his observations on the parchment he'd brought with him. The Library would have new additions when he returned to Avii Castle.

"I'm surprised the journey is so smooth," I responded to Berel's observation. "The last portion of my journey to Avii Castle aboard Orik's boat was uneven at best."

"Smaller boats ride the waves. Something this size merely plows through them," Berel shrugged. "I saw your landing at the castle—I looked through past satellite recordings until I found it."

"I know." It didn't matter, now. Berel knew much of what the Avii had kept secret for years uncounted. That knowledge would count for nothing if all of Siriaa died of the poison.

"You are the High President's son?" Kaldill and Daragar had come looking for Berel. Kaldill turned to smile at me, however, while waiting for Berel's response.

He already knew who Berel was. What he was doing was amazing —at least to me. Asking questions was his way of measuring whomever he studied. Kaldill intended to measure the father by the son.

I could have told him that Edden Charkisul was the best leader Kondar could hope for. I also hoped that his life was safe—I knew Berel had information from the last vid-meeting with the High President, and news of the usurper's escape worried both, I could tell.

"I am, sir," Berel nodded respectfully. "I understand you are Kaldill Schaff, King of the Elves. I have never heard of elves, sir. Will you enlighten me?"

Without aid of any mechanical object, an image of forests and flowering gardens appeared among us. They appeared so real I wished to touch petals, stems and trunks. I'd never seen such healthy growing things in my life. Without realizing, I'd breathed a sigh of desire-filled pleasure at the sight.

People—elves—began to walk through the images. Like Kaldill, they had pointed ears. They wore embroidered robes that complimented their surroundings perfectly, and were content to be where they were.

"We have a library and a seat of learning here—these grounds surround it," Kaldill smiled. "It is called Gaelar N'Seith, Garden of the Elves."

"It's beautiful," I breathed. I couldn't help myself—I wanted to go there. In my mind, no taint of the poison would be found in that soil.

"You are correct," Kaldill smiled at me again. "Perhaps we should discuss your wings, and why they are different from all others."

"I have no information to give you," I shook my head.

"I understand that. I merely wish to examine them, I think, and attempt to solve that riddle for both of us. Daragar has already visited the Larentii Archives and spoken to Nefrigar, their Chief Archivist. He knows of none such, either. If a Larentii has no records, then there are no records to be found."

"Do they have records of Fyris and Kondar? Of Siriaa?" I asked.

"Yes, most certainly," Daragar replied with a smile. "After each of my visits, I give information to Nefrigar, who stores it in the Archives.

Other Larentii visited before I came. Kondar, Fyris and Yokaru are all there, from their beginnings on this world."

That stopped me in my tracks. He knew of their origins? The question of why Fyris was hidden and so backward compared to the other continents tickled my tongue. I dared not ask it; Omina, Amlis, Rodrik and Beatris walked through the door.

Midday had arrived and they'd come for their meal—as scheduled.

Larentii Archives

"This is information I would refuse most others," Nefrigar handed copies of heavy volumes to Kooper Griff, Head of the ASD. "It includes current maps and conditions, all of which were supplied by Daragar through his many visits to Siriaa."

"Lissa and the others are just as interested in this," Kooper nodded to Nefrigar. "You have my thanks."

"The Hidden had influence upon many things," Nefrigar replied, his words enigmatic. "None of it good."

"Let's hope it doesn't end up killing us, then," Kooper replied.

Le-Ath Veronis

"Even the Larentii don't know what it is," Lissa shut the book with a sigh. "Or where it came from. They've studied the effects and the efforts made by the winged guardians to hold it at bay, but the guardian queen is dead. According to this—she was only able to disrupt the spreading of the poison. She didn't neutralize it."

"You know the Larentii collect everything. They wouldn't collect that poison—whatever it is," Kooper jerked his head at one of the books. "That means even they don't trust their methods of collection or containment. What in the name of the fire pit is this?"

"I'll attempt to sort out who Liron is—or was," Lissa fumed. "It looks as if he were at the bottom of all this."

"The people of Fyris—and the guardians—Daragar notes that they're not native to that world. Where did they come from? There's no evidence they arrived on their own. This is a huge mess," Kooper grumbled.

"We have imported people, a hidden continent, a poison nobody can define and a dead god, in all probability. Anything else?"

"The guardian queen—how did she interrupt the poison's spread?"

"Where's Daragar now?" Kooper asked.

"Daragar is there—on Siriaa," Ildevar Wyyld appeared in Lissa's study, where she and Kooper held their private conversation. "Kaldill went with him."

"If anybody can bring a planet back from the brink, it would be Kaldill," Lissa nodded. "Although I'm having my doubts about this," she tapped the borrowed book.

"Has Marid of Belancour been apprehended, yet?" Ildevar asked Kooper.

"Not yet, Founder," Kooper shook his head. "Local authorities attempted to take him before my agents arrived. Their effort was unsuccessful and Marid fled with his family and everything they owned. We're searching now, but there's a cloud about his location. We know he's no longer on Shaaliveer, but we can't pin the location down."

"If I learn that jackass has a Sirenali, I'll kill him myself," Lissa snapped.

Kooper refrained from responding; his worry was the same as Lissa's. Only a Sirenali could defy his searches and that spelled disaster, in his opinion.

~

The waters of Fyris

Quin

This time, I was conscious while we navigated the straits. It was as if we traveled through a wall of very dense fog for several moments before coming out on the other side to sunlight glittering off the waters. I had no idea what might create the fog, let alone the shortening of our journey.

Berel attempted to contact his father in Kondar shortly after. At first, there was no reply—I can only imagine that the wall of fog prevented communication in some way, but once the fog lay far behind us, Berel's tab-vid worked perfectly.

He and I both breathed happy sighs when Edden Charkisul's face appeared on the small screen.

"We're getting close, Father," Berel smiled at his parent. "At our current speed, we should arrive in four hours. The Captain reports that most of the sharp rocks and other obstacles have disappeared off his scanners and they've mapped a clear path to the city Quin calls Lironis."

"Have you seen any of the inhabitants, yet?" Edden asked.

"No. We are far enough offshore that we cannot see land yet. The scanners now indicate it is there, though. Isn't that exciting, Father? I feel like an explorer from centuries ago."

"You are an explorer, Son," Edden smiled. "I will receive reports from the science officers, but I prefer your reports above theirs. Keep me informed."

"I will," Berel nodded enthusiastically.

Berel couldn't see it, but I could; worry clouded the High President's face. Civil war threatened Kondar and he was preparing for battle, should it come. When Berel ended the communication with his father, I asked my questions.

"Will you show me everything you have on the one who imprisoned you?" I begged. Berel nodded and requested information from the tab-vid's store of knowledge. Before long, both of us pored over images and reports concerning Dorthil Crasz.

The urge to fly about the Western spires overwhelmed me when we passed them. Amlis and Rodrik had never seen them from the west, so they stood at the railing with Berel and me as we passed. Berel held his tab-vid aloft, recording images for his father.

Farther east, past the spires, I could see the darker outline of the cliff where I'd sat on Stepper's saddle, gazing at the wonder of the tall, spiked formations. Birds still wheeled about them; the spires were home to them and the sharp rocks held many nests.

"We will arrive in less than two hours," Kaldill joined us at the rail. "So much might be done with this world," he breathed. "I worry that it may not be possible."

I knew Kaldill was old—I merely couldn't comprehend how old he could be. To him, the Larentii who now stood beside him was very young. I found it amazing that neither Kaldill nor Daragar showed any signs of age. Both were more than ancient, yet they appeared quite young.

Had Kaldill not been immortal, I imagined his face would be covered with the lines of his worries throughout the millennia.

"You see too much," Kaldill reached out a hand and tucked hair behind my ear. At least my hair had grown out along with my wings— it was now down to my shoulders. Where Kaldill's hair was a golden color, mine still contained gold, copper and silver strands. Most days, I had no idea what to make of it.

"It's beautiful," Kaldill reassured me. "Never berate yourself or what you have because it is different. Rejoice in it, instead."

"Not always an easy thing to do, King Elf," I nodded respectfully to him. I didn't want to say it—was almost afraid to think it—but his touch had sent a wonderful shiver through me and I wanted to savor it as something that belonged only to me.

Instead, I turned my thoughts to Tamblin and how he'd proclaimed himself King of Fyris. A real King stood humbly beside me and thought to brush hair away from my face when the wind blew it into my eyes. Tamblin would only take his pleasure from a lowly servant, never thinking of her—only of himself.

Vhrist

"My King, we saw terrible things," Captain Herth of the fishing vessel Grunt, reported to Tamblin.

"Terrible things?" Tamblin sounded bored.

"Where the strait begins—you know of it?" Herth trembled, a fisherman's cap held tightly in his fingers as he addressed the King.

"I know of it." Tamblin shifted on his temporary throne and cut his eyes toward Yevil, who stood nearby. Tamblin had never seen the fog representing the strait—he'd only heard reports and knew of the written accounts of many sailors. He'd also heard of it from his brother, Tandelis—who'd visited the glass castle several times.

"Anyways," Herth swallowed with difficulty, "we saw three huge things. Perhaps they were boats, I know not, as I cannot imagine anyone making anything so large. They appeared to be made of metal, but how can metal float? It is sorcery, my King, I have no doubt. They passed through the fog and as we were half-covered in it ourselves, I don't think we were seen."

"How large?" Tamblin's attention was now captured.

"Too large to describe, my King."

"Did you attempt to follow?"

"Too afraid, sir. Fast, they traveled. I doubt we could have kept up."

"Where were they heading?"

"Down the western side—toward the spires."

"All of your crew saw this?"

"Yes, my King." Herth now doubted his decision to come to the King with this news. After all, Tamblin could act irrationally and kill him and his crew. It wouldn't be the first time, Herth realized. He swallowed again—hard.

"Does any of your crew have a drawing talent? I wish to see what these things look like."

"One sailor, sir. The youngest."

"Fetch parchment," Tamblin shouted. "Bring your sailor," Tamblin's hard gaze settled on Herth.

~

Lironis

Quin

The ships were forced to anchor far from the old docks in Lironis, as the waters were too shallow for their bulk and the planks and pilings had rotted over the years. None thought to repair them for any reason; still, people of Lironis gathered when the ships arrived, as they could be seen quite a distance from the shores.

"I must arrive by boat," Omina snapped before Daragar could offer his skills at relocation. "The people must see Amlis and me returning thus."

That's how all of us prepared to leave the ship—by smaller boats lowered to the water by the ship's crew.

"Truly archaic," Kaldill whispered at my side as he gazed at the city beyond. Berel, breathing short, excited breaths, recorded more images on his tab-vid as we awaited our turn in the boats.

"Quin and I will arrive as we should—by flying," Justis' hand dropped to my shoulder. That meant Ardis would fly with us. "We will accompany the boat carrying Omina and Amlis. It is proper that they be guarded by Avii upon their arrival."

"I will place a shield, then," Daragar nodded to Justis. "To ensure your safe arrival."

"You have my thanks," Justis ducked his head. He knew—as did I— that Daragar thought to protect me, first. Kaldill, standing nearby, hid a smile.

You have my thanks as well, I silently sent to Daragar. He smiled, then.

You are welcome, he replied.

~

Lironis

Yann, Varnell's man-at-arms, shaded his eyes as he gazed westward. A minor noble, Yann had been assigned to Varnell ten turns earlier, when he was still a stripling. Yann hated the old man—and the King—but hid his feelings as well as any other inside the castle.

Many times, he wished himself strong enough to murder Yevil, but realized his death would come swiftly should he try—at either Yevil's hand or the King's guards'.

Instead, Yann spent most of his days barely speaking and obeying Varnell's every whim. Today, Varnell had sent him to the old docks to see what the fuss was. Yann resolved to never forget the way the Prince-Heir and the Queen arrived—in a sturdy metal boat manned by strange sailors and guarded by three Avii, whose wings beat a steady rhythm as they flew about it.

Omina and Amlis stood tall at the center of the boat while it raced toward the shore. Several of the men aboard the vessel held strange weapons, too—to Yann, they appeared as thick, metal sticks. He had no idea what their purpose might be, other than to strike another with their weight.

Shoving his way to the front of the crowd waiting on the rotting dock, Yann was the first to drop to his knees and pledge support to Amlis the moment the Prince stepped onto the old pier, the Queen right behind him.

Quin

"Make way for the Prince. Make way for the Queen," the crowd took up the chant as Amlis strode forward, his boots making the wooden planks creak beneath his feet while Omina walked a step behind at his shoulder. Rodrik watched the crowd warily as he had no sword—it had stayed behind at Avii Castle.

Justis, Ardis and I landed lightly behind; the crowd pulled away from us automatically. I would have too—the gaze Justis leveled upon them relayed his accusations—in his eyes, they'd all murdered Elabeth and Camryn.

When Daragar and Kaldill appeared from nothing, the crowd gasped and shrank farther back. They knew nothing of those who might appear and disappear at will. The sight of a very tall, blue man was also something they might never expect; therefore, the Larentii frightened them.

"It's Finder," I heard someone whisper. Jerking quickly, I turned to see who'd spoken.

Eyes ahead, dear Quin, Kaldill spoke into my mind. *We will make discoveries later.*

He was right—it wasn't my purpose to search for those who might recognize me—I was there to guard the Prince and Queen.

More gasps came as additional boats disembarked behind us; I didn't turn to look. Berel, Wolter and the others would be coming ashore guarded by Kondari soldiers, all of whom carried weapons.

The walk from the docks to the castle took half an hour, and half of Lironis arrived to watch as we strode unhindered through the palace gates. I didn't fail to notice, however, that the people who watched were more starved and sickly than they'd been when I left.

The sight of it grieved me much.

It wasn't until Amlis and Rodrik approached the main door that Varnell's guards appeared; they'd hastily dressed in old armor and faced us with their swords drawn. Varnell himself pushed through them until he stood six paces from Amlis, a blade drawn and pointed threateningly at the Prince.

"You think to delay me?"

It wasn't Amlis who spoke, or Rodrik or the Queen. Varnell blinked at his empty hand and then at Justis, who'd snatched the blade from the old man's grip. "I tell you this, old man," Justis held the sword to Varnell's throat and hissed in his face, "If any are still living who participated in Elabeth's murder, I will kill them myself."

Justis tossed Varnell's blade onto the courtyard stones, where it rang its metallic protest into ensuing silence.

"I wish to send a message to my father in Vhrist," Amlis said. He'd found his quarters much as he'd left them, aside from the thick layer of dust that covered everything.

"Unwise, my Prince," Rodrik scolded. Amlis nodded after a moment and I released the breath I'd held.

Dena, who'd followed me, now supervised the maids who'd shown up to clean Amlis' chambers while the rest of us attended to other duties.

Across the hall, more maids and servants did the same for Omina. Wolter and Deeds had gone to the kitchens to see about food and supplies while Berel, who sat at the Prince's desk conversing with his father, offered supplies from the ships if needed.

"Son, allow me to speak with Quin, please," Edden said.

"Yes, High President?" I moved to stand at Berel's elbow, so Edden could see my face in Berel's screen.

"There are airchoppers on board one of the ships," he said. "I understand that someone must accompany my pilots to get in and out again. Who will you recommend to guide us?"

"Orik," I said immediately. "He has sailed the waters around Fyris for many years and knows how to locate the strait. Fen, also. Perhaps one or two others, depending upon how many airchoppers you wish to send."

"Two, I think, for a preliminary relief delivery," Edden said. "I'll have supplies delivered to Avii Castle, and the airchoppers can fly them from there."

"That would be greatly appreciated," I said. "The people are starving—the harvests have been very poor and far from what they should be."

"Yes, we've analyzed the images Berel sent and that's our conclusion as well."

"I hope the people will agree to allow the ships' medical staff to examine those who are ill," Berel said.

"That may take time—they are quite distrustful at the moment, as your technology appears to be sorcery to them. They don't understand it at all."

"Will you heal them?" Berel asked.

"I may do some," I allowed my shoulders to droop. "I worry about depleting my energy in the face of so many."

"Not everything is your worry," Wolter walked in and dropped a hand on my shoulder. "Do what must be done and in private. We don't need all of Fyris at the castle gate when they learn what you can do."

"Quin, many of them are treatable through other means. Save what you have for the worst off and most deserving," Edden said. I knew what he wasn't saying—that he'd had to pay for that privilege for Berel. I wanted to apologize, but it hadn't been my greed that demanded payment. I would have done the healing for nothing, because it was deserved—by father and son.

"Halthea is dead—she tried to kill the King," I blurted instead.

"I have already heard that news so I know why you tell me this," Edden nodded. "It is none of your fault, child. We understand this."

"Thank you, High President," I ducked my head in a gesture of respect. Edden smiled at me in return. "I shall make you a citizen of Kondar. Immediately," he replied.

~

Vhrist

"Do you know anything about this?" Tamblin tossed a hand-drawn picture through the bars of Rath's cell.

Rath stood slowly—the mattress he'd been given was barely an improvement over the stone floor beneath it; the straw bedding had flattened long ago. It did nothing to help the joint disease he'd developed after sixty years of life.

Lifting the parchment drawing before straightening with an effort, Rath blinked at the strange image. "What is this?" he turned to Tamblin. Yevil stood at Tamblin's shoulder, glaring.

"Glare all you want, it won't offer insight into what this is," Rath handed the drawing to Tamblin through the bars and shook his head. "I've never seen such. Is it a ship?"

"That's what the fishermen say who saw it," Tamblin snorted.

"Where is it now?" Rath asked.

"We don't know. The sailors were too frightened and too slow to chase it."

"Then you know more than I," Rath said. "Has it attacked, or provoked attack?"

"We have no word of such," Tamblin replied. Yevil shuffled angrily at Tamblin's side.

"It is an enemy, that is plain to see," Yevil's words exploded in an angry growl.

"Are you taking these sailor's words for truth, then, without seeing this for yourself? Were they drunk, perhaps?" Rath lifted an eyebrow at Yevil. "Were they attacked? How do you know it is an enemy?"

"Why would they be here, then?" Yevil demanded.

Rath, even in the dim light of the dungeon, saw the spittle fly from Yevil's mouth as he spoke.

"Just because your ships plan an invasion doesn't mean that anyone else might possess such an insane notion," Rath observed.

"What other reason would there be?" Yevil hissed, his voice harsh and accusing. "You and the filth you call your sister planned this, somehow."

"We planned nothing," Rath snapped.

"No? What is this, then?" Yevil jerked a message from an inner pocket of his jacket and tossed it through the bars.

Rath didn't need to pick it up—he knew what it was. Hirill had been instrumental in this bit of treachery. The message he'd sent to the winged guardians had never left Fyris. "I hope I live long enough to witness your deaths," Rath hissed.

~

Lironis

 Quin

Rodrik took his usual quarters in Amlis' suite. I think he wanted me to stay with the Prince, too, but Justis insisted that I stay with him —he'd been given a suite next to Amlis'. Ardis and Dena took a suite next to Omina's, while Kaldill and Daragar had temporary rooms at the top of the castle.

I resolved to visit them when I could—I'd never been to the upper levels of the castle, after all; Tamblin kept them closed off to all. Berel chose to stay with his guards on the flagship; Wolter and Deeds went with the Queen to provide a guard for her.

Sophie and Yissy had also gone with the Queen; I had a feeling that Sophie would find herself named as dressmaker to the Queen and maid-in-waiting before two days had passed.

I had no idea who was running the kitchens now that Wolter had taken another position, but food was provided according to a regular plan. A delivery of food and supplies had already come from the Kondari ships—the castle cooks had never seen packaged food before and had to be shown what to do with it.

The Kondari language also escaped the kitchen staff; therefore, three Kondari were dispatched with the supplies to assist in food preparations. I doubted they'd ever seen such archaic methods of cooking, but they mimed much to make themselves understood by the kitchen help.

I knew, too, that things were deteriorating in Vhrist, but dithered over whom to approach first with the news. Rath was still alive but that wouldn't be true for much longer. "The airchoppers are flying toward Avii Castle, with Orik and three others aboard," Berel said after he arrived and flopped onto a settee near the window.

I'd stared, unseeing, through a suite window while considering the problems facing us. If Tamblin were a rational man, and were Yevil even half as evil as he was, we could come together and discuss the greater problems facing Siriaa.

As it was, neither of those things were true. While Rath might be a womanizing noble at times, he still recognized the danger Fyris was in and knew that sending an invading fleet toward an unknown country was more than foolish.

"The Queen's brother is in a dungeon in Vhrist—on the northern border of Fyris," I turned to Berel, then. "Yevil and the King promised him thirty days while they awaited a response from Amlis. I fear they may void their promise and execute him anyway."

"Does the Queen know?" Berel sat up straighter and studied me with interest.

"No. Neither does Amlis or Rodrik. Rath is Rodrik's father, and I worry that if I tell any of them, they'll race toward Vhrist, only to get caught in Yevil's net."

"What's this?" Justis stalked in. He'd overheard part of my conversation with Berel. Hoping he'd react in a rational manner, I explained what I knew.

CHAPTER 4

*L*ironis
   Quin

"Airchoppers will make too much noise," Berel pointed out. "They'll know we're coming. My concern, of course, is that innocents may die attacking Kondari troops, who have body armor and advanced weapons. I want no deaths," he added.

"I want Yevil's death," Amlis hissed. Rodrik kept his silence as he sat next to the Prince, but his face revealed a terrible anger. As much as he and his father disagreed, he still loved him.

"Riding horseback will get us there far too late," Deeds offered. Amlis nodded his agreement.

"The waters surrounding Vhrist are very shallow," Daragar offered. "A ship cannot get close enough to facilitate an escape. You'd be dependent upon the airchoppers again, and that, as young Berel has so aptly pointed out, will result in unnecessary deaths."

"Fly in," Dena suggested. "We have six black-wing guards, a Yellow Wing, a Green Wing, a Blue Wing and the White Wing. Surely we can get in and out silently enough and carry away one man."

"Black Wings only," Justis began.

"You will waste time searching for the proper cell," I said. "I will go as a guide."

Kaldill and Daragar exchanged glances when I spoke, but neither offered comment. "How long will it take to fly from here?" Ardis asked.

"Less than two hours," Justis replied. I knew then that he'd made this journey before.

Gurnil, who sat at the meeting table writing notes swiftly across parchment, glanced up and nodded to Justis. "I will expect a report upon your return, Commander," Gurnil said.

"You will have it," Justis agreed. "Come—Black Wings and Quin with me. We leave at nightfall."

Vhrist

The drawings Tamblin held this time defied explanation. Along with the drawings came descriptions of loud noises accompanying the contraptions. Who knew what they could be, and this, so shortly after their conversation with Rath in the dungeons?

"We will have the execution tomorrow," Tamblin nodded to Yevil. "In public. Then we will send his head to Lironis—to my wife. If she's there, as Rath claims, then it's only right that they should see one another," Tamblin laughed.

"Tell the bitch to bow to you or she'll be next," Yevil's voice was sly.

"Sounds reasonable enough, only include Amlis in that charge. Place extra guards around Rath's cage, too."

"I'll see it done, my King."

Lironis

Quin

"If you tire, let me know. I'll have Ardis carry you," Justis said. "Regardless, before we reach Vhrist, I'll have him carry you anyway, to hide your white wings. Black is not easily seen, and we've drilled for this many times. All we need is your locating skills."

"I know," I nodded. "I worry that he may be moved, in case any of his men make a rescue attempt."

"They'd be better off fighting Tamblin's troops," Justis huffed.

"They're outnumbered, and the King's troops fear Yevil," I explained. "I fear that he may have more weapons like the one Amlis took to Avii Castle. Sadly, the thing exploded when their ship was attacked by Kondari airchoppers, which also caused the boat to explode. Beatris barely had time to leap from the deck before it was incinerated."

"He had a weapon that exploded?"

"You should ask Amlis about it—he carried it away from Vhrist," I shrugged. "I think it was the one used to kill Elabeth and Camryn."

That admission stopped Justis cold. "What did it look like?" His voice sounded deadly.

"Ask Amlis—he and Rodrik held it," I said.

"Come," he snapped. I followed him out of our suite.

"It looked something like this," Amlis hastily drew a sketch with pen and ink upon a scrap of parchment.

"That cannot be. Nothing like that should be in Fyris," Justis breathed.

"It made a hole in Brin's chest," Rodrik indicated the size of his fist. "Yevil killed him with the infernal device after Brin stabbed Timblor."

"You know what it is," I gazed at Justis, who looked grim.

"These are supposed to be hidden in Jurris' private treasury," Justis claimed, studying the sketch again.

"What is it, then?" Amlis, asked.

"An ancient weapon," Justis muttered. "A dangerous one. How did such as this come to Fyris?"

"I believe that may be determined by Yevil's parentage," I said. "I know Tamblin allows him sway in most things, and I wonder at that.

I also wonder what Yevil's back looks like when he removes his shirt."

"What are you saying?" Rodrik asked.

"I've never seen Yevil without a shirt," Amlis admitted. "Even when sparring with swords."

"A half-blood?" Justis lifted an eyebrow.

"Perhaps. I feel too much of a connection between him and another that I know of."

"We are in deep trouble," Gurnil sighed.

Kondar

"Dorthil, this is useless. We need collaboration, not civil war," Edden said. He'd placed a vid-call to Dorthil, who was currently a guest of Sector Two's President and his advisors. Edden didn't point out that Sector Two was experiencing upheaval regarding heavy-handed legislation churned out by the current President and his staff; that would ensure Dorthil's continued fomentation of civil war.

"Fourth Sector is with us," Dorthil snapped. "You merely wish to save your skin. I should have disposed of you when I had the chance."

"You realize those words are treasonous?" Melis Norwal's face appeared behind Edden's shoulder. "Sector Two has not yet declared its secession from Kondar. From where do you expect to import grain? Sector Two holds a shoreline and its chief exports are fish, shellfish and vid components. Stop this foolishness now and help us find a cure for this poison. Sector Two's fish are already contaminated with it."

"Your policies have angered the gods," Dorthil thundered. "It will not take long before Sectors One and Three follow Two and Four. They will rally to my call and that will leave you on the island that is Sector Five."

"I spoke with both One and Three before calling you. They advised me to mobilize troops to Sector Two and haul you into custody. Shall I follow their advice?" Edden asked.

Dorthil cursed before offering a reply. "I will prevail. I have a powerful ally," he stated.

"What powerful ally? The Yokaru think you're a joke."

"He calls himself a wizard," Dorthil hissed. "He can kill you with a thought."

"What thought is that?" Melis asked calmly. "Who is this man—this wizard?"

"His name is Marid, and he is from Yokaru. You should fear that name." Dorthil terminated the communication.

"They have no wizards—and no Yokaru citizens have such a name," Edden discussed an earlier conversation with the Yokarun Emperor over dinner. "They have no dealings with Dorthil—there are no records of his leaving and no records of anyone arriving here to visit him. I have no idea if this is merely lies and posturing on Dorthil's part, or whether someone who identified himself as Marid from Yokaru actually approached him."

"Few things are offered for free if this is true—I imagine the wizard asked for something in return for what he purportedly gave to Dorthil," Melis said. "I hesitate to place another communication, but it may become necessary. Strange things are happening upon our planet as you know—Berel says a very tall, blue man and another who claims to be a King we do not recognize are there with him and Quin, although he cannot record images of them, for some reason."

"More wizardry? I thought such only happened in children's tales."

"Perhaps we have fallen into one of those tales," Melis shook his head in confusion. "I find no explanation for any of this."

"That means we're back to what Dorthil wanted from this so-called wizard."

"We have spies in Sector Two—they are reporting the current unrest among the people. Shall I ask that they get as close as possible to Dorthil?"

"Close, but not too close—I want no deaths," Edden sighed. "If he is visited again by this wizard, I wish to know it. Immediately."

~

Le-Ath Veronis

"I have a message," Kooper arrived in Lissa's office with very little notice.

"From?" Lissa, smoothing back strawberry-blonde hair, studied Kooper Griff.

"Daragar. He says his nexus echo received a hit."

"On whom?"

"Marid's name was mentioned."

"Cripes," Lissa rubbed her forehead. "Who said it?"

"Someone on Siriaa who recently attempted a coup against the Kondari government. Seems he wanted the High President's position. He had it—for a short time. He's been chased away for the moment, but it looks as if he's plotting civil war from one of Kondar's Five Sectors."

"He wants a civil war while the planet is dying beneath his feet? That's preposterous."

"He's a bona-fide difik," Gardevik Rath appeared beside Kooper.

"How do you know about this?" Lissa's hands went to her hips and her eyes narrowed at her High Demon mate.

"Our son, Torevik, has apparently had a conversation with Salidar, who spoke with Trajan."

"Of course he did," Lissa tossed up a hand in resignation. "Is there anybody who doesn't know by now?"

"The information is kept among the powerful," Garde defended himself.

"Except that King Jayd knows it, Queen Glinda knows it and likely half the High Demon population on Kifirin knows it. Are you trying to panic everybody in the Alliance?"

"Not intentionally. You know High Demons are impervious to

poison. That makes us a logical choice to visit this planet—I've never heard of it before."

"Siriaa, and it's almost at the space travel stage. If this weren't happening, Ildevar would likely approach them for membership in the Reth Alliance."

"That's an interesting offer though—if that's what it is," Kooper interrupted thoughtfully. "A few High Demons as guards—they can protect anyone within a few feet by the natural shields they have. We can dig for this poison and take samples, but I hesitate to take it off the planet. Can we build a facility there, to study it?"

"That sounds logical," Lissa blew out a breath. "Will Daragar consent to construct something with Kaldill's help, or should we send someone else? How many High Demons want to go?"

"I do. Tory wants to go. Reah, perhaps, and Kordevik Weth."

"Don't you think we need more than four?" One of Lissa's eyebrows rose as she asked the question.

"Kifirin. Kifirin wishes to come." Garde hung his head.

"Fine. Is this your way of trying to get back in my good graces?"

"I—yes."

"We'll talk if things go well on Siriaa."

"Really?" Garde's head jerked up and a smile tugged at his lips. "I'll make sure of it."

Fyris

Ardis moved to fly above me as we approached Vhrist. Pulling in my wings, I dropped until he caught and held my body against his while his wings continued to work above us.

I could tell Justis and the black-wing guard had practiced this maneuver many times. It was a method of collecting a wounded comrade in midair and I couldn't fault Ardis' execution of the tactic.

Perhaps a mile to the north under a half-moon's light, I could see Vhrist and the sea beyond. It was time to tell Justis where we were going.

The dungeon is near the docks—the one where drunken sailors are often held, I sent to the Commander. I knew Justis imagined Rath would be held in the palace dungeons, but Yevil, in an attempt to keep Rath's loyal troops from fighting to free him, had moved the prisoner under cover of darkness to the new location.

I also knew this dungeon had its share of water-covered floors and rats that swam in and out with the rise and fall of tides. Rath, who'd fought with Yevil's troops, had received a damaging blow to his head and now lay unconscious on a stone floor with filthy water rising about him.

Yevil hoped Rath would die of the head wound or drown while unconscious. I hoped we'd arrive in time to prevent either.

"Tell Ardis where to fly—we'll follow," Justis hissed as he flew close.

I will, I responded silently. I'd been compelled to tell Justis before we flew away from Lironis that I could send mental messages. He'd promised to have a discussion with me later concerning withheld information.

You could attempt to speak to me, mind to mind, I added. He hadn't tried before, but the Orb had spoken to him—not Jurris.

What? Immediately inserted itself into my brain.

You have mindspeech, I said. *I heard you easily.*

Several curse words lodged inside my head, few of them aimed at me. I was grateful.

When Justis took the lead after I explained how to get to the sailor's lockup in a mental conversation, we wheeled far to the west and came in low over the water, instead of risking flight past the palace guards. Justis and his Black Wings flew silently as we made our way into Vhrist.

Three of the five weapons Yevil still possessed wouldn't fire.

Two, though—he smiled at the deep holes he'd made in the castle's outside walls. These two operated more silently than the other he'd used. Who knew where it was now? Yevil didn't care, as long as he had weapons that would work.

"My Lord, we suspect an escape attempt—a guard reported a shadow between him and the moonlight overhead," one of Yevil's guards reported breathlessly. He'd run all the way from the docks to deliver his message.

"Get horses," Yevil snapped. "I look forward to killing another winged devil."

~

Quin

I was terrified. Yevil was on the way and we had just gotten past the guards at the entrance. All four lay unconscious after Justis and his Black Wings delivered head blows. More guards stood along corridors barring the way, waiting to attack anyone who might attempt a rescue.

I learned that night how ineffective Tamblin's guards were against the Avii. Justis, Ardis and the others were faster and better trained than any in Fyris. I also discovered that each Black Wing carried two knives that proved deadly to those who chose to come against them.

Still, Yevil was on the way and the weapon he carried didn't require hand-to-hand combat. My breaths trembling in my chest when we reached Rath's cell, I informed Justis of what was coming.

~

Lironis

"Is it time?" Kaldill drained a cup of wine. It was Fyrian and substandard, but he disregarded the taste.

"If you like," Daragar shrugged. "What is your intention?"

"Benign, for the moment," Kaldill replied. "That could change if Quin is attacked."

"Then I will allow you to handle this," Daragar inclined his head.

"Your reaction is likely to be less destructive than mine, should that happen."

"I applaud the restraint you have shown thus far," Kaldill agreed. "Yes, I will handle this."

~

Vhrist

Quin

After fighting our way through the last six guards, I took the lead and the others followed. Water was halfway to my knees and sloshing noisily against stone walls as I waded through it, terrified that Rath would drown before we reached him.

Rats squeaked and swam or skittered about us, making me grateful that Justis and the others wore tall, black boots to prevent bites. The rats, like every living creature in Fyris, were starving. Me they wouldn't touch—I'd already warned them away from my feet and legs, but Justis and the others had no such talent.

Rath's head bobbed upon swirling waters when we reached his cell. I wanted to cry out—metal bars stood between us and a dying man. Years of saltwater had taken a toll on the metal, however, and when six Black Wings placed their hands upon the bars and pulled, they bounced backward as the metal gave way with a sickening screech.

Ardis almost dropped into the water, but was pulled back by a hand from Justis. Rushing around Justis' bulk, I ran inside the cell and knelt beside Rath, pulling his head up so he wouldn't breathe putrid, salty water.

I had to deliver a warning before I could offer Rath any healing, however. Yevil arrived at the outer gate and was making his way through the sailor's dungeon, a weapon capable of killing any living thing held in his hand. We still had to get out again; Yevil and the weapon he carried would be blocking our path.

~

Wyyld II

Father, I could handle this for you, Lendill sent mindspeech.

I know you still handle special projects for the ASD, but I am not without resources, Kaldill pointed out. *See?* He sent the mental image. *The buffoon has no idea we're following him.*

Pap, that's a ranos pistol he has in his hand, Lendill pointed out.

I have shields, Kaldill replied. *Quin, on the other hand, does not.*

Quin?

I'll bring her soon for introductions.

Not if that weapon hits her. Unless I miss my guess, that one is ancient and has no safety measures.

Then I hope it blows up in this miscreant's face, Kaldill said.

You can't count on that.

I count on few things. Besides, Daragar is with me, and he is eyeing this device with skepticism.

You have the Larentii with you? Pap, what do you have up your sleeve?

My arm—on both sides.

Should I send for Kooper? He can bite the bastard and be done with it.

Tell him to save his venom for a more worthy adversary. This one is mentally unstable; I can feel the warped vibrations from here.

Pap, please be careful, Lendill begged.

I will.

Quin

How well can you see in the dark? I asked Justis.

Well enough—better than those from Fyris, he replied.

Then put out the torches, I said. Ardis knelt next to me, holding Rath's head up while I attempted to heal his head wound. Hoping that Yevil couldn't see as well as Justis in the dark, I prayed any shots he fired would fail to find a target.

Justis lifted the first torch from the wall and dropped it into the water at his feet. It died with a hiss, leaving us in dimmer light.

Nodding to two more Black Wings to do the same, torches came down and went out in a sizzle of smoke and fumes.

That left only one light in Rath's cell—mine. It shone golden as I continued my healing efforts. *Move away—stand by Justis*, I instructed Ardis mentally. *Take the evil when he arrives and aims his weapon at me.*

Water swished about Ardis' feet as he stood and went to find Justis. I knew Yevil would arrive very soon.

In a few moments, Rath would be healed. My light would dissipate then, but would it be swift enough? Shoving my fears aside, I continued my efforts.

~

Le-Ath Veronis

"An elf and a Larentii stalking a killer? I don't believe this," Lissa dropped her face in her hands. "Why didn't they ask me? I could take care of this in seconds. Neither one has experience in these matters— what do you suppose they intend to do?" Lissa lifted her gaze to Kooper, who'd just gotten word from Lendill Schaff.

"I can't help but think this is going to be the case of the rabbit stalking a wolf. Not that they don't have power—we know better. They've never handled anything like this in their lives. Kaldill has an army of trained elves to fight his battles."

"You could go," Lissa suggested.

"Lendill offered my services. Kaldill refused."

"And it just gets better," Lissa muttered. "Keep me posted. I want to know how this turns out."

~

Vhrist

Light reflected off rising water and flickered against stone walls— the fools still had torches burning. Yevil grinned at the thought. They'd be easy targets for his weapon. Motioning for the guards who strode ahead of him to step back, he took the lead, his weapon poised to fire.

～

Only Quin's light remains inside the cell, brother, Daragar sent to Kaldill.

Agreed, Kaldill responded. *I have a plan, since this filth will aim at the one he sees first.*

Ah, Daragar smiled as the mental image came to him. *An elf should never be underestimated, or so Nefrigar says,* he added.

The Chief Archivist is well known and highly respected by my people, Kaldill said. *Now—it is time.*

～

Quin

Rath moaned—the first sign that he still lived. I worried that he and I would both die, however—Yevil was poised to walk into view and Rath still needed help. Strange, that it took only moments for Yevil to make his way through the maze to find us.

Of course, Justis and his Black Wings had to fight their way to Rath's cell, rather than striding swiftly in that direction. Healing, in my experience, could not be rushed if I wanted the patient to survive.

Yevil's voice sounded and I jerked my head up to see the weapon pointed at me. He laughed, too, while he aimed it at my head. "The mute girl grew wings. That's too bad. You're dead."

The weapon fired.

CHAPTER 5

*V*hrist
Quin

I may never see again what I witnessed that night, while Rath woke after his wound was healed.

Yevil, as if he'd been surrounded by the glass of Avii Castle, screamed as the blast of light emitted by his weapon bounced like lightning inside the sphere about him, before striking his right leg below the knee and severing it.

His screams erupted louder and higher past that point as three guards dared to rush Justis, Ardis and four black-winged guards.

Yevil's men died quickly while Yevil dropped to the bottom of his sphere, weeping from the pain and loss of a limb.

"I must admit, I didn't see that coming," Kaldill muttered as he appeared and stepped around Yevil's transparent prison. Daragar lifted an interested eyebrow at Yevil's plight before moving around him and following Kaldill.

"I think we should take that filth with us," I jerked my head toward Yevil, whose howls could still be heard.

"If you wish it," Kaldill shrugged. "I believe your theory could be tested if we carried him back. Is this what you wish, Cheah-mul?"

"Yes," I shrugged, although the unusual language he employed at the end evaded my interpretation skills.

"Then it shall be thus."

"I will take him," Daragar offered. "I'll leave the others to you." He nodded to Kaldill.

"Very good. Remember to add air in his sphere—with the way he's howling, he'll run out quickly."

"The weapon managed to cauterize the wound, so he needs little care," Daragar leaned down and examined Yevil in a clinical fashion.

"Guards are coming," Justis pointed out.

"Then we should leave," Kaldill replied. In a burst of brightness, we were inside Amlis' suite in Lironis. Amlis, shocked beyond comprehension, shouted when we arrived. Rodrik slipped on the stone floor, rushing to defend the Prince. He landed on his knees, finding himself face-to-face with Yevil's sphere, his nose pressed against the solid transparency.

It was then I noticed that Daragar had left Yevil's severed leg behind in Vhrist—as food for the rats.

Le-Ath Veronis

"Kaldill said he was only attempting to protect all involved. It merely happened that the weapon fired and severed the murderer's leg while he was shielded."

"Where's the leg now?" Lissa asked Kooper.

"I believe it was consumed by rats, but I can double check if you'd like."

"No, thank you," Lissa held up a hand.

Lironis

Quin

"Do they have any more of these weapons?" Amlis asked.

"Not now," Daragar replied. "The two Yevil carried are deactivated —I saw to it myself. The others still in Vhrist will no longer operate, either. When someone chooses to target Quin, they will be treated to the same."

"How is Rath?" Wolter asked.

"Recovering well—after Quin tended him. That healing could have gotten her killed," Kaldill replied. "Omina is with Rath and they are discussing Tamblin's plans."

"Can we remove this—whatever it is? I wish to see Yevil's back," Amlis studied the sphere around the one-legged enemy.

"Deeds and I will hold him for you," Wolter volunteered.

"No. Ardis and I will handle this—he meant to kill more Avii, and would have without the help of Kaldill and Daragar," Justis nodded his thanks to both.

I went still—he'd called me Avii. My breath stopped for a moment.

Kaldill smiled grimly as he released Yevil from his transparent cage. The moment he was free, Yevil attempted to stand and fight.

He should have known better.

Amlis ripped the shirt from his shoulders after Yevil dropped to his knees with a yelp of pain. I peered at Yevil's back as he snarled his hate.

There, on his shoulder blades, were nubs. At the base of those nubs, next to his skin, grew the smallest, downy feathers.

They were red.

Yevil was half-brother to Jurris. Justis jerked Yevil about and punched him senseless with a single blow.

"How old would he be?" Ardis asked. I was weary but refused to leave while Justis, Ordin, Gurnil and the others discussed this half-blood child of Treven's.

"Old by Fyrian standards," Gurnil replied. "Treven went through the gate fifty turns past, and I imagine this one was old enough to understand that Treven wanted his bloodline on the Avii throne instead of Camryn's."

"Then he has enough Avii blood to stay young for an extended period," Ordin said. He'd remained quiet through most of the conversation, but chose to speak now. As a healer, he'd seen the sickness about him the moment he'd stepped onto Fyrian soil. I knew it pained and angered him in ways only a healer might feel.

"He has to be near seventy turns, at least," Justis said. "Treven was watched carefully his last ten turns and he made no flights to Fyris during that time—Camryn forbade it."

"The question now is what are we to do with him?" Gurnil asked.

"I know what I want to do with him," Justis snorted.

"My question is what will Tamblin do now?" I blurted.

"He has a choice, doesn't he?" Dena offered. She sat next to me, quietly attending to the conversation. "He either attempts to follow his plan of invasion, or he returns to defend his throne. He must know by now that we've rescued Rath."

"Without Yevil at his side to pour poison in his ear, perhaps Father will see reason, now," Amlis grumbled.

I preferred not to rely on Amlis' hopes—Tamblin had his own demons and they drove him much of the time. I held no illusions that light would shine upon his blackened mind now that Yevil was gone. After all, he'd asked his eldest son to kill Yevil, likely knowing somewhere in the recesses of his soul that the Prince could die at Yevil's hand.

Then, after knowing Yevil was responsible for Timblor's death, he still allied himself with the known evil. Tamblin's senses had twisted long ago and there were no delusions in my mind that he would find rationality at last.

He'd killed his brother, too, as well as the Avii King and Queen. That act had started the sickness overtaking Fyris. Whether at Yevil's coaxing or by his own desire, he'd effectively killed the people of his kingdom. His desire to sail away from Fyris and attack the unknown was ludicrous.

"Look, we're exhausted. There will be time enough to discuss these things when we're rested," Amlis rose and stretched. "I'll speak with my uncle in the morning and we'll decide what to do then."

I waited until I'd shut the door of Justis' suite to work the kinks from my neck and shoulders. Justis stretched out his wings to relieve cramping from the hurried flight to Vhrist.

"I can probably remove the knots in your neck and shoulders," I offered.

"Please," Justis sank to his knees and allowed his wings to droop beside him. Placing my hands on the affected areas, I healed them of their aches. His skin was smooth and strong beneath my hands. I pulled away the moment I knew he felt better.

"Thank you—I have never had relief so quickly." Justis stood and without a backward glance, strode into his bedroom and shut the door.

"I intend to clear out the old healer's quarters and set up a clinic there for those who wish to seek treatment," Ordin announced over a late breakfast the following morning. "Medics from Berel's ships have offered to help and with their knowledge and the medicines they carry, it is my hope to relieve some of their suffering."

"That is an excellent idea," Kaldill agreed. "It will help in our investigation of the poison, I think. I wish to send samples to some I know, so they may work on the same problem from afar."

"I have word that some will come who are immune to all poisons," Daragar interjected. He sat with us, making himself smaller to fit the chairs about the long table in the King's chambers.

Except there was no King, and never had been. Tamblin named himself such, but he'd been deposed by his wife and son. Amlis would never call himself King, but I was concerned that Omina would consider herself Queen no matter what. I worried that things were moving too swiftly toward a less than ideal conclusion, but I had no authority and less desire to share that particular concern.

Who is coming? I ventured to send mindspeech to Daragar.

You will see, he replied.

He was right—I would see. All I had to do was look at them, after all. I'd seen what Daragar and Kaldill were, and they were very powerful. So far, none had defied what I could read in them.

Justis had been silent throughout the meal, choosing to listen to the others talk. I learned that Kaldill and Daragar had imprisoned Yevil—not in the dungeons beneath the castle but on the highest level, where the Avii once landed when they visited Tandelis.

I hadn't been to see the prisoner there, but many from the castle had already made their way up repaired steps to look upon a one-legged aberration. Yevil had no friends among the residents—he'd killed too many of their friends and family to have allies.

Varnell and his loyal guards, on the other hand, were in the dungeon—at Amlis' command. I hoped they weren't being mistreated, but had no desire to walk down stone steps to find out. I'd had enough of dark places for a while.

Instead, I considered helping Ordin clear out the old physician's quarters on the ground level in the older section of the castle. He'd ordered my nubs cut away every spring, and while that was always painful, Tamblin would have killed me if he'd known what they really were.

It made me wonder that Tamblin never knew about Yevil's nubs. Shaking that vision away, I turned back to the conversation.

Dena and I stood inside the physician's quarters later, staring at the piles of papers, shelves of glass bottles with who knew what inside them, furniture—broken and whole—scattered about and the windows tightly covered with wooden shutters.

"Worse than I imagined," Ordin sneezed at the dust covering everything. "Nevertheless, shall we?" He nodded at the task that lay before us. "Save all writings and anything you think may be of interest or have a bearing on the poison," Ordin added.

Lifting a wooden crate, I began to clear bottles off a shelf. These things would be left outside and carted away by castle servants—Amlis had decreed it.

～

Cloudsong

"Father, the ASD is here," Morid hissed. "Give yourself up and beg for leniency. Surrendering to them is preferable to capture, torture and death at Cayetes' hand."

"Surrender yourself. I don't intend to hand myself over to the ASD or those criminals," Marid snapped. "I have another place to go and plans to carry out. I care not what you and the rest of my family do."

"They are weary of running from the ASD, and even more weary of looking for Cayetes' thugs at every turn," Morid said. "They have no guilt in this matter."

"But you do," Marid's eyes narrowed. "Do you wish to die at the Vampire Queen's hands? She hates us still, you know."

"If you'd been honest at the beginning," Morid pointed out.

"Faugh, what would that have gotten us? We'd be dead."

"Cloudsong might have lived."

"How was I to know the bastard warlock would tap the core?"

"Give up, Father. Ask for mercy from the Founder, then. It will keep Cayetes away."

"He believes everything that witch tells him. She was a witch, you know, before she was vampire. That's why her son sits the throne of Karathia."

"We don't have time to discuss lineage," Morid complained. "They are getting close. They've already tripped my two outer sensing spells."

"Then stay and face their justice. I'm leaving. Come, Geng," Marid motioned for the Sirenali to follow him while pulling a leather bag into his arms. "Good luck, Son. I hope you live past sundown."

Marid and Geng disappeared, leaving Morid to shout after them.

～

Sector Two

Dorthil's Quarters

"Where is this Yokarun wizard you claim to know?" Sector Two's President Pragg demanded. "If he is powerful as you claim, we need his help now. Did he merely intend to trap you? If that's the case, I want no part of this."

The tap at Dorthil's door interrupted the standoff. "Master Crasz," Dorthil's guard appeared after Dorthil called out. "There's someone here to see you. He says his name is Marid of Yokaru, but he bears no resemblance to any Yokarun I've ever seen. He also has a strange one with him."

Le-Ath Veronis

"Morid, your crime is not reporting this sooner. Surely you realize this is madness," Lissa shook her head at Marid's eldest son. "Do you know where the spheres are buried?"

"No. Father sent them out and only told me he could find them later."

"You say he has a mute Sirenali with him?"

"Yes. Geng's tongue was removed long ago by one who wished not to have a Sirenali's obsession placed upon him."

"That would make sense," Kooper sat at the end of the table, helping Lissa question Morid. "You don't have to speak to hide criminals from everybody including the powerful, and there's no obsession if you can't speak the words."

"Fuck." Lissa uttered the one-word expletive and rose from her chair. "I have a good guess as to where Marid has gone; I've already asked Kaldill and Daragar to *Look* for the blank spot. Since Siriaa is a governed non-Alliance world, however, we have to ask permission to actively hunt for Marid and the Sirenali."

"I suggest we approach them soon—Marid may have plans to overthrow the government there—again. Once that happens, we'll never have permission because he'll be running the planet."

"And selling that poison crap to anyone who wants it, no matter the consequences," Lissa turned to level a gaze upon Morid. He shrank from her anger.

One does not anger a Vampire Queen. It would be wise never to anger Lissa, as she was so much more than that. Morid was only beginning to have an inkling as to what she was.

"I'll contact the Founder—we have to approach Siriaa soon or all may be lost," Kooper rose and nodded to Lissa. "Let me know if more information comes to light."

◈

Lironis

Quin

New guests arrived at sundown but I, covered in dust and filth from cleaning the old physician's quarters, went in search of a bath before meeting them. Dena followed, as did Ordin, and I missed the availability of water from pipes as servants heaved hot water and a tub up castle steps so I could clean myself.

Wolter led Dena and me to the kitchens after I was clean and dressed, to meet our new guests. I wondered at the location of our meeting, until I met the ones who'd come.

The men gravitated about the woman who'd arrived, and I could see why. She was beautiful, with long, silvery-white hair hanging to her waist. As powerful as Kaldill, too, although she was a quarter High Demon—a race naturally impervious to any poison, just as the Larentii were.

"You can see that, can't you?" She approached me. I almost cowered away.

"No," she touched my shoulder and then fingered my hair gently. "You have nothing to fear from me or any of these," she gestured toward the men behind her.

"She has nothing to fear," Kaldill appeared at my side. "By my command."

"The Elf King has spoken," Reah laughed. That was her name—

Reah. It was a lovely name—to speak and to hear.

"Reah is mated to my son—the Prince-Heir," Kaldill grinned, his eyes lighting with mischief. Reah swatted at his shoulder, deliberately missing. I could tell they were old friends, as well as related by marriage.

I wished I knew others like them, I realized. Friends who might tease one another and share many things without fear. Dena joined us in the kitchen and stopped short at the sight of Reah and the others.

"This is Reah," I began my introductions. "This is her mate, Torevik, his father, Gardevik, Kordevik, a guard, and this one—I know not his name." I stopped at the last man inside the kitchen, realizing that I couldn't see what or who he was; that had never happened before and I wondered at it.

"I am Kifirin," he nodded to me and smiled. "If the Elf King has you under his protection, then I shall uphold and strengthen that."

"Thank you, Lord Kifirin," Kaldill gave a respectful nod. "Your offer gladdens my heart."

"All of us have mindspeech," Reah continued. "Do not be afraid to speak with us in this way. No matter how far away we are, we will hear."

Good, I responded. *Something terrible has happened in Kondar's Sector Two. I felt it while bathing. I fear Lord Dorthil has a terrible ally at his side, and an even worse ally to hide behind.*

Le-Ath Veronis

"I think I scared her to death when I disappeared like that," Reah said, lifting the cup of tea Lissa offered.

"You think she can see through a Sirenali's fog?" Lissa shook her head.

"I hope that's what this means," Reah agreed. "Kaldill is sending mindspeech, telling me he is attempting to calm her, with Daragar's help. She thinks she did something wrong."

"That poor girl," Lissa rose to pace. Reah had arrived in the middle of the night, but then darkness was the rule on that half of Le-Ath Veronis. The planet rotated on its side to produce constant darkness for the vampires. Lissa and a few other vampires were able to walk in sunlight, but that was a tiny exception in the vampire world.

"She can read most anyone, but she couldn't read Kifirin," Reah went on. "These scones are good—who made them?"

"Cheedas—he found new recipes somewhere," Lissa mumbled, naming her chief cook. "Do you think I should come and take a look at this girl?"

"I don't want to frighten her more than she already is," Reah said. "She hasn't had an easy time of it, and those fool Avii tried to kill her when she was dumped on their doorstep."

"You say Kaldill is trying to help her?"

"He and Daragar both."

"Then I'll hold off—Ildevar is planning to approach the Kondari High President in two days—is there any chance we can clear the way on that?"

"The High President's son is there in Lironis, now, sending messages to his father."

"Then we'll use that," Lissa sighed. "I'll let Ildevar know. Kooper intends to travel with him, along with a few others."

"I'd ask him to choose his companions carefully," Reah said.

"I will."

Lironis

Quin

"I didn't want to make a mistake," I assured Kaldill, who fussed about me as if I really mattered. Wolter waited to bring me dinner, telling Dena that she'd worked hard all day and asking her to sit at the table in the kitchen to be served with me.

"Reah made this," Wolter set a wide bowl of food in front of me. "She calls it noodles in mushroom sauce. I've tasted it—it's wonderful."

Dena was served a fish course with her noodles, and both of us were in raptures at our first taste of the food. Whatever Reah was, she was also a master cook. I'd never tasted anything I liked so much.

Wolter, a fine cook himself, was very impressed by her skills. Kaldill continued to sit beside me while I ate, and Wolter offered a cup of watered wine with our meal. "This is worth cleaning out dusty old rooms any day," Dena smiled and sipped her wine.

We weren't finished with the physician's quarters, or even half finished. It would take two more days to clear everything out, and then another day or two to scour it and make it clean enough for Master Ordin's patients.

"We've made good progress," Ordin nodded his thanks to Dena and me. "It won't be long before everything is cleared away and cleaned well enough."

"When we get the bedroom and sitting rooms clean, I'll move equipment into it and start seeing patients," Ordin said.

"Not without a guard present," Justis said, striding into the kitchen. "We've just returned from a reconnaissance mission—Tamblin is making preparations to ride this way."

"Another mystery solved," Torevik said. "Bringing all his troops, I suppose?"

"Yes, and how is it that you speak our language?" Justis muttered, taking a seat next to Dena and accepting a plate of food from Wolter.

"We speak most languages," Torevik shrugged. "Call me Tory. Everybody does."

Justis was tall—Torevik—Tory, just as tall. I wondered if Tory could fight as well as Justis. If Tamblin were bent on causing trouble, that question could be answered soon.

Vhrist

Tamblin was furious and shouting at anyone who came close. Omina, whom he'd sent to Lironis to hold the throne for him, had brought winged devils back to Fyris and convinced them to fight for her.

He'd seen them himself—their black wings flapping far to the south as they spied on *him*—the King of Fyris. Rath had disappeared from his dungeon two nights earlier and ten guards were dead, another four wounded. Yevil was also gone; whether dead or captured, Tamblin didn't know. None remained to stand at his elbow; none that he trusted—or even half-trusted.

That had been Yevil's position. Half-trusted and dangerous. Tamblin's mind wandered to the case of weapons Yevil always hid in his quarters—surely he'd had one with him when he went to fight the winged ones. Those weapons had killed their kind before; why had they not worked this time?

Any guards who'd witnessed Yevil's failure and Rath's subsequent disappearance were now dead—most cut across the throat for a swift death. What had Yevil told him about the winged devils and the oath that kept them from killing anyone from Fyris?

Had that been a lie all along?

Perhaps he should have read some of those books in Tandelis' library before burning all of them. Yevil said they weren't needed. Until now, that had held true.

Tamblin could no longer sort truth from lie, and it made him angrier, still. "I want to leave now," he shouted at the servants, who scurried to pack faster.

~

Kondar: Sector Two

"What do you mean, Sector Four has withdrawn support?" Dorthil hissed at President Pragg's assistant.

"The communication is quite long, explaining all their reasons for pulling away from secession," the assistant handed a tab-vid to Dorthil. "President Pragg desires a meeting with you within three hours. He suggests bringing the Yokarun wizard with you." He nodded to Marid, who stood nearby.

"Do you need a healer?" The assistant gestured at Marid's nose.

"Have you never seen a nosebleed before? It is nothing," Marid waved a hand in dismissal. "Arrange the meeting. I will certainly come."

~

Lironis

"There is nothing I can do," Kaldill fingered the small plant in his hand. Its leaves were sparse and yellow where they should have been green. The limp stem bent over his fingers, as if it hadn't seen rain in a while. The ground was damp, however, so there was plenty of moisture. The soil itself was the problem. "The poison is too firmly entrenched in the land. Even if it were eliminated tomorrow, I couldn't cleanse the soil and begin again for millennia," he added.

"I suspected as much," Daragar agreed as he shortened his stride to walk beside the Elf King. They'd traveled a short distance from Lironis to examine the plants and animals outside the city. "Too much damage has been done to this small country, and the fact that it was hidden away from all others had already caused it to go stale."

"The farmers and herders know little about conservation," Kaldill agreed. "This is a lost cause."

"I will place that report in the Larentii Archives. May I attach your name to the assessment?" Daragar asked.

"Of course. It will please me to know that the Larentii trust my judgment."

"We do."

~

Quin

I wanted to keep working on the old physician's quarters, as that would take my mind off Tamblin's decision to attack Lironis. The moment Justis said the one who called himself King was preparing to ride for Lironis, I understood his intentions. If he had his way, Omina and Amlis would die.

I wondered to whom he'd assign the task of their killings—Yevil was no longer at his side and thirsty for blood.

I'd spent a long night, either sleepless or experiencing disturbing dreams that I couldn't recall upon waking. All of it left me unsettled and grateful for the dawn. The prospect of hard work would hold my fears at bay—at least I hoped it would.

Breakfast occurred in the kitchen, just like dinner the night before. Amlis had ordered the large table in Tamblin's suite brought down and the old table that wasn't nearly large enough was removed from the kitchen and stored in my old sleeping quarters.

Wolter and Reah had put their heads together and food appeared —I had no idea where the eggs had come from but I cared not—they were prepared in such a way that I savored the taste with much pleasure.

"We brought supplies from Le-Ath Veronis," Reah smiled at me as I gaped at the plate of fruit set near my elbow. "The Queen sends her regards."

"The Queen of Le-Ath Veronis is my mother," Torevik grinned. He sat across the table from me and then turned his smile on Reah.

Someday, I wanted to meet her, I think; she cared enough to send fruit and eggs for a lowly vegetarian. "Thank you," I nodded respectfully to Reah and Torevik. "I've never had food I liked so much."

"You should have food you like every day," Kaldill arrived and took a seat beside me. "Our prisoner on the roof tried to refuse his plate this morning, but the scent of eggs and ham finally convinced him otherwise."

"What about those in the dungeon?" I asked. In my mind, Varnell, on his very worst day, wasn't half as bad as Yevil on his best.

"They are receiving food and care—Varnell suffers from joint disease. Ordin has already provided medicines to relieve the pain. They also have clean blankets and pallets, plus a change of clothing every other day," Gurnil informed me.

"The whole palace is gossiping about us," I said, spearing a fat, red berry and stuffing it in my mouth. The flavor of it burst across my tongue and brought forth an unexpected smile.

"Many have never seen Avii—either too young or conscripted to work in the palace after Tamblin killed half the servants in the purge following Elabeth's death," Wolter muttered. He set a plate of ham on the table, in case anyone else wanted more before he took a seat at the end to eat with us.

"That's when you came, isn't it?" I asked.

"It is. My home was in Vhrist—the same as Chen and Fen's," he nodded. "I knew them before. Chen came with me; Fen followed quickly, at Rath's request."

"I couldn't stop Chen's death," I hunched my shoulders. "I barely sent mindspeech in time to save you and the Prince."

"That came from you." Wolter stilled for a moment. "Thank you. I had no idea."

"You thought me dead—and mute before that," I shrugged. "I'm sorry you ruined a good knife taking Hirill down. I knew he was dangerous, but couldn't tell anyone when I was here."

"The message you watched us write never left Fyris," Rath hobbled into the kitchen, helped along by Omina and Sophie. "I hear you're well-spoken as well as able to read and write."

"Any language," Berel, who sat across from me, nodded. In some way, Daragar had given Berel access to the Fyrian language. I had no idea how that was accomplished, but it made me glad—he would understand all conversations about him, which enabled him to relay swift information to his father.

"You're the one—the son? From the land Tamblin thinks to attack?"

"Yes, but Commander Justis says he has changed his mind and is now riding this way to reclaim the throne."

"Has a plan of attack been drawn up?" Rath dropped into an empty chair. Wolter rose to find plates for him, Omina, Sophie and Yissy, who appeared from behind Sophie's skirts with a mischievous smile.

"He should think twice before attacking ours," Torevik said, spreading butter over a thick slice of bread. "We're here to provide protection, no matter what type is needed."

"Troops from the ships will also fight," Berel agreed. "Does this Tamblin understand what he may be facing if he attacks?"

"No," Omina snorted. "He hasn't understood anything for a while. One moment he's ordering my death; in the next breath he's telling me to come to Lironis and hold the throne for him. He's mad and getting worse, I think. Have we gotten any useful information from Yevil?"

"Nothing we don't already know," Kaldill replied. "Daragar and I wish to set up a laboratory to study the poison consuming your lands. It is our hope to find a way to keep it from spreading too heavily to Siriaa's other continents. Is there a place that might be suitable for such?"

"You may have the area between the castle and the docks—it will provide easy access to those on the ships—they wish to help," Omina said. "I grant access to any ground you wish to excavate as well."

"I've had to place a shield about me—I can feel the land groaning with the disease if I don't," Reah said. I jerked my head in her direction —it was exactly what I felt daily.

"I feel the same," I ducked my head. "There will be no more harvests in Fyris and the people will die." I didn't tell her that in the last two days, the disease affecting the land had gotten worse. I couldn't explain it, so I kept the knowledge to myself.

"Yet Tamblin thinks to start a war with the Prince and me," Omina sighed. "He focuses on the wrong things and has since he took the throne."

"I worry that innocent men will die in a war, when we should concentrate our efforts on defeating the poison. If we don't, all of Siriaa faces extinction," I said.

"Has the poison passed the boundaries of Fyris, then?" Rath asked.

"It has," Berel confirmed. "My father's best scientists are at a loss as to what it is and how it might be neutralized."

"Elabeth knew," Justis snapped.

He was right—Elabeth had somehow kept it at bay in the past. Now she was dead and the poison threatened everything.

Again, I wished for the book Jurris kept from all. Perhaps it could tell us what we needed to know.

CHAPTER 6

L *ironis*

    Quin

Perhaps I should have expected it—with the Larentii and the Elf King involved. That evening, when I walked out of the old physician's quarters after a long day of cleaning, I could see the top of it past the castle walls. Gleaming in the late afternoon sun, it was constructed of metal and glass, much like some of the buildings I'd seen in Kondar.

To me it looked pristine—a clear surface upon which a study of the poison could be performed. Berel, walking down the stone path leading to the healer's quarters, offered a smile as he watched me gaze at the new research facility. I knew I was covered in filth, but couldn't help smiling back at him. "Daragar says there are showers in the new building, if you'd like to make use of them," Berel said.

"Really?" Dena stopped beside me and gave Berel a hopeful glance.

"Yes—there are several," Berel laughed. "Come. I think clothing can be found for you while you bathe."

"There are tales that Avii Castle was constructed in a day, but I never really believed it," Dena shook her head as we followed Berel toward the castle gate. "I believe it now."

"I watched it appear from nothing. Daragar says the Larentii and the powerful can manipulate atoms, so construction presents few problems to them."

"Atoms?" Dena failed to understand.

"I'll explain it later," Berel grinned. "Come on, I'm hungry. You must be, too."

"It will take Tamblin fourteen days to arrive with his troops—they cannot travel without rest," Rodrik said over dinner. This time, we'd gathered in the dining area of the new research building, which was equipped with a solar-powered kitchen.

Kaldill asked Reah to design it, and it was better than anything I'd seen—in Kondar or Avii Castle.

"I fear he'll take what he wants from the people along the way, and kill them if they refuse," Rath mused. "Whether it be food, beds or grain for the horses."

"Do you know the origin of your name?" Torevik asked Rath. "My last name is the same, and I wonder if there is a common root word in our pasts."

"I know little of our past," Rath shook his head.

Berel ducked his head—he knew something. I merely had to wait until later to find out what it was.

"The people of Fyris have no connection to either Kondar or Yokaru. They do have some connection to the Avii, although you can see the vast differences between the Avii and the Fyrians easily enough," Berel explained while pulling up a private file on his tab-vid. "Father received this information from his science staff."

Within the information given to Berel was a void, where other information had been removed. That worried me—why was it necessary to remove any information from the report?

"Did you see what the missing information was?" I turned to Berel.

"No. Father said it didn't have a bearing in their findings concerning the Avii and the Fyrians."

Still, I wanted to know what it was but didn't say it. Berel had already given me everything he had, and that was a very kind act of faith. Did Rath and Omina know that they might not be native to Siriaa? After all, that's what Berel thought, and I agreed with his assessment.

Where had the Avii and the people of Fyris originated?

How did they arrive, and why?

With the arrival of a Larentii, an elf and half and whole High Demons, I had no idea how many other worlds there might be, or what the Avii and Fyrians might have been before they were brought to Siriaa.

I had little information with which to comprehend any of those things.

~

I began cleaning the old physician's bedroom on the third day, while Dena worked in his library and Ordin began seeing patients in the outer rooms—those who were brave enough to approach a winged healer and his volunteer staff from the large ships anchored near Lironis. That meant he was seeing those who were worst off or in the most pain.

The old physician had died in his bed, which left a smelly mess behind. Rolling up covers first, I dragged them to the window and shoved them through and outside—I doubted Ordin wanted the bedding dragged past those who waited to see him at the door.

The old, straw-filled mattress came next, and I was grateful to get the smell of it shoved outside the room. This was the reason I'd offered to let Dena clean his library—the bedroom was an untidy clutter she shouldn't have to clear away.

We had cleaning supplies courtesy of the ships, and I was grateful as they helped clear away the smells. Next, I began to dismantle the bed—it was constructed of heavy, carved wood and slats.

That's when I found it.

The box was smooth on all sides and shut tightly. I might have thought it a child's coffin, except it was made of metal.

This metal shone in the dim light, letting me know it had been manufactured far from Fyris—they had not the skill to make something of this quality. It bore a strange, flat keyhole, too, but wasn't locked. What had the physician kept inside it? Cautiously I lifted the lid.

What I discovered revealed some truth about me, but I lacked sufficient knowledge to reason it out completely.

Within the box lay a strange material, with parts of it removed. The missing part was in the shape of a large doll—or a child. Upon closer examination, I found several hairs where the head would have lain.

Those hairs were the same colors as mine—gold, copper and silver. Nobody else had hair such as that—these were mine. Sometime in the past, when I was very small, I'd lain in this box.

Shutting it hastily, I shoved it away from me in horror.

"Quin, you seem distracted," Berel observed during lunch. I'd been forced to bathe after clearing out the bedding earlier, and after my discovery, had to force myself to keep working.

I'd also never taken anything in my life. I'd done so that day, hauling the metal box up castle steps until I reached Justis' suite. There, I hid the box beneath my bed in the tiny room next to his.

Nobody thought to stop me; perhaps they imagined the box was for Justis or another in the royal wing. Only servants saw me as it turned out, and they had their own duties. They'd never bothered with me before and that habit continued, although I now wore wings.

"Just reflecting on the old physician. He cut my wing nubs away when I lived here before," I offered to stave off Berel's curiosity. Yes, I was thinking about the physician, but I was thinking more about the box.

"Forget those times, Quin. They are in the past," Gurnil coaxed. He sat next to Dena, and they'd discussed what she'd found in the physician's library. Perhaps Gurnil would carry those old books back to Avii Castle with him, or perhaps he already had copies of those outdated medical texts.

Before, I would have been interested in any book. My mind had been taken over, however, by the mystery of a metal box found beneath the physician's bed.

I forced myself to pay attention during the rest of the meal, then made my way back to the physician's quarters to finish cleaning.

By the end of the day, Ordin's healing quarters were as clean as we could make them, and more supplies and equipment was ordered. Guards were assigned to Gurnil—both Black Wing and Fyrian. One of those guards was Yann, who'd pledged his loyalty first when Amlis and Omina arrived in Lironis.

He stood straighter and prouder, now, I noticed. In the past, I'd seldom seen him unless Varnell wanted something from the kitchens outside mealtimes.

"Quin, I'll ask you to spend time with me," Ordin said after dinner. I understood what he meant—he'd be asking me to heal those he deemed worthy. I nodded—we agreed on those things much of the time. I knew he'd listen, too, if I told him otherwise.

"Tomorrow morning, Master Ordin?" I asked.

"Yes, after breakfast."

I found it humorous that there was a balcony outside the third-floor kitchen in the research building—built not just for dining outside on a nice day, but as a landing space for those who could fly to get their meals.

An elevator was inside for those who had to walk and chose not to take the stairs. I also knew—whether anyone else did—that the research building could become a fortress if Daragar and Kaldill chose to make it so. It was powered by Siriaa's sun and was self-sufficient—including a machine that desalinated and purified drinking water from the sea.

Work had already begun on the lower levels of the facility and soil samples, brought in by residents of Lironis, were examined with equipment most of them had never dreamed of. They were paid, too, these contributors—with food and clean water kept in reusable metal jars.

Some of those jars bore a finish similar to that of the strange box I'd found. Storing that information away, I turned to the business of flying from the research building with Ordin after breakfast, to begin healing those we could.

～

"Prince Amlis, your father is killing many in his path. People are deserting villages far ahead of his army, now that they know he's coming," Justis stalked into Amlis' study, followed closely by Ardis.

"How do the villages know he's coming?" Amlis shook his head, confused by Justis' words.

"Two of our guests—Torevik and Kordevik—told them," Justis replied. "I see no reason to stop them; they're saving lives."

"I agree with you," Amlis rose from his seat and held up a hand. "I don't want people to die, either. Had I an army, perhaps we could convince Father to stop this madness."

"What would happen if he died? Would his army continue his quest?" Ardis asked.

"No, not since we hold Yevil," Amlis turned to look out his window. "Yevil would have commanded the army had my father fallen, but without his presence, I imagine that many, especially recent conscripts, will merely desert and ride homeward."

"Then there's a simple solution to this problem," Justis muttered. "You don't have an army and it will go badly for all if the Kondari are forced to fire upon your father's troops."

"You're talking of killing my father," Amlis hissed, turning a swift, angry gaze upon Justis.

"Who has killed too many already, including your uncle and the Avii King and Queen. He is also responsible—with that aberration we hold on the roof of your castle, for killing an entire planet. That's what is happening, or have you not reached that conclusion yet?"

Justis' anger frightened Amlis, but he refused to back down. "Can we not capture him instead? We hold Yevil already—I blame him most for the crimes you listed."

"We can attempt a capture, but I warn you now—should it not be successful, his death will be warranted. He's cutting a swath through an already sick and threatened population, employing murder and theft wherever it pleases him."

"Do you have a plan of capture?" Amlis took his seat again with a troubled sigh.

"Not yet. I believe something can be arranged. I'll let you know." Justis rustled his wings and swept from the room.

Amlis was left to wonder whether Tandelis had ever witnessed the anger of the Avii.

"Father, I have received word that you should expect visitors," Berel began. He held his tab-vid aloft while a smiling Reah and Kaldill stood behind him.

"What visitors?" Edden smiled at his son. "Those two behind you, perhaps?"

"If you'd like us to come," Kaldill nodded. "Although more important visitors are scheduled to arrive. We merely wanted to coordinate with you to find an acceptable time."

"I'd like to meet you," Edden said. "Is it possible to bring Berel and Quin, too? I can arrange for an airchopper from the ship to deliver you to Kondar."

"We have our own transportation, but yes, I will be happy to bring Quin and your son for a visit."

"I will clear my schedule for tonight; will that leave you enough time to arrive?"

"More than enough," Kaldill agreed.

"Will you arrive in time for dinner? How many guests should I expect?"

"Reah and I will bring Quin, Daragar and Berel. Ildevar Wyyld, Founder of the Reth Alliance, will arrive with two others. That makes eight guests, although only seven will be dining," Kaldill chuckled.

"I'll make arrangements, then," Edden nodded. "A Founder of an Alliance, you say?"

"Yes. You have nothing to fear; Ildevar is one of the finest people I know."

~

Sector Two

Dorthil's Quarters

"You think I don't have spies in Kondar? Think again," Dorthil hissed at President Pragg. "Charkisul is being approached tonight by the Founder of the Reth Alliance. We must act quickly to destroy both. Once we're in charge of Siriaa, they'll never get their claws locked on it."

"Founder? Reth Alliance? What are you talking about?" Pragg growled. "There is no Reth Alliance, unless Yokaru has hidden something from us all along." He spat his last words in Marid's direction.

"Yokaru? Faugh," Marid gestured angrily. "I only told you Yokaru before, because you have no idea what lies beyond this planet. The Reth Alliance swallows planets and demands they conform to their rules and standards. Is that what you want for Siriaa?"

"They will make us slaves? Is that what you mean?"

"Slaves to their will," Marid blustered. Dorthil realized then that the wizard had lied to him all along, but as the lies fell in with his own desires, Dorthil kept the information to himself.

"What can we do? Shall I contact the other Presidents?"

"Too late for that—they'll dither while we must take action," Marid said. "I will take you to the High President's dinner tonight. If you choose to kill him and his guests while we're there, I'll be happy to lend a hand." Marid wiped blood away from his nose with a dark handkerchief, its red color hiding the blood it already bore.

Lironis

  Quin

"Quin, we're going to Kondar for dinner tonight," Berel beamed at me. He'd run down castle steps to arrive at the healer's quarters as quickly as he could. He looked forward to seeing his father, I could tell.

"Who is going with us?" I asked. I had to know—I felt growing danger about the High President, but didn't wish to alarm his son.

"Reah, Kaldill and Daragar. Father will see a Larentii for the first time. Kaldill says others will arrive; he named the Founder of an Alliance. Isn't that exciting?"

My shoulders sagged in relief when he listed those accompanying us. Too many things troubled my mind of late, and some of them, understandably, swirled about a metal box.

"I will find Daragar, then. I wish to speak with him," I said.

"I heard my name," Daragar appeared magically at Berel's side. He smiled at me, and that served to slow and warm my heart. It was beating too quickly, and I felt chilled and terrified by all I knew.

"Sit here," Daragar settled me on a bench on the research building balcony. "Do you wish to only speak with me, or will you allow Kaldill to attend?"

"He can come," I hunched my shoulders. "It's only fair that he hears this, too."

"Hear what?" Kaldill appeared. He'd been called, I suppose, the moment I gave Daragar permission to include him.

"I keep hearing the name Marid. In my dreams and at other times. Do you know of such?" I asked.

Daragar glanced at Kaldill before turning back to me. "I do. Do you have other information?"

"I feel the High President is in peril because of this name," I stuttered. "I feel better, knowing you will be there with him tonight, but I feel this Marid is more than dangerous."

"Dangerous only to the High President?"

"Dangerous to all of Siriaa," I shuddered. At that moment, I wanted more than anything to tell Kaldill and Daragar about the metal box, but was terrified by what I might learn. I kept my lips pressed tightly together as I'd often done in my past, shoving that desire away.

"Quin, I have asked that something appropriate be brought for you to wear," Kaldill said. "If you wish to have more clothing than that, Daragar and I can provide it."

"What I have is good enough to work in." I ducked my head as heat warmed my cheeks.

"That is not what we meant," Kaldill was up and kneeling before me, lifting my chin. I blinked into eyes that were neither gold nor green, but a mixture of both. Now, they were filled with concern —for me.

"You know even the lowliest servant here has something to wear for special occasions. Why should you be different?" Daragar asked.

I'd been different all my life. Was different now. The box I'd found might tell a tale of just how different I was. Nevertheless, these two deserved an answer, and appreciation for their offer.

"Yes—I'd like something pretty," I confessed. I'd never had anything that qualified as such—even Amlis' uniforms had been utilitarian. Nowadays, I was grateful to have clothing I didn't have to scrub myself.

"You shall have pretty things—I command it," Kaldill waved a hand and smiled.

"Is that all it takes?" I couldn't help smiling back at him. As ancient as he was, he had a young heart.

"Quin," he placed both his hands on my face, then, and held it gently, "the flowers in spring bloom beautifully, even if they've been trampled during the winter by those who have no care for such. It is hope, I think, that keeps it so."

He placed a kiss on my forehead, then, before disappearing.

Reah identified the color of my dress as turquoise, and it fit snugly beneath my arms and wings, hugged my breasts and then fell in graceful folds down to my ankles. Soft shoes completed my outfit in a pale, golden color.

I'd found the dress lying across my bed when I finished helping Ordin with his patients. More people had shown up than had come the previous day, so word was spreading that the winged healer and those who assisted him could indeed relieve their aches and illnesses.

We'd had a few who needed dental care; those were handled by some from one of the ship's crew. I was grateful that was so—merely watching them numb sore mouths made me shiver.

Pushing the events of the day aside, I walked out of my bedroom to find Justis waiting. He appeared uncomfortable, for some reason. "Make sure you stay safe," he said abruptly and left the suite in a rustle of feathers.

Breathing a sigh, I walked out behind him to meet with Kaldill and the others.

"Are you sure you wish to embroil yourself in this quest?" Justis asked. He watched as Torevik cleaned blades that were longer than he was tall. He could tell they were heavy, too, by the way Tory handled them.

"Absolutely. We went to two villages Tamblin's army hit on their journey from Vhrist. I have no qualms about taking him into custody. I believe there are some who wish to question him—aside from you," Tory nodded in Justis' direction.

"Can you wield those—with effectiveness?" Justis ventured to ask.

"Not as I am now. Pray that you don't see what I can become to wield these properly."

Justis held his questions back; he had no desire to anger Tory. "I'm nearly ready," Tory said in the silence that followed. "Say the word and we'll go."

⁓

"Are you sure this is a good idea—going without Quin to guide us? She led us straight to Rath the last time," Ardis observed.

"It's why they called her Finder when she lived here," Justis explained. "She can find things. Torevik assures me he can do much the same, using one of his talents. We will see how effective it is."

"We could wait until Quin returns," Ardis began.

"I want this usurper in custody tonight," Justis growled.

⁓

Avii Castle

"A message from Commander Justis," a black-winged guard bowed to Jurris before handing the parchment to the Avii King.

Jurris examined the seal on the rolled message, determining that it hadn't been tampered with. "Very good, that will be all," Jurris waved the guard away before cracking the seal.

My King, the message began,

My men and I have killed Fyrians when they attacked us, with no adverse effects. Liron either chose not to interfere, or supports us in our efforts. Tonight, we go in search of the usurper. The Prince has asked us to take him into custody rather than killing him and for now, I will honor that request.

I ask that you search your private treasury for the weapons stored there by Camryn. It is my belief that they were transported to Fyris in the past. Even if your treasury is intact, other weapons of a similar nature have been found here and that should not be. The Larentii assisted in rendering them harmless, which is a welcome relief.

Already we have in custody the one Quin spoke of—the one calling himself Yevil. He it was who had the weapons in his possession. We have discovered through evidence attached at the end of this message, that Treven fathered him. I hope this does not upset you, as he is directly responsible for Camryn and Elabeth's deaths.

Your brother and Commander of the Guard,

Justis.

Affixed to the bottom of the message was a tiny, red feather. Jurris cursed and flung the message across his study.

∾

Kondar

Quin

"Welcome," Edden Charkisul beamed at us the moment we were ushered into the entry of his residence. Berel wanted to run but chose to walk sedately toward his father, before Edden enveloped him in a warm embrace.

I was grateful that such love existed between them. Grateful, too, that Edden had seen to Berel's education—he was impressive in his role as temporary Commander of the fleet anchored near Lironis.

"Where are the others?" Edden asked when he and Berel stepped away from one another.

"We are here, High President." I blinked in astonishment at the three who'd come.

∾

Quin says Marid intends an attack of some sort, Kaldill sent to Ildevar as Ildevar gripped Edden's hand and offered polite greetings.

The High President fears something as well, but his fear is less focused, Ildevar replied as he offered the gifts he'd brought with him—Tiralian crystal and ripe gishi fruit.

Where did the Tiralian crystal come from? Kaldill asked.

I have friends, Ildevar sent a mental laugh. *Does Quin say when the attack might occur?*

I believe the attack is in flux—perhaps he is gathering his courage or his power. Reah believes he is aging, although he still appears young to most. Belancours have always been adept at illusion.

With Reah here, his wizardry will be neutralized if he comes close enough, Ildevar pointed out. "This is my trusted advisor, Willem Drifft," Ildevar made the introduction aloud. "And this," he indicated his other companion, "is Kooper Griff, my security for the evening." Edden greeted both and then gestured for his guests to join him in the dining room.

With Daragar here, Marid may as well give himself up before he starts. Kaldill said as they walked to the dining room with the others.

The Larentii are wonderful when they're given permission to intervene, are they not?

I believe the Wise Ones may have weighed in on this decision, Kaldill responded. *Daragar's feelings for Quin play a part as well. He cares very much for her.*

Let us hope all goes well, then, and we capture Marid without bloodshed. Lissa wishes to speak with him most urgently.

Master Norwal, I sent mindspeech to the High President's Chief of Security, *one of the High President's servers is a spy.*

"Quin?" Melis Norwal barely blinked as he turned in my direction. We'd already been served the first course, and I'd determined that the food was safe. The young man who looked uncomfortable in his uniform had drawn my attention immediately, and I knew he'd fed information to the Sector Two President and the one who called himself Marid.

I mentally described our server to Melis as the young man in question walked out of the dining room. Melis was on his feet, reaching for his weapon when the assassins landed in the vestibule outside.

~

Fyris

"Follow me," Tory said as he walked toward the army encampment. Makeshift tents and campfires dotted the landscape before Justis and his Black Wings as they followed cautiously behind Tory.

Justis almost backed away when they were attacked by ten soldiers wielding blades; Tory changed before his eyes. Became taller. Black-scaled. His face flattened and horns appeared, curving around his ears and revealing sharp tips extending past his forehead. He had wings as well—similar to those a bat might have. Smoke drifted from his nostrils as the long swords he carried were drawn into his hands. Deftly handling both blades, Tory killed two attackers swiftly before the others backed away.

The second attack was laughable when it came; three men died before another dozen chose to run from Torevik Rath's High Demon Thifilathi. The third attack was merely a gesture—one died while his companions raced away. After that, soldiers and commanders alike gave way as six black-winged men and one tall, bat-winged creature stalked through their camp toward the King's tent.

Tamblin and a few personal guards stood outside the tent eventually, watching the seven approach. Tamblin's sword was in his hand but he trembled, whether with rage or fear, Justis cared not. This was the other half of his intended revenge—the second plotter in Elabeth and Camryn's deaths.

He intended that they would pay for their crimes—when he could convince others that it should be so.

"I name you murderer," Justis now strode beside Tory and pointed a finger accusingly at Tamblin. "Lay down your weapon and we will not hurt you—at Prince Amlis' request."

"That bastard is no Prince," Tamblin hissed, shaking with rage. "He is not my son. Ask anyone."

"He is your son," Tory breathed smoke, his voice low and guttural. "It has been verified scientifically. It is your mind that is weak, not your child."

"Scientifically? What word is that?" Tamblin spat back. Tory, Justis and the others halted, barely four steps from Tamblin.

"Something I doubt you'll ever understand," Tory replied, lifting one of his blades to rest the tip against Tamblin's throat. "Drop your weapons and you will not be harmed."

Tamblin's guards dropped their swords and pulled daggers from boots, letting them fall to the ground before stepping back with their hands raised.

Tamblin refused to give up his sword.

"Do you wish to do this, Commander Justis?" Tory turned to Justis, his dark eyes narrowing as he jerked his dark-scaled head in Tamblin's direction.

Justis knew his own expression was locked in a furious snarl. "I wish it," he hissed. Before Tamblin could protest, Justis wrenched the sword from his hand, tossed it away and shoved the self-proclaimed king against the center pole of his tent. The angry Black Wing Commander then held Tamblin's arms ruthlessly behind his back so Ardis could shackle him.

"This is what happens when your people see you as a tyrant," Justis hissed in Tamblin's ear before letting go.

"We must go," Tory snapped suddenly. "I've received a message from Reah. Things are not going well in Kondar."

Official Report
Kooper Griff, Director, Alliance Security Detail
The meal was in progress; the Founder was deep in conversation with the Kondari High President, describing how the Alliance was formed and how it worked. Quin, the young woman previously listed as a witness, sent mindspeech to the High President's security chief, alerting him to the presence of a spy posing as one of our waiters.

The security chief, Melis Norwal (also listed as a witness), stood to go after the suspect when Marid of Belancour arrived with Sector Two President Pragg (see attached list of Kondari rulers and politicians), a mute Sirenali and two others, all except the Sirenali heavily armed.

Marid, head of household and chief wizard of the Belancour clan, held a ranos pistol, which I recognized quickly. He'd come prepared and armed, in case his wizardry didn't work against any of us. Reah Desh Silver, of High Demon ancestry and formerly an agent for the ASD (see records), prevented Marid's wizardry from having any effect and protected the rest of us in the dining hall with the neutralizing ability a High Demon possesses.

Marid and his companions fired their weapons, then, never expecting that Daragar (a Larentii) would provide an impermeable shield to protect us. At that time, Marid discovered that he and the others with him were trapped —Reah kept him from using wizardry to escape and the Larentii placed a second shield to keep him from running away.

What Marid did then, none of us expected. His smile was touched by madness as he pointed the ranos pistol at himself and fired before anyone could stop him. Quin, the young woman, shrieked and fainted as Marid's head exploded and his blood bathed anything nearby—so violent was his death and Quin's reaction to it, that it took some time and effort to revive her afterward.

Sadly, the news she delivered when she awakened was not good. See attached witness report, labeled appropriately with her name and the date it was recorded.

≈

Lironis

Omina studied Tamblin, who now shared the shielded cell with Yevil atop the castle in Lironis. She wished to spit upon him, but the shield kept anything from traveling through the clear, impermeable surface.

Torevik and the others who remained, including those from Avii Castle, had been in private meetings since their return, with only a few hours' sleep in between. Omina had no idea what they were discussing; she only cared that Tamblin was safely held away from her, Amlis and any other.

She wondered at that moment how many deaths Tamblin had ordered, and how many of those deaths were by Yevil's command or suggestion. "You always were a pig," Omina hissed at him.

Tamblin, sitting cross-legged on the stone floor of his invisible cage, refused to raise his head or acknowledge Omina's presence. He and Yevil had barely spoken to one another, too; they'd taken opposite ends of their cage and both sat on the floor of it.

Yevil's remaining leg kept him from standing for long periods, although he did stand upon occasion, to stretch.

"Filth," Omina flung at Yevil before gathering her skirts and whirling to stalk away. She cared not what happened to either, but death would be her first choice.

~

Kondar

Quin

Ildevar Wyyld, Founder of the Reth Alliance, was an honorable man. He was also many other things, but an honorable man was what I told Edden Charkisul when he asked me about him the following afternoon.

"You think the Reth Alliance is also honorable?" Edden asked.

"I can see that in him, too," I nodded. Ildevar had already offered teams of scientists who would travel to Fyris and study the poison. It was in his best interests to do so—Marid, just before his arrival at the High President's palace, had released hundreds of spheres containing the poison on hundreds of worlds—many of those worlds members of the Reth Alliance. Those worlds were now infected with the same poison that threatened Siriaa.

Marid had been a fool—a treacherous one—and, as he'd managed to ensure the murders of too many people to count with his final act of perfidy, I silently cursed his name.

CHAPTER 7

Le-Ath Veronis

Queen Lissa studied the ranos pistol taken from Marid's hand—it was relatively new and had likely been bought on the black market. The five others lying beside it in evidence trays were older. Far older.

"Ancient," she sighed before lifting her eyes to Kooper Griff's. "This is the worst possible outcome, isn't it? Do we have any idea which worlds are now infected?"

"Quin could only give us a partial list, and we're verifying what she gave us. She was only able to read a few things in Marid before he blew his head off."

"How many did she give you?"

"Twenty-six—that number is good and bad. Good that we have names for them, bad because she claims there were hundreds of those containment spheres that Marid spilled before traveling to Sector Five."

"Morid has no idea where his father put them—I've already tried compulsion. He knows nothing."

"The Sirenali is in your dungeons, but he's so happy that he's no longer under Marid's thumb that he doesn't mind being locked in a cell."

"Can anyone communicate with him?" Lissa asked.

"We haven't really tried—all we've done is mime eating and sleeping," Kooper shook his head.

"Ask Morid, then. Maybe he knows. I'm hoping the Sirenali will have information the others don't. He may be able to lead us to other worlds Marid infected. If we can find the infection points, we can quarantine the area until we find a remedy."

"If we don't find them, the entire planet could die and we'll be looking to relocate as many as we can."

"We don't have enough planets to effect mass relocations," Lissa pointed out. "Quarantine is much better if we can get to it in time."

"I'll get on it right away," Kooper promised.

Lironis

"You're needed," Justis stepped inside Amlis' study after knocking twice.

"For what? I've already been to the roof and spoken to my father. He chose to remain silent."

"For a meeting, and then to lead your troops back here before dispersal—I hear many of them are still heading this way and stealing what they don't have funds to pay for," Justis snapped.

"May Liron have mercy," Amlis scrubbed a palm over his face before rising. "Lead the way—let's get this meeting over with. Rodrik!"

Kondar

"Father, Kaldill says there's an important meeting happening in Lironis, and he says Quin and I should be there. May I have your permission?" Berel gazed hopefully at his father.

"Of course. Quin assures me that the threats against my life have been neutralized for the moment; therefore, it is imperative that you go. Report back to me as quickly as you can."

"I will." Berel moved forward to embrace his father. "This is terrible news—that other worlds are now infected," Berel said after pulling away. "Perhaps this is what the meeting is about."

"I hope some cure can be found—the images you sent of the land and the people of Fyris tell my scientists that the poison will kill them soon if things do not change. The samples we're collecting from seawater shows the poison is increasing. Siriaa will be engulfed in it if something isn't done soon."

"I find it interesting that some still wish to engage in self-serving political pursuits while the fate of their planet is of no concern and its people are dying."

"It will always be thus," Edden's brow furrowed with concern, "As much as we think it should be otherwise."

~

Lironis

Quin

I felt as if my wings dragged the floor behind me when we returned to Lironis. Events from the evening before haunted me still and Berel was nearly as troubled as I concerning the aftermath.

He, Daragar and Kaldill surrounded me as I made my way to the Prince's chambers—he'd taken Tamblin's suite for himself and had his library and clothing moved over. As yet, he hadn't officially taken control of Fyris, but it needed to happen soon—the people required a steady hand and a wiser head than Tamblin's in the coming days.

I understood, too, that Amlis had to take jurisdiction over the remnants of Tamblin's army, to keep them from plundering the farms and villages between them and Lironis. Rodrik would take charge of the troops, I guessed, once Amlis appeared and named himself Prince of the people.

There would be no king in Fyris—Justis would make sure of that—

at Jurris' command. Omina would no longer call herself Queen—Justis would see to that, too.

Once we arrived in Amlis' new meeting room and took our seats at the table, Reah rose to speak. "I've asked two others to come at Kifirin's request," she announced before nodding to Kifirin. "I believe they may be able to shed light on Tamblin's behavior in the past. It is my hope we can explain everything before the meeting ends, but the news will be troubling, to say the least."

Two people appeared beside her. One was another of her mates—his name was Gavril, although most people called him Teeg. The other Reah saw as a father, although they were not related by blood. I could see this in her, as I could read nothing from him—he was too powerful.

"This is Karzac, the best physician I know," Reah introduced him, first. "Anything you hear from him will be truth, no matter how difficult it may be to accept."

Until Reah's announcement, I had no idea the prisoners would be brought to the meeting. Justis, Ardis and two other Black Wings brought them in. Yevil cursed but quieted immediately when Justis sent a dark look his way. Yevil was then seated in a chair against the wall while Tamblin was brought forward.

Tamblin growled softly but refrained from expressing his opinion with words anyone could understand. "Seat him here," Karzac pushed a stool toward Justis, who, with Ardis, held Tamblin between them.

Justis shoved Tamblin onto the stool when he attempted to resist. Tamblin sat, his anger apparent as his face darkened. Karzac approached him, gesturing for Justis and Ardis to back away.

Tamblin thought to escape when they took their hands off him. With an unconcerned wave of a hand, Karzac's power shoved Tamblin down again. He didn't attempt to rise a second time; instead, his body trembled at the power employed to hold him in place.

"Please observe," Karzac turned toward the table and nodded.

Reaching out a hand, he held it for a moment at the back of Tamblin's neck. Tamblin shrieked as something burst from his neck and slapped into the physician's hand.

Ordin, sitting across the table, gasped at what Karzac had done. I blinked in astonishment—something had been buried in Tamblin's neck, for who knew how long? He wasn't aware of it, I knew that much. I'd have seen it in him, otherwise.

After using his other hand to heal the bloody wound left on Tamblin's neck, Karzac strode toward the table and set the tiny object before Teeg. Teeg examined it closely for a moment before lifting his gaze and nodding to Karzac.

"It's a controller," Reah's voice trembled.

"Where did that come from?" Justis strode forward and lifted Yevil by burying a fist in his shirt collar and jerking him from his seat against the wall.

"My father," Yevil spit in Justis' face.

"This device is so old it operated intermittently, which ensured that Tamblin at times had control over his thoughts. At other times, when the controller worked, he was under Yevil's spell," Karzac explained.

"At this point, there isn't enough of his mind left to heal," he added. "It appears that many of Yevil's commands coincided with Tamblin's desires, so it would be more than difficult to sort controlled actions from uncontrolled ones."

"It matters not to me—a murderer is a murderer," Justis growled.

"I feel the same," Karzac nodded. "It is not my position to interfere —I merely wish to explain what I know. The decisions based on those facts will be yours to make."

"I want to know where it came from; I've not heard of such in Camryn's treasury, which now belongs to Jurris," Gurnil fumed. "I doubt you can believe anything that liar Yevil says. He is the same as his father, who also spoke nothing but lies."

"We know those ancient weapons used by Yevil to kill the Avii

King and Queen were kept there," Justis said quietly. "While I know of nothing like this controller device, that doesn't mean that it also didn't come from there. My question is this—why were those weapons in Camryn's treasury in the first place? Berel says there are none such as these created on Siriaa, and neither Fyris nor the Avii have the technology required to produce them."

Silently I sat and listened to the debate as it went on; Amlis and Rodrik had left only a few moments earlier, after ordering as many men as they could muster to travel with them. I had the idea that someone might transport them to the army so any damage caused by that now headless horde could be held to a minimum.

Somehow, in my mind, I understood that the unusual weapons and devices had arrived when the Avii and Fyrians did, but I had no guess as to when that was or from where. It was a puzzle that I had few resources to solve, after all, no matter how much I wanted to do so.

Had the metal box been transported at the same time? That thought was so far-fetched I discarded it immediately. I was no ancient object, after all. I was flesh, blood and bone; I bled when cut or whipped and my bones had broken—I'd experienced all those things in my brief lifetime.

"It is clear that Treven stole from Camryn," Justis said. "And Yevil used that stolen property to kill. I would prefer that we take him to the King and allow Jurris to pass sentence. If I know my brother, he will force Yevil through the gate."

"What about Tamblin?" Omina asked. "I'd prefer that Jurris pass judgment upon him as well."

"Amlis asked us not to kill him," Justis muttered.

"Amlis is on his way to the army Tamblin conscripted. Tell me Tamblin didn't order them to perform heinous acts against the people of Fyris," Rath spoke for the first time. "He attempted to kill my sister and me. How do you think we feel about that?"

"He and Yevil tried to kill Amlis—several times," I spoke without realizing. "By poison, twice by ambush; these are the acts of mad men," I concluded. "Both are responsible in some way for Timblor's death."

"I have no doubt those things are true," Omina wept. I knew she cared for her eldest, but he'd aptly followed his father's lead, rather than taking a stand against his injustices. I would speak no support of Timblor, whether he was loved or not. He'd taken pleasure in my beating when I'd acted to save Amlis' life. He would have made a cruel king, had he taken Tamblin's place.

My dear, I see the sorrow on your face. Do not fret—all will come right, Kaldill spoke in my mind.

At that moment, I knew two things—first, I wanted to huddle against him while past memories plagued me and new ones troubled me more. Second, I wanted to tell him those things, but dared not. The answers to the ensuing questions could harm me more than the questions themselves.

"I suggest we wait for Amlis' return; he will make the final decision on his father's fate," Justis decided. "Yevil will go to Jurris for judgment."

Le-Ath Veronis

"They had a controller, Mom," Teeg dropped onto a chair next to his mother's in the arboretum atop her palace. "It's not modern and larger by comparison to the one I created, but it worked well enough to do what Yevil wanted."

"I guess you'd know what one looked like, then" Lissa huffed. "I'm grateful they're outlawed everywhere, now. They're an abomination."

"I know," Teeg held up a hand. "That's the past and I understand my mistakes. We won't visit that again. Reah glared at me the whole time I was there because of it."

"You think she's not justified?"

"She is, but there are extenuating circumstances. You have to believe I'd never do that when I'm completely sane. Besides, Tybus would kill me. He wouldn't bother to think about it first; he'd just do it."

"I know. He'd probably have help."

"I understand that."

"From me."

"Mom!"

"Come on, it's time for dinner," Lissa stood and jerked her head toward the door. "You coming?"

"I'm coming."

~

Lironis

"You may want this," Ordin handed a leather-bound book to Gurnil.

"Have you read it?" Gurnil accepted the book and examined the cover. The leather was darkened by age but still pliable—the old physician had kept a personal journal throughout his life.

"No. I have no idea who could be interested in it; I may offer it to Quin to read and ask for a more legible report to be handed to me afterward. She seems depressed after the events in Kondar; perhaps a reading assignment will help."

"A good idea. She's always happy to read," Ordin agreed. "We'll have patients again tomorrow, but I'll only keep her four hours. She can read after the midday meal."

"Good. How are they, by the way? The citizens of Lironis?"

"Starving. Sickly. Many of them suffer from the early stages of the wasting disease. I've held Quin back from healing that—they'll only get it again."

"That's my fear, also. When does Justis plan to take Yevil to Avii Castle?"

"Tomorrow."

~

Quin

"Will you read this for me and provide a report for the Library records?" Gurnil handed a leather-bound book to me after dinner.

"This is the old healer's journal and I feel you would better understand it, as you've spent most of your life here. Something you may find important I might discount altogether."

"When would you like your report?" I asked, taking the softbound book from Gurnil.

"Whenever you have time," he waved a hand and smiled. "I hope it is interesting reading."

A part of me hoped it was, too. Nevertheless, I was glad to get it —and worried at the same time. *What if the answers to my question about the metal box lay within its pages?* Recalling my manners, I stammered polite thanks to Gurnil and went to find Berel and Dena.

"Ardis says they're leaving tomorrow to take Yevil to Avii Castle," Dena said. I'd found her and Berel inside Berel's suite—he'd moved to the research building as he was more comfortable there.

His guards from the ship were also more comfortable there, although they hadn't complained about quarters in the castle. They stood outside the suite door, allowing us to talk.

"Are they flying or taking an airchopper?" I turned to Berel.

"I offered an airchopper. They prefer to fly him in," Berel shrugged.

"Do you think it will be a form of torture, to hold him aloft over the sea for hours?" I asked Dena.

"If I were unable to fly, I'd think it torture," she blew out a breath.

"Then it will be awful for him," I said. "Perhaps he deserves it. Will they continue to fly if it rains?"

"They'll only search for land if hail falls, and that seldom happens at this time of year."

I recalled riding in a hailstorm with Amlis and Rodrik, but didn't say that. I didn't envy the journey Justis was determined to make, but it was evident that he'd kept his troops trained and ready, no matter the circumstances.

I doubted Jurris cared whether the troops were trained or not—all he cared about was himself most of the time. He hadn't really cared about Halthea—he'd only cared about the color of her wings.

Justis—as did I—hoped that one day, Jurris would be half the King Camryn had been. I hoped for all the Avii that the day would come soon. After all, when I worked in the kitchen at Avii Castle, Justis had no care for me but he ensured that the Black Wing who'd pulled my wing nub and drew blood was punished. Jurris wouldn't have done anything to help a half-blood girl, dumped on his doorstep as I was.

Even Ardis recognized that fairness in Justis and gave him respect. Dena still slept in Ardis' suite, in her own bed—for now. I could see his eyes following her at times. I also knew he would never hurt her, or ask for what she wasn't willing to give.

Dena was beginning to care for Ardis, and as I didn't want to interfere in any way, held back from asking. She would tell me when she was comfortable with the new feelings she carried.

"Quin?" Reah tapped on Berel's open door.

"Reah?" I slid off Berel's couch, grateful I didn't stutter her name. She was the most beautiful woman I'd ever met, and with the power she held, she was magnificent. It was difficult to comprehend that the others failed to see these things in her.

"I have a request," she smiled at me. "From Torevik's mother, Queen Lissa. She would like you to visit—the Sirenali that Marid had with him in Kondar cannot speak and neither of us can read anything from him. We'd like to see if you can tell us anything about him."

"I'm not sure whether I can," I shook my head. I hadn't bothered with him—I'd focused on Marid because he held vital information. I'd only gotten a little of the knowledge needed from him before he killed himself.

"Will you try?" Reah's green eyes begged me to say yes. "Besides, the Queen would like to meet you. Gurnil and Ordin have volunteered to come with you, as have Kaldill and Daragar."

"May I go?" Berel asked. I realized then that we'd be traveling far away from Siriaa. Berel was excited by the prospect; I was terrified.

"Kaldill and Daragar will come?" I quavered.

"Yes. There is nothing to fear, I promise."

"Then I'll come. I don't wish to disappoint anyone; I can only promise to try to read this man."

"Sirenali," Reah corrected gently.

"As you say," I hunched my shoulders. "How should I dress?" It was a valid question—I didn't wish to offend a Queen.

"Dress nicely, but for comfort," Reah smiled. "The Queen isn't particular."

"I'll help," Dena stood with a smile.

Not long after, I was herded back to the research building where Berel, Kaldill, Daragar, Reah, Gurnil and Ordin waited. Torevik intended to come as well—the Queen we would visit was his mother.

As quickly as Daragar could transport me to Kondar, this trip was just as swift. I marveled at the ability to fly through the stars and arrive far away in less than a blink. Nevertheless, I'd closed my eyes for the journey, opening them once my feet settled on a solid floor.

Avii Castle was a wonder; buildings in Kondar, including the High President's palace home, were amazing. What met my gaze when I arrived at the palace on Le-Ath Veronis took my breath away.

Dark marble, with veins of gold and silver in its depths, covered the floor. A lighter version covered the walls. All of it was so carefully designed and beautiful I wanted to touch it to make sure it was real.

A woman—small and slender—waited for us. She was lovely, with blue eyes and reddish-gold hair. I discovered quickly that I couldn't read anything in her, either. The Queen of Le-Ath Veronis, dressed in a silk tunic and pants, smiled at us and lifted her cheek for Torevik to kiss.

Kaldill held a hand at my back and Daragar walked beside us as we were led inside the Queen's library. As massive as Gurnil's Library was at Avii Castle, this one eclipsed it. My fingers itched to open a single book—*surely I could read it*—and lose myself in other worlds and cultures.

I couldn't—it hadn't been offered and I'd been invited for other reasons. Others waited in the library for us to arrive—many of them mated to the Queen. Some of them made me want to shrink away—one of them could become a huge wolf whenever he wished.

Perhaps he guessed at my discomfort—he offered a gentle smile, convincing some of the tension to fall from my shoulders. Another there frowned at me, making the tension rise again.

It was Kaldill's son, Lendill. I knew it before Kaldill introduced him.

"Don't be a fucking dick," Kaldill scolded his son. I jerked to a standstill—I'd never heard Kaldill curse before.

"Lendill, stop being a fucking dick," Reah echoed Kaldill's words. They were mated; I could see it when Lendill turned in Reah's direction.

"Lendill, stop being a fucking dick," Queen Lissa repeated. Winkler—the man who could become wolf at will, burst into laughter.

A woman stood with the many men in the library; she, like several others, was fascinated by winged people. "You really fly? I mean, Roff flies, but he doesn't have feathers."

"What Renée's saying is that she's used to winged vampires, but not winged people," Lissa said. "I don't know of another winged race such as the Avii in all the known universes."

"Renée is a pretty name," I offered. I was at a loss to comment on the wings—I hadn't had mine long, after all. Gurnil or Ordin would be better to ask about the Avii. A name—a real one, anyway—was also something I hadn't had for long.

"Thank you," she said. If she hadn't been described as a vampire, and if I hadn't seen it in her already, I would have thought her the same as any other. She had feelings for the one she believed had made her vampire, when the one who'd actually made her vampire stood nearby. The Queen had offered her blood for the turn and one named Montrose had taken over, teaching her the ways a vampire should behave and comport themselves.

Lissa lifted an eyebrow as all those things flew through my mind but didn't say anything; I couldn't read her but I could read the others about her.

"May we offer food or drink before we make our way to the Sirenali's cell?" the Queen suggested. That's how we came to have tea and tiny cakes in her library, while I was ensconced on a comfortable sofa with Kaldill and Daragar.

Berel was in raptures, I think. After getting permission to record images, his tab-vid was held aloft more often than not while the library, the people and everything else was captured for his father's perusal.

Eventually, however, it was time to visit the prisoner. Rather than clumping down many steps to the Queen's dungeons, we were transported there by someone with the talent for such.

Instead of a dark, rat-infested place, I found a clean, well-lit row of cells with adequate bedding and climate control. "This way," the Queen led us to a cell near the end. The man they all called a Sirenali was inside, his head in his hands as he sat, hunched over, on a cot.

Without prompting, I read everything I could about him. He had no information on the spheres—Marid the wizard had given him no information as to their location.

I knew what Marid had known and cursed about in this one's presence, however. "The wizard's containment spheres weren't completely effective," I announced. "The poison leached out of them somehow and now the world of Shaaliveer is also contaminated. Marid had the wasting disease," I added. "This one believes it made the wizard's spells too fragile to hold back the poison."

The last thing I read in him troubled me greatly, but I had no real knowledge of what it meant. "What does tapping the core mean?" I turned to Queen Lissa.

"Did you see where he came from—the Sirenali?" Lissa thought to ask. She'd asked me, Kaldill, Daragar and a handful of others to come to her private study, where we could discuss what the Sirenali knew. I could tell my question concerning the tapping of the core disturbed her, but she ignored that subject for the moment.

"He only knows his mother moved about after he was born. He has no idea who his father was or what happened to his mother—she sold him to a wealthy criminal when he was very young. He hates her for that, and the fact that she had no objections when his tongue was removed prior to the sale."

"Does he remember her name?"

"Erithia. He curses her daily."

"Is he evil?" I could see that the mother's name meant something to the Queen, but as I couldn't read her, I had no idea what it could be.

"He bears no malice against you or most others—I only saw anger against those who've harmed him in the past. That included Marid and the criminals who owned him before he fell into Marid's hands."

"I don't know what to do," Lissa flung out a hand in a gesture of confusion. "We let him go, he could end up with another Marid. We keep him here and it's similar to imprisoning the innocent."

"What about Avendor?" Reah suggested. Yes, she was one of the few inside the Queen's study.

"Interesting idea. Do you think they'd mind?"

"Probably not. Can he use fingerspeech?" Reah turned to me.

"He knows it," I nodded. "He learned when he was young."

"Had to, I suppose," Lissa grumbled. "What's his name? Did you see that?" she asked me.

"His name is Terrett," I replied, "Although the ones who bought him called him Geng. Nobody has called him by his proper name in a very long time. It is my hope," I began, working to keep my trembling at bay, "that you treat him kindly. He has never known such his whole life."

"Of course she'd ask that," Kaldill sighed later, after Quin and Berel were transported to a local shop to buy treats to take back to Siriaa. "She hasn't been treated well, either. I've seen it from Amlis and his man-at-arms Rodrik—those of the higher class believe the only way to show their displeasure to those they consider beneath them is by beating them. Quin suffered at their hands, and then at the hands of a few Avii before she became useful to them. Word is she can heal almost anything; the Avii King and his now-deceased Red-Wing Princess demanded millions from the Kondari High President to heal Berel from a rare and deadly form of cancer. Of course, Quin received nothing for her efforts."

"This is preposterous, and I'd pull her away from there immediately if I didn't feel she had some role to play in all this. Nobody else can read the Sirenali—apart from my sister. That alone makes Quin more than valuable and I only want to see her protected in all this." Lissa grumbled.

"What progress has been made on the poison?" she continued. "If Siriaa's core has been tapped as Terrett believes, it'll only die faster."

"The Kondari have already done some research and have determined it is a living organism that produces the radioactive poison by excreting it."

"Can we kill the organism? We have to do that first or repairing the core will be useless. Reah won't attempt it unless the world can be saved, somehow."

"The Kondari scientists say early samples taken from sea waters rendered dead organisms, but the poison, like any other nuclear waste, has a life of centuries at best."

"Do they still have these dead organisms?"

"I believe they do. Should I ask to borrow them?"

"If you could. I'd like Karzac and a few others to take a look at them. I also want more information on Liron—the god the Fyrians and Avii worship. Did he have a hand in the creation of these creatures, or did someone else do it?"

"A question for one of the Three, perhaps?"

"It would be, if we could find any of them," Lissa frowned.

"Their time is different from ours," Kaldill observed.

"I'll make sure to point that out the next time I see any of them."

"Do you believe it will do any good?"

"Probably not."

~

Quin

I'd never seen so many cakes, pies and cold or frozen treats in my life, and all of them sat proudly on shelves inside the same treat shop. A sign outside the shop, lit in bright colors against the constant night of the Le-Ath Veronis city, read *Niff's*.

I'm sure there was a story behind the name, I merely couldn't decipher it at the moment. Regardless, Berel had no trouble pointing out what he wished to take back to Siriaa, so all of it was carefully packaged for the trip.

I chose several things, thinking of Dena and the others we'd left behind in Lironis. Before long, we had a rather large crate filled to the top, which Reah promised to transport without any of it melting.

Daragar and Kaldill arrived when everything was ready, so we were transported back to Lironis with barely a thought.

CHAPTER 8

"I brought these back for you," I placed the small, white box in Justis' hands after I walked into our suite. "The berries are covered in what they called dark chocolate, and when I saw it, I thought of your wings."

"They look good," Justis opened the box and lifted out a red berry dipped in the dark, cold chocolate. He closed his eyes in pleasure the moment he bit into it.

"Did you have one?" he asked, holding the box out to me.

"I was still too full after tea and cake, but I'll try one now," I lifted one of the three remaining berries from the box. They were quite large and one would have filled the palm of my hand had I chosen to squeeze it.

After my first bite, I considered that it was just as good as Justis thought it was—cold but not overly so—to keep the chocolate crisp until it melted on my tongue.

"Thank you for this," Justis lifted a second berry from the box and devoured it.

"You're welcome," I smiled and shrugged at him. "You should have seen the Queen's palace on Le-Ath Veronis. It was incredible. When are you flying out tomorrow?"

"At first light. If all goes well, we'll only be gone three days."

"All right. Please be careful. I don't want anything to happen to you or the others."

"Do you see something?" Justis had the last berry in his hand.

"No, I merely desire your safe return, that's all. Good-night," I said and walked toward my tiny bedroom.

~

"Marid knew he had the wasting disease, else he'd never have taken his own life," I told Dena over breakfast. Justis and the black-winged guards had left early at first light, after a quick meal. They wouldn't eat again until their arrival at Avii Castle, which concerned me.

"I wish I knew how to do that—to know things," Dena shook her head at me.

"At times it seems a terrible curse," I responded. Berel sat beside me then, setting his tab-vid and his plate of food on the table.

We'd chosen the balcony to eat while the others had breakfast inside. I knew they were discussing recent events, which included Marid's death. Gurnil and Ordin chose to join Reah and the others in that discussion, but after another troubling night of fitful sleep, I avoided a meeting and more disturbing news.

"I left a second tab-vid with Tory—he said he'd make sure the meeting was recorded for my father," Berel informed us before spearing scrambled eggs with a fork.

"Your father's shoulders must bear a terrible burden," I sighed. I knew from reading Berel that Sector Two was demanding an inquiry after the arrest of their President. I wanted to laugh—they'd demanded an inquiry into his actions and practices shortly before he'd traveled to Sector Five to make an assassination attempt.

"You know there's a saying in Kondar—that someone is as fickle as Sector Two," Berel grinned before shoving eggs into his mouth and chewing.

"I find that humorous," I smiled at him.

"You're supposed to," he swallowed and grinned. "I heard the army is on its way back, but as they're riding instead of skipping—that's what Tory says he can do—skip somewhere, it'll take them more than a week to get here."

"What are they doing for supplies?" Dena asked.

"I heard that Vhrist was cleaned out before they left, but that didn't stop Tamblin from stealing anything he could along the way."

"How are the people of Vhrist faring, then?" I asked.

"Orik was at breakfast with the others—Fen too. They say that the news they have is that Vhrist has been forced to ration everything, because the army took their surplus."

"You've learned a lot about Fyris in a very short time," I said.

"It's fascinating, and I have to present good information to my father," he shrugged modestly. "Gurnil found maps for me—I can't tell you how happy I am that the Larentii gave me the ability to read as well as speak the language. Everything is so much easier because of it. I've interviewed a few castle servants, too. Father was appalled by the descriptions of their treatment at the hands of the nobles."

"I believe Tamblin and Yevil saw to that," I said, toying with my fork. "I can't say how things were when Tandelis had the throne, but it had to be better, didn't it?"

"Books on the old laws are in Gurnil's private library," Dena said. "I dusted his shelves and saw them there."

"Gurnil can probably tell you if you want to know, then," I nodded at Berel.

"I'll ask after breakfast." Berel went back to his food.

If Siriaa weren't in so severe a crisis and its people in such peril as a result, I would think that having breakfast with two whom I'd come to love was joy incarnate. As it was, I felt as if the weight of the planet had settled onto my shoulders, much as it had for Berel's father.

"Quin, are you ready to start the day?" Ordin walked onto the balcony and nodded to my companions.

"I am." I rose and allowed my wings to pull away from my back.

"I'll join you there after I speak with Master Gurnil," Berel promised. "Father is asking after the health of the people."

~

The physician's staff from one of the ships followed Master Ordin and me into the physician's quarters. Already there was a line waiting to get inside. Two medics from the ship began their trek down the line, making a swift evaluation as to which ones needed to see us first—a process they referred to as vital assessment.

The large, examination room at the front had been divided into five cubicles—the one at the back equipped for dental surgery, as the ships' staff named it.

Ordin had one of the first cubicles, I had the one behind his. Two ships' surgeons had the two opposite ours.

It was no secret that the worst of the patients were brought to me. Many more were asking to see me than I could comfortably handle; those were directed to Ordin and the others.

My first patient was a young woman with the wasting disease. I felt a great deal of pity for her and after a brief consultation with Ordin, healed her of the sickness. She was the first whom I considered for such—all my other patients had been elderly up to that point and only wished for respite from the pain.

When the young woman was helped from the room by her mother, I worried that I'd only see her again. I wondered that the people couldn't feel the disease of the land beneath our feet—it bled through the stone floors of the healer's quarters and disturbed me as I worked.

Ordin said I'd work for four hours, as Kondar measured time. I ended up working the full nine, with only a sandwich brought by Dena at midday.

Berel had come as promised, recording images of patients waiting outside the quarters while we worked as swiftly as we could inside it. Word came that people were either riding in from outlying villages or were carried inside wagons pulled by horses or oxen.

Even the animals appeared sickly to me when the carts were parked outside and the horses and such led away for water and what grain could be found for them.

"I can get supplies," Reah arrived with Torevik behind her to survey the increasing crowd.

"I fear we need another building, just to house those who are too ill to return to their homes," I pointed out. "If we had that, we could also dispense food and supplies there, if we had such."

"A good idea. Let me see what we can do about it."

I'd been covered in blood, filth and vomit when Reah came to visit —I'd have been ashamed if I weren't so near exhaustion by that point. I knew Ordin was in the same shape—he merely snapped at a castle servant to bring a clean smock and went back to work.

Holding my wings out to invite cooler air against my back, I accepted the smaller smock the servant offered to me and motioned for the next patient to be brought forward.

"They're fighting a losing battle—the entire population is sick—or will be soon," Reah sighed. "I know the core is tapped—I opened my shields long enough to check. Marid didn't have the finesse of a warlock when he tapped it and the breach is extensive. Energy is pouring out at an alarming rate."

"Is there any place on Siriaa where those people can be taken—so they can be treated away from Fyris? I gather that's where the poison is concentrated the most," Lissa said.

"There are only two major continents, Kondar and Yokaru, then Fyris and the polar caps. These aren't built for the harsh winters the caps will force upon them—especially with so many sick."

"How many are we talking about?" Lissa asked. "In Fyris?"

"Not that many, considering. Perhaps one hundred thousand or a little more, at most."

"While Kondar and Yokaru hold millions," Lissa shook her head.

"Cloudsong is uninhabited," Reah pointed out. "After the Belancours were arrested and removed recently."

"You may want to check it—Terrett's information revealed that

Marid's containment spheres weren't working. Cloudsong may contain the poison now."

"That bastard," Reah muttered.

"I can think of worse things to call him," Lissa agreed. "When I told Trik that Marid was dead, he nodded. I think he already knew."

"It's tough when your own grandfather gives you away, isn't it?" Reah asked. "Just because Trik had a withered hand? Foolishness."

"If Marid had bothered to spend money on medical care, Trik would have been fine."

"He's better off where he is, and with the Larentii helping, he's whole, now."

"Do you want to go with me to Cloudsong? We'll see what Marid did to it."

~

Lironis

Quin

"Quin?" I hadn't seen Kifirin for at least two days. He stood outside my cubicle, now.

"Lord Kifirin?" I nodded respectfully to him.

"You should stop for the day and rest. Ordin is waiting for you to accompany him to the research facility. A bath, fresh clothing and a meal are waiting."

Hunching my shoulders, I lowered my chin and nodded. It would do the sick no good at all if I weren't rested enough to do what needed to be done. "Come then," Kifirin said. I followed him outside, where Ordin waited.

We didn't have to fly, Kifirin transported us.

~

I nearly fell asleep in the shower after leaning my head against the cool, tiled wall. Water ran over my back and wings while I wished for a bed. My stomach growled, telling me I needed food, first.

Pulling myself away from the tiles and forcing my eyes open, I finished cleaning myself and walked out of the cubicle. I'd learned the first day that the water shut off automatically when I left the shower.

Clothing, no doubt left by Dena, lay folded over the chair in front of the mirror and vanity. Drying off as quickly as I could, I slipped underwear on that I'd never seen before. Then, lifting the top garment, I examined it carefully.

The fabric was smooth and soft as a baby's skin. I found it to be very like the tunic I'd seen Queen Lissa wear, only in a much more suitable garment for where I was. Slipping the neck hole over my head, I tied the back, noticing that the tunic hung halfway to my knees.

The trousers matched and flowed softly about my ankles when I walked. Had I not been so weary, I'd have taken a great deal of pleasure from wearing such fine garments.

My hair came next—I finger-combed it in the mirror until it looked somewhat neat in appearance, then walked out of the bathroom toward the kitchen and dining room.

"Quin, you look lovely," Kaldill smiled and indicated the chair beside him.

"Did you bring this for me?" I asked, touching the fabric of my tunic.

"I asked, yes, but Queen Lissa offered her designer. The results are quite breathtaking," the skin around his eyes crinkled as he smiled wider.

"Then I thank you. It was a wonderful gift after a long and trying day. I was obliged to dispose of my work clothing—I had no hope of washing stains and such out of it after healing so many."

"That is of no consequence—I will ask for a healer's wardrobe for you," Kaldill waved a hand imperiously.

"You've been King for quite a long time, haven't you?" I asked, as a plate of food was set before me.

Kaldill threw back his head and laughed.

The meeting after dinner should have put me to sleep. It didn't. Reah, after being gone for a few hours during the afternoon, was back, with word from Queen Lissa. "We'd hoped to transport those from Fyris to Cloudsong, only to learn that Marid managed to poison it while he was there. We're looking for another suitable world, but nothing has presented itself."

"You're looking to take the people away from Fyris?" Omina almost came out of her seat, her anger evident. Rath, sitting beside her, was just as angry but didn't say anything. "Amlis will be furious," Omina insisted.

"My lady, your people are dying. This is merely a temporary shift, to keep them from getting sicker than they already are. If the poison is cleared away from Fyris, they may return."

"That's why we were looking for a deserted world—where the Prince can rule without hindrance from other inhabitants," Reah attempted to soothe Omina's anger and distrust. "Our other option— and the most expedient—is Harifa Edus, the werewolf planet. Only a quarter of it is occupied, leaving much open ground for your people to live. Once the cities and villages are built with help from the powerful, the people of Fyris would be free to ply their trades and sow gardens and such—spring has arrived on that sector of the planet."

"Werewolves? I've never heard of such," Omina huffed.

I wanted to speak, then, but held my tongue. As long as Omina left them alone, the werewolves would not be a bother. I had the idea that she'd have to travel many, many miles and many days to reach even the closest werewolf, if Reah had her way.

"They've never heard of you, either," Kifirin snorted. I stared— smoke had come from his nostrils. To me, that indicated he was upset in some way. "Reah offers you a gift beyond price and it makes you angry? It will cheat your people if you and your son refuse it."

Lord Kifirin, they have little care for the people, except that it affects them in some way, I sent mindspeech to him.

I know this, he responded gently. *The measure of any monarch is in how he treats the lowliest of his subjects.*

I felt Omina's character was being weighed in the balance and

wondered upon which side she'd fall. Tensions rose in Amlis's study—
I regretted that he and Rodrik weren't present for this meeting.

"Very well," Omina flung up a hand in surrender. "Take the people.
I shall stay here."

"It will kill you, just as it will kill them," Reah said softly.

"I am aging and have seen too much already," Omina huffed. "Amlis
is the ruler of Fyris, as it should be. I will return to Vhrist and die with
it, unless a remedy is found in time."

Quin

"Quin, we will discuss these decisions soon—you and Ordin need
rest, first," Gurnil advised when the meeting was over. I imagined that
he wanted Justis present, too, and that wouldn't be possible for two
more days.

I wondered, too, how the people as a whole would be transported
—would their animals and such travel with them? The whole thing
made me more than curious, and I wished to speak with Reah and
Kifirin about it when I had an opportunity to do so.

Avii Castle

Jurris had already passed sentence on Yevil—the gate waited. He
was spending his last few hours in a cell beneath the castle, until the
midnight hour came. He'd be shoved through, then.

Justis stayed behind with Jurris, after the Council was dismissed.
Justis carried Gurnil and Ordin's votes with him when he and the
others bore Yevil to the King—both had voted for the gate.

"You wished to speak with me alone?" Justis asked after the last
servant left Jurris' quarters.

"Yes." Jurris dropped onto the chair behind his desk and allowed
his wings to droop. "Tell me, brother—will I become that?"

Justis understood Jurris meant Yevil, who'd shouted obscenities at all the Avii while Jurris held his trial and announced the charges brought forth by Justis. He'd ended by calling them filthy, dead birds, nesting on a useless piece of glass. Jurris had ordered the criminal gagged after that, and only allowed him to speak before sentencing.

Those words hadn't been kind, either. Justis doubted if Yevil realized just how short his time had become. Regardless, he'd been gagged again and taken to the dungeons, where—no doubt—the now ungagged Yevil was likely shouting at the guards there.

"My King, if you had shown any evidence of becoming what that aberration is, I would have told you already," Justis muttered.

"You say Tamblin is in custody? He still lives?"

"Yes, although I doubt it will be for long. Had I not seen the device pulled from his neck myself, I'd have doubted such a thing existed. Nevertheless, several at the meeting recognized it. I cannot say whether Yevil dictated Tandelis' death, as well as Elabeth and Camryn's, through that infernal creation, or whether Tamblin went along with the plan willingly."

"Camryn always said there was friction between the brothers; Tandelis held much back from Tamblin as a result."

"I worried when Tandelis' wife died in childbirth, and the child with her," Justis rustled his feathers. "Tamblin already had an heir—Timblor was three years old when that happened. Tandelis believed he had enough time to find another wife and get an heir, but that's exactly what he didn't have."

"Did you get information from either as to the exact events that day?"

"Only that Yevil employed one of those weapons to kill Elabeth, Camryn and their guards first, then turned it on Tandelis, who sent guards to attack Yevil. Tandelis and his guards died, too."

"What about Lirin—their daughter?"

"Yevil claims he killed her. We know a body was delivered here, but it was damaged too badly to identify."

"What was done with the remains?"

"They lie in a glass casket inside the main vault. You were

overcome with grief and melancholy at the time, so I didn't tell you what was done with them. Why do you ask?"

"I wish to see them now."

"Very well. Shall we go there, before making our way to the dungeons?"

"It would please me greatly."

~

Yevil had barely drawn breath between shouting at the guards; Justis ordered him gagged again when he was dragged from his cell. He and Jurris, followed by a dozen Black Wing guards, would usher Yevil to the gate.

Ardis walked steadily behind Justis—Justis couldn't help thinking that this trip could have been the former Captain's, had Quin not asked for his life.

Instead, it gave him grim satisfaction to be executing the one who'd killed Elabeth with joy in his heart at the deed.

What poison had Treven whispered into his half-blood son's ear before he was also forced through the gate? Justis shook his wings, angered by the thought. At least Treven stayed out of his path in the past—he'd been afraid of the black-winged Commander of the Queen's Guard—with good reason. If Treven had threatened Elabeth in Justis' presence, he would have died—with Camryn's blessing.

Instead, he'd stolen weapons from Camryn's treasury and instructed his half-blood child to do harm, instead.

"I watched your father pass through the gate," Justis leaned forward and whispered in Yevil's ear. "It will please me greatly to watch you pass through as well."

Justis stood beside Jurris, Black Wing next to Red, as Ardis and two others lifted one-legged Yevil and tossed him through the stone cavern.

It looked shallow, that cavern, but that was deceptive. Once anyone entered, they disappeared.

~

Tiralia

Yevil cursed when he landed, then looked about him. The ruins of a city lay in the distance. Around him, too, he could see bones— stripped clean of everything except feathers. The last pile was red—his father lay there.

What had killed him and the others? Yevil cared not. The broken city lay in the distance and he was determined to go there.

"You won't get far."

Yevil blinked. Tall, the creature was—more than three times the height of a tall man. Black scales gleamed in weak sunlight, and the tips of curved horns on the creature's head glinted brightly.

"Did you eat him?" Yevil nodded to the pile of bones and red feathers that had once been Treven of the Avii.

"I have no appetite for evil, with or without wings," the creature replied. Smoke poured ominously from his nostrils and massive, muscled arms crossed over the huge chest. "The very air here is poison," the creature added. "Already it is eating your lungs as you breathe. A fitting end for a poisoner of an entire planet, I think, to be poisoned himself."

"Take me away from here," Yevil begged. "I will repay you."

"Your death will be payment enough." The creature disappeared.

"Wait, come back," Yevil shouted, then coughed. Blood poured from his mouth; he stared at the strangeness of it before falling.

His last thoughts were for himself.

~

Lironis

  Quin

"Quin, I have a suite in the research facility, which has an extra bedroom. Do you wish to spend the night there?" Kaldill asked. "You may return to your room in the castle when Commander Justis arrives. Berel's suite is across the hall," he coaxed.

"If that is your wish," I agreed. I was exhausted and he knew it. "I'll get something to sleep in, first."

"No, your closet has been suitably stocked," Kaldill smiled. "You'll find something there, I think."

"All right." Without further discussion, I allowed Kaldill to transport me to his suite. He escorted me to the second bedroom doorway, kissed my forehead lightly, pushed me gently inside and shut the door between us.

I slept better that night than I had in a long while.

Another of Reah's mates appeared at breakfast the following morning. I was forced to clench my teeth to keep my mouth from dropping open.

He was Larentii.

He was also Chief Archivist for his race.

I found myself staring at the ultimate librarian, who stored much of the information kept in the Larentii Archives in his head. Bright-blue eyes turned to regard me before they lit even brighter with his smile.

"You are welcome at the Archives anytime," Nefrigar chuckled. The universe should stop in wonder, I decided, whenever a Larentii laughs. "Ask Daragar to bring you whenever you wish," he added.

"When there is time enough to enjoy it," I replied as solemnly as I could. After all, I had healing to do the moment I finished breakfast, and hadn't touched the old physician's journal yet, to write the report Gurnil requested.

"Nefrigar wishes to study your wings," Reah said. I blinked at her, confusion tinged with worry clouding my mind.

"I only wish to touch briefly, to memorize the colors and texture so a report may be written for the Archives. I have never seen such, and there are no records in the Archives of any like them."

"That's fine," I agreed. I'd worried that he wanted a sample, and I'd experienced having feathers plucked already.

"Young one," Nefrigar knelt beside me, "No Larentii will ever bring you harm. Will you stretch out your wings for me, so I may measure them?"

"We should go to the balcony," I said. I didn't realize that everyone else waiting for breakfast would come with us, Ordin and Gurnil included. There, in the early morning sun, I stretched my wings as far as I could for the Chief Archivist of the Larentii.

Somehow, he could measure without using a tape or a stick. Daragar appeared, nodded to Nefrigar and smiled as the Archivist touched my feathers carefully.

"The sun makes a lovely color when it shines through the bands," Nefrigar informed me. I'd never thought to look, to be honest.

"She doesn't stand for long before the mirror," Daragar said softly.

"You may fold your wings, now," Nefrigar said. "I have what I need. Come see me at the Archives, young one." With that, he disappeared.

"I received a message from Father this morning," Berel said as plates of food were passed around the table moments later. "I recorded audio from the meeting last night, so he discussed it with Melis and a few others."

"What did he say?"

"I'll tell you later," Berel promised.

Later came during a hasty midday meal—a sandwich again, while I sat atop a castle turret to get away from the sick ones clamoring to see me. I'd desperately needed the respite—healing was exhausting work.

The sick had learned there was no medicine to take, no stitches in torn skin and no pain if someone were fortunate enough to be brought to my cubicle.

Berel was forced to climb many steps to get to the window beside my perch. "I'm sorry I made you come so far," I apologized. "I worried that there would be a riot in the courtyard if I attempted to walk away. I flew, instead."

"There must be more than five hundred people down there," Berel agreed, leaning his elbows on the windowsill. "I asked some of mine to walk through and distribute small packages of food and water while they're waiting, and Master Gurnil asked for benches to be brought so they wouldn't have to stand so long."

"I know. You have kindness in your heart, Berel Charkisul. I hope it always remains so."

"I know what it's like to be sick," he said with a shrug. "If I could, I'd be down there, helping you heal them. Such is not my gift."

"What did your father say about the meeting last night?"

"He says that if you leave Siriaa, I am to go with you."

"Berel, I don't know whether I'll go or not," I stuttered, shocked by his words. "I mean the Avii will still be here, your father will still be here, the people of Kondar and Yokaru will still be here and the poison will still be here. It is a wondrous gift Reah and Queen Lissa are offering, to take the people of Fyris away to a safer place, but there is so much work to be done here, still."

"I understand that, but my father's scientists have discovered what you already know—that the core is somehow leaking and its energy is feeding the poison. While these findings are preliminary, they worry that Siriaa will die faster because of it. Carrying two hundred thousand people away will be nothing compared to the millions left behind in hopeless circumstances. Already, stored food prices are up, merely based on rumors."

"Tapping the core. Now I understand what he did," I muttered.

"Who?"

"The wizard who killed himself. He was sick and his power was failing, so he tapped the energy of the planet's core to provide power for what he wished to accomplish. In the end, because he faced Reah and Daragar in your father's palace, he could not do what he intended."

"What did he intend?" Berel's voice was sharp and fearful.

"He intended to kill your father and bend Kondar to his will. President Pragg would have died, too, had he known it. Marid of Belancour wanted the whole planet to rule, so he could sell the poison to criminals everywhere. What he didn't realize is that there is no known cure for the poison, once it escapes. I know not how Queen Elabeth kept it from spreading, but she did. That secret died with her, and I have no idea if there is written information anywhere as to how she accomplished that feat."

"So many other worlds are now contaminated with this poison," Berel shook his head. "I don't understand the depth of malice required to do such a thing."

"I believe it came down to jealousy and greed," I shrugged. "I've seen that all my life. I have to go back, now." I stuffed the last bit of sandwich into my mouth and chewed before taking flight to the courtyard below.

CHAPTER 9

Lironis

"She needs a day off, but that could cause a riot. You should see the looks the rest of us get when patients are brought to us instead of Quin." Ordin rustled his wings in frustration as he stalked past Gurnil—he'd arrived in the suite where their bedrooms were now located, to have a shower and change clothes before going to dinner.

"They should understand that Quin will see the worst off," Gurnil began.

"We've told them that, many times. Still they complain. Is Justis back, yet?"

"He's expected at any time."

"If Jurris keeps him longer than necessary," Ordin huffed. "We need him and his guards to help with the crowds. We have to inform him of the planned move; Reah tells me that she and several Larentii have volunteered to construct schools and other necessary buildings in the section of Harifa Edus they've carved out for the Fyrians. I still don't know what the reaction will be, however, when they're dumped in a strange place with no prior knowledge."

"Take your bath," Gurnil sighed. "We'll discuss this over dinner. Perhaps Justis will arrive in time to join us."

~

Quin

I wobbled into the shower, exhausted. This was my routine, now—work until I was exhausted every day, with barely a few moments to eat a meager midday meal. At least Kaldill's quarters had the shower I'd come to love so much, to wash away the sweat and grime.

My clothing went into a special hamper Kaldill supplied—it had a tightly-closing lid so the smell wouldn't permeate my bathroom until someone could collect it to wash.

A bench had been brought and placed inside the shower; Kaldill had known, somehow, that it provided welcome relief for one who'd stood most of the day to heal the sick.

I wished, too, for a way to give Ordin and the others time off—all were showing signs of wear as they treated an endless line of patients.

Forcing myself to dry off after my shower, I dressed in the first thing I could find in the closet and walked toward the door. Yes, I should have been looking forward instead of down—I stumbled through the door and walked straight into someone.

I shrieked—it startled me so badly.

"Here, now." Hands—and a voice—soothed.

Justis was back. I looked up into his face and burst into tears. I may have wrapped my arms tightly about his waist, too—I don't remember.

~

"Set the trays here," Kaldill instructed softly. I heard his voice—he'd come to our suite shortly after Justis carried me inside, still sniffling like a child. Daragar followed on Kaldill's heels.

Pulling my face away from Justis' black shirt, which was now soaked with my tears, I saw that Kaldill had asked for our dinners to be delivered to the suite. I wanted to hug him for thinking of it—there wasn't any way I wanted to show tearstains to anyone else.

"Overworked," Kaldill said softly, offering a glass of milk to me with a gentle smile.

"I'm sorry. I didn't mean for that to happen," I mumbled, accepting the milk. I realized I sat on Justis' lap and felt embarrassed because of it.

"No need," Justis wrapped fingers around my hand that held the glass. "Drink this—you're probably half-starved, on top of everything else."

I was, but I didn't want to admit it to the Commander of the King's Guard, who'd just flown for hours to return to Lironis. If anybody needed something to eat or drink, he did.

"We have food and drink for all of us, except Daragar, who's already soaked up enough sunlight to do him for a while," Kaldill laughed gently. "Come, we have enough seats. We'll sit and eat and talk, if you want to talk."

That's how the four of us came to have our dinner in Kaldill's suite that night, while Justis described Yevil's trip through the gate and his screams and cursing beforehand. He also described Jurris' apparent depression and worry that he could become what Yevil and Treven were—careless murderers whose only concerns were for themselves.

"Should we send Ordin back to Avii Castle?" Kaldill asked. He recognized Justis' worry for his brother.

"I want to, but Quin is already overworked as it is. If we take even one healer away, it will place a heavier burden on those left behind."

"If it will help Jurris, then I won't mind," I said. "I doubt he could ever become what Yevil and his father were, but he needs reassurance, just the same. If Ordin can provide that, then he should go."

"Quin, I don't want to see more of your tears," Kaldill offered gently.

"I know, but everything is in such a delicate balance on Siriaa," I said. "Yes, we need to get the people of Fyris away, or they'll die quickly. The poison is getting worse—much worse. I can feel it. If one monarch or president or trusted leader falls, the balance will collapse and Siriaa will die an even quicker death."

"You see the civil wars and riots that will come, because the poison will consume everything and leave the people without food or clean water, don't you?" Daragar interjected. Until that moment, he'd been content to listen while the rest of us talked.

"Yes. I wish I had access to your Larentii Archives and time enough to read and study the problem; I feel it has happened many times before. A part of me wants to move all the people away, but this is their home. Another part of me realizes that Marid, before he died, managed to infect many other worlds with the same malady. Should we move to another world, only to find the same difficulties facing us there? We need a cure for it," I allowed my wings to droop. If the powerful couldn't find a remedy for the poison, then all could be lost.

"If Amlis were here, he'd say no," Rath pointed out.

"My son will say yes," Omina countered. "He will see the reason behind it—Tamblin will not be taken to safety with the others and he will die eventually, because the poison will ensure it. I have no desire to live my last days in Fyris, worried that a madman is on the loose. He should be executed publicly for his crimes, before the people leave this world behind."

"I'll wait to speak with Amlis."

"You do that," Omina flipped her skirts and stalked away.

Quin

"Move your things into the suite next door," Kaldill suggested when Justis rose to leave. "You and Quin. Daragar and I have this building protected—none will approach her here—I fear the residents will attempt to find her when she is eating or sleeping if we do not."

"That sounds reasonable. I'll move my things tomorrow, and

arrange for Quin's things to be moved as well. Sleep here tonight," Justis nodded to me. "I'd feel better if you did."

I swallowed my concerns—I'd find a way, surely, to move the metal box without anyone asking questions.

The morning brought breakfast and a debate. Ordin wanted to stay in Fyris. Justis wanted him to leave for Avii Castle after the meal.

"We're only waiting for the Prince to arrive with his troops—the population will be moved after that," Gurnil argued Ordin's case when Ordin's face darkened with anger.

"If the people can be moved, why can't the troops be moved as well?" Justis stood and rustled his wings—he was just as angry as Ordin—perhaps more so.

"The healers here are overworked as it is, and you're suggesting we take one of them away?" Gurnil hissed.

"Please stop—this disagreement is doing more harm than good," Kaldill held up a hand after a swift glance in my direction. "If you wish the troops moved, Daragar and I shall do it—with the Prince's permission. I warn you, however, another debate will ensue, I think, over whether he should allow this exodus."

He was right—I wasn't sure what Amlis might think of relocation. It could take time for him to see what a dire state Fyris was in before he realized that he would have no kingdom if the people were all dead.

Time was growing short. Whatever the wizard had done to the planet's core was making the poison grow exponentially. I couldn't grasp the how or why of it—I only knew that it was.

"Have any new soil samples been taken recently?" I stood and blurted.

"No—they're working on what they already have," Berel said. Until now, he'd listened to the debate without comment. "Do you think we should?" he asked.

"Yes. It's so much worse, now," I hugged myself. "Fyris will die in a moon-turn if we don't get the people away from here."

Kaldill didn't bother to ask how I knew that. Daragar appeared at his side—I'm sure he'd been listening to the conversation from elsewhere. Someday, I hoped to understand how he did that.

"Tory and Korde are with the Prince—they carried rations in so the troops wouldn't raid villages," Reah spoke to Kaldill.

"I'll bring them back," Kaldill nodded, standing and drawing himself to his full height. At that moment, I saw the true Elf King—stern and authoritative. Amlis would have a battle he couldn't win if he disagreed with Kaldill in any way. A sigh escaped my lips the moment he and Daragar disappeared.

"Three found dead in their tents this morning," Rodrik muttered as he settled on the makeshift stool inside Amlis' tent. "The ones reported as sickly yesterday."

"They're dying of the poison, Rod," Amlis shook his head. "They'd have died of starvation without the rations brought by Torevik and Kordevik. Have there been any messages from Mother or Uncle Rath?"

"Nothing today," Rodrik shook his head. "What has changed, Amlis? It's as if the poison quadrupled overnight."

"I know. I don't understand how it has no effect on Tory or Korde, but whatever they have transfers to me when I'm near them—I can feel it."

"Tory indicated that he has an immunity to all poisons," Rodrik began.

"I know. And the creature he becomes? The troops are terrified of him, even when he appears normal. I pray that he isn't angered enough to become the creature again."

"He is frightening, and I suspect Korde can also become one of those creatures. I have never heard of such, although it serves to protect us and ensures the troops follow our commands. Do you believe Tory and Korde are wizards, too?"

"Not wizards," Tory lifted the tent flap and blinked into the dimness. "Kaldill and Daragar are here. They say it is imperative that we move you and the troops to Lironis now—a decision must be made before all of Fyris dies."

~

Lironis
   Quin
   Amlis and his troops arrived and the ensuing debate went on while Ordin (who'd stayed for now) and I did our best to heal the sick, whose numbers had tripled overnight. Some of those we saw were troops from Amlis' army.

   Rodrik, who stopped by for a short time and asked for something to cure Beatris' headache, let me know there was no clear winner yet in the continuing argument. I merely shook my head at him as he accepted the small bottle from Ordin and strode away.

   Beatris had done her best to stay away from anyone who wore wings once we arrived in Lironis—she felt embarrassed and inadequate around us. Instead, she chose to keep close to Omina, who now had a circle of minor noblewomen about her. Both Omina and Beatris were tended by Sophie, with Yissy receiving much attention from all of them.

   Except for Yissy, there were no other children in the castle. Breaking away from that thought, I turned to my next patient, a man who should be young and strong, but who'd broken his leg and contracted the wasting disease. I hoped the decision to leave Fyris behind came soon.

   Very soon.

~

"Lironis is far better off than the lands between here and Vhrist,"

Amlis argued. "I could feel it the moment I landed. Leagues away, the ground beneath my feet groaned with the poison. I hear that most of those who are waiting in the courtyard for treatment are from outlying villages, not here."

"How do you explain that?" Justis asked, his voice frosty and his dark eyes narrowed in speculation.

"I can't, I just feel it—the difference," Amlis shrugged.

"How long will that remain true?" Gurnil asked. "You don't know, and neither do any of us. All your people cannot live in Lironis—and without sufficient crop harvests and healthy animals, they will starve if the poison doesn't kill them first."

"This is our land. My concern is that we will not be allowed to return, once we leave it."

"It may never be safe to return," Gurnil exploded. "Need I remind you of the reason we stand here today, debating your exodus? Queen Elabeth kept the poison at bay, yet she died here, with none to come to her aid." His wings snapped out, indicating the depth of his anger.

"Fold your wings, Master Librarian," Justis said quietly. "The Prince realizes he has no choice. He merely doesn't want to say it."

"My Prince," Rodrik interrupted.

"What is it?" Amlis turned toward his man-at-arms.

"Do you recall the old physician's words?"

"What?" Amlis was confused by Rodrik's question.

"Do you remember when I went to him, asking about Quin? When we believed that she was Lady Rinda's child after I spoke with the old man?"

"Yes," Amlis shook his head. "But what bearing does that have on this?"

"He said 'have you asked yourself why the deaths and deformities affecting Fyris have failed to touch Lironis?' He told me to ponder that question, before telling me that you and I should leave Lironis behind. He also said that your father believed he sent Lady Rinda's child to the kitchen. I realize now that the old physician knew better."

"Are you suggesting that Quin is Elabeth and Camryn's daughter?" Amlis grasped Rodrik's meaning quickly.

"I don't know," Rodrik began.

"We don't have a clear answer either," Gurnil began. "We had her DNA tested by scientists in Kondar. Their response was that the tests were inconclusive. We have no concrete evidence as to whom Quin may be."

"I have asked the ships' technicians to do a test on the child's remains sent to Avii Castle," Justis announced. "I believe we will know soon whether Lirin, Elabeth and Camryn's daughter, died here or lives, still."

"Either way, do you think Quin has something to do with holding the poison at bay here in Lironis? If she goes to Vhrist or elsewhere, will that also hold true?" Berel asked. He had his tab-vid set on the meeting table, recording the debate for his father.

That's when the call came. "Son?" High President Charkisul began.

"Father, what is it?" Berel asked.

"I also have a confession to make. Tell those people to leave Fyris behind. We've already done DNA testing on Quin, and the tests were not inconclusive as we said. At the time, I only thought to save her life and spare her pain—from those who could do harm. Quin has no connection to anyone on this planet."

~

Quin

Something was different—I could feel it. Since it concerned me, however, I had no idea what it might be. Forcing those thoughts away, as worrying as they were, I went back to healing the sick.

~

"My question is this—does this change how you feel about her?" Kaldill demanded. He and Daragar asked for a few moments with Justis when the meeting broke for the midday meal.

Kaldill knew the attendees would break into groups—he'd already seen Rath, Omina, Amlis and Rodrik leave together.

"No. At least—no." Justis scrubbed his face with a hand before turning back to Kaldill and the Larentii who stood behind him. "I know not what my brother will think, however."

"At least he'll know she's not the half-blood he thought she was," Kaldill muttered and turned away. "You heard the High President's words—he's made her a citizen of Kondar. She is welcome there if not with the Avii she resembles."

"I worried that she'd leave with you," Justis sighed.

"She is welcome to go anywhere with me, and welcome to stay wherever I am. She feels responsible for helping Siriaa, or have you not realized it, yet? I'm not sure you could pry her away unless there is no hope left at all. Yes, I can take her away for short trips, but I cannot and will not interfere with her choices."

"I will send a message to my brother when the results come back from the tests on the remains. I know not what his reaction may be to the fact that Quin does not belong to us in any way."

"Why do you say that?" Daragar spoke for the first time. "Perhaps you should consider that she may belong to all." He disappeared with a disgusted sniff.

Quin

Midday had arrived, bringing Dena with a sandwich. She offered to sit with me while I ate, but I hugged her and told her I needed time alone.

With a nod, she watched me walk out of the healer's quarters, and before anyone else could touch me, I lifted my wings and flew upward, toward a high turret.

If I were lucky, I could eat while I walked down steps to Justis' old quarters, retrieve the metal box and fly it to the research building with few noticing. It would involve sneaking through the royal wing to do it, but I felt I could—everyone should be eating elsewhere.

The upper levels of the palace were almost deserted—I could hear a maid and a servant coupling in one room as I passed by. When I thought the rest of my journey through wide, stone halls would be uneventful, I heard voices coming from Omina's suite.

Stopping short, I held my breath as I listened, making sure they hadn't heard my footsteps. They hadn't—because they were talking too loudly to hear them. When I stopped, however, it ensured that I'd hear them clearly enough.

"We don't know who or what Quin is," Amlis snapped. "What difference does it make? She's saving lives. Tell me those people wouldn't be dead or nearly so that she's helped."

"I'm not sure I want her here—not after what I heard," Omina's voice was cold.

"All you heard, Mother, was that she bears no connection to anyone on Siriaa."

"We thought she was half Avii, at least," Omina huffed. "Even that's not true. She could be a monster, for all we know, and turn on us."

"A monster? That's ludicrous," Rodrik's voice intervened. "I've seen nothing of the kind from her."

"Go tell the people in the courtyard that you don't know what she is, then," Omina shouted.

"Mother, there are servants everywhere. By now, they may already know what you've been shouting since we've come to your quarters. Is that what you want? She saved your life, for Liron's sake. Have you forgotten that?"

"That's another thing," Omina snapped. "Who on this planet holds that kind of power? Nobody. Why didn't I see this before?"

I'd heard enough. Wiping tears away, I ran as softly as I could for the nearest window and flew away from the castle.

"Lord Justis?" A castle servant tugged on his arm. He'd been deep in conversation with Ardis and hadn't noticed the man's approach.

"Yes?"

"We've moved everything out of your quarters—and out of Finder —er—Quin's quarters. Except the box beneath her bed."

"There's a box there?" Justis offered the man his complete attention.

"Yes. It's a strange box and I wasn't sure I should touch it."

"Show me," Justis growled. The man almost ran while Justis strode purposely behind him. Ardis followed Justis as they made their way through the castle and up steps leading to the royal wing.

∾

"Quin is missing," Ordin said. "That's why I sent for you. I don't think she'd shirk her duties or refuse to heal the sick on a whim," he added.

"Quin is missing?" Gurnil's heart increased its rhythm. "Has anyone seen her?"

"I've asked everyone here; nobody knows where she is." Ordin jerked his head toward the door of the healer's quarters, indicating he'd already asked the ships' healers and castle staff in the courtyard.

"This isn't good," Gurnil muttered. "We were discussing her in the meeting earlier, where, ah, certain things came to light. I hope someone hasn't let that slip—without proper explanation, it could prove emotionally devastating."

"We have problems," Justis shouldered his way inside the door of Ordin's cubicle. "A servant saw Quin flying northward away from Lironis, and a strange box was found beneath her bed in the castle."

∾

"Daragar, have you seen anything like this before?" Kaldill tapped the lid. The metal box lay on a table inside his suite, after he asked Justis to leave it there.

"The hair inside is hers," Daragar sighed. "This frightens me. Shall I go looking for her?"

"We can't find her by the usual methods—I recognized that in her when I saw her the first time," Kaldill pointed out. "I don't know what to do. This has weighed on her—I can see it now. Likely, either someone told her that she was a topic of discussion at the meeting or she overheard it afterward, somehow. Dena spoke to her last when she brought Quin's meal—she reports that Quin wished to be alone."

"I will send mindspeech," Daragar said.

"I hope it works," Kaldill replied.

Quin, Lara'Kayan, where are you? Kaldill, Justis and I are worried. Daragar's voice sounded in my mind.

Tell me Justis worries, I returned. *I'm not even half Avii.*

"Where did you hear this?" Daragar appeared beside me. I watched as he reformed sharp rocks so he could sit comfortably at my side.

I'd chosen the Western spires as my place to weep. "It is known as nexus echo," he observed conversationally as he made himself at home. I'd selected the highest point on the center stone, thinking only another Avii could reach me there.

Obviously, the Larentii could, too.

"What is known as nexus echo?" I scrubbed stubborn tears off my cheeks.

"The way I can hear someone speak my name from afar, or find them if they reply to my mindspeech," he smiled and drew me onto his lap. "Larentii do not lie—as a matter of choice," he added.

"But others do it every day," I pointed out.

"Who spoke the words within your hearing, my love? Are you sure they spoke complete truth?"

"They said I had no connection to anyone on Siriaa. That sounded like truth to me."

"That much Kaldill and I have guessed already," Daragar sighed. "We worried that the knowledge could upset you. As it turns out, you'd already determined that on your own, or mostly so. Didn't you?"

"Yes." Images came unbidden of the metal box beneath a bed in the castle.

"We found the box, dearest. We are working on that puzzle, now. Don't let it trouble you; do not allow words to harm you that are spoken out of fear and prejudice."

"You didn't hear her," I mumbled. Omina's words stung, but that was the way my life had always been. I'd been different from the moment I was dumped in Wolter's kitchen as a child.

"Age doesn't cure foolishness—it only tells everyone that someone is an old fool rather than a young one," Daragar tilted his head and smiled at me. "I hear that the High President is demanding that you be brought to Kondar if Lironis fails to treat you better."

"Edden Charkisul is a good man. A kind man, too, as is his son. Do you find it odd that they hold power, when many who do so are quite self-serving and cynical?"

"You should see politicians on other worlds, or visit one of Queen Lissa's Council meetings. Most people have become jaded and expect the squabbling that goes on continuously."

"It is so wearying," my wings drooped as I sighed. Daragar stroked feathers with long, blue fingers. I found it soothing and settled deeper into his embrace.

"You never looked at me as anything other than a person or being in my own right, rather than something alien," he said. "Whereas I only have a fragile truce with most of the Avii at the castle, because Camryn and Elabeth allowed a curious Larentii to read through the Library. Gurnil is a sympathetic friend, as is Ordin, and Justis is getting used to me, but few others see me that way."

"Does it bother you?" I looked up at his chin. Like the rest of him, it was a sunny blue.

"No. There are no others in all the known universes like the Larentii. We were created first, you know, by the Mighty Heart."

"Is that a religious belief?" I asked, curious.

"No. I have met her," Daragar smiled. "Now, shall we go back to Lironis? I hear people are clamoring to be healed."

"I suppose I should go," I sighed. I wanted to huddle in a corner somewhere and feel sorry for myself. I had no idea what I was, where I'd come from and realized, after a moment or two, that the Avii and the people of Fyris were the same in that respect. None of them knew where they'd originated, either.

I wondered if Omina understood that.

Daragar laughed—he'd seen the emotions cross my face. In less than a blink, I was back in Lironis and escorted to my healing cubicle by a tall, blue Larentii.

~

Dinner was a quiet affair. Again I was tired, but Kaldill and Justis made sure I sat between them during the meal. Omina, Rath, Amlis and Rodrik were absent. Berel kept looking at me, begging me to speak to him. Finally, I did.

"What does your father think of Fyris still being hidden?" I began. After seeing Marid for the few brief moments I had, I'd known it was his spell that kept Fyris' existence hidden from the rest of Siriaa.

"It's somewhat annoying to be forced to carry someone from Fyris back and forth in the ships and airchoppers," Berel said. "And if they leave, where will we be?"

"That's why we should take the ring from Tamblin's hand and carry it to Jurris," I said. "He can keep it in his treasury."

"I can send it on an airchopper," Berel offered. "Orik won't mind making another trip, I don't think."

"This will allow free passage between Kondar and Fyris, to study the poison," Gurnil observed.

"Master Gurnil, I think everyone should leave Fyris. If they don't, they'll die." The words burst from me before I could stop them.

"I agree with Quin," Kaldill said. "I can feel the earth beneath our feet putrefying. The poison is spreading faster than I ever thought possible."

"We are not the ones to convince," Ordin pointed out. "The Prince must be convinced first."

That night, we went to bed with nothing resolved. The following morning, after breakfast, Ordin and I walked to the research facility balcony to fly to the healer's quarters.

I could see the crowd waiting in the courtyard, once I took flight to follow Ordin. My focus was on the sick waiting for us when the arrow pierced my wing and I dropped from the sky with a shriek.

CHAPTER 10

L ironis

"We should be grateful for the difficulty in hitting a moving target," Kaldill sighed. "And for Ordin's quick actions to pull Quin from the air before she hit the courtyard below. Daragar has placed her in a healing sleep after repairing the arrow wound in her wing."

"I will find who did this," Justis' fist closed on empty air.

"Find the source of the poison behind the act," Kaldill said. "Regardless, we have little time. Nearly a hundred people died last night and many more are showing signs that they won't wake tomorrow. The Prince needs to let them go or send them home to their deaths."

"I will find him and present him with those choices." Justis walked swiftly toward the door of Kaldill's suite.

"Tell him we leave tomorrow, and I intend to move Quin if she'll allow it."

"What about the ring?"

"Take it from the fornicating bastard's hand—by force if necessary. I'm inclined to grant Quin's wish in this. Carry it back to your brother the King with my best wishes."

"I will see it done." Justis jerked his head and shut the door behind him.

"Beatris is ill, Amlis, and Quin lies injured in Kaldill's suite. How do you suggest I approach him to ask Quin to save my lady wife? The headache she had has become something far worse." Rodrik raked fingers through his hair in fear and frustration as he spoke to the Prince.

"I hoped that Lironis wouldn't fall to the poison. I see that it has overwhelmed everything at last," Amlis buried his head in his arms. Rodrik sighed as he looked past the Prince and through the window in the meeting room, while Amlis sat dejectedly at the table.

"You know that arrow came from one of ours—Mother couldn't keep her mouth closed or her words quiet," Amlis looked up again at Rodrik.

"Then send the people away and let her and my father stay here to rot," Rodrik tossed out a hand. "Just don't let Beatris die."

"I don't intend to allow your wife to die, Rod, but I hesitate to approach the King of the Elves. While he is courteous and well-spoken much of the time, I can't imagine that there isn't the hardness of a diamond in him, should someone break his laws or harm those he loves."

"Then allow me to send for a litter to carry Beatris to his door. Surely he cannot refuse her."

"We will go after dinner—they will wake Quin to eat." Amlis jerked his head up at the knock on his door. Rodrik moved away to open it. Both were surprised to find Justis on the other side.

"You'll agree to send the people away and allow me to take the ring from your father's hand, in exchange for Quin's healing of the lady Beatris?" Justis' eyes narrowed.

CONNIE SUTTLE

"If Quin feels well enough and agrees," Amlis held up a hand. Justis looked angry enough to throttle him, and he doubted Rodrik and he together could fight off the determined Avii Commander.

"Then I agree. I will fly back to the research building. Bring the lady and meet me there at your earliest convenience." Justis turned swiftly and walked out the door, leaving Amlis staring at Rodrik in near-shock.

~

Quin

"Quin?" Kaldill's voice was soft. Coaxing.

"Hmmm?" I responded, still half asleep.

"Amlis and Rodrik are here. Beatris is sick. They say they'll allow the move if you'll heal Beatris."

He and I both knew I'd heal her anyway, but if Amlis wanted an excuse to do the proper thing, then I would keep my part of the bargain.

"Where?" I sat up, blinking in the dim light inside my bedroom.

"Outside—in the sitting area. Fluff your wings, *deah-mul*, you look as if you've slept in them."

"Because I have," I mumbled and stood unsteadily for a moment before balance returned. I realized I was dressed in nightclothes, but it didn't matter—Beatris needed my help.

"How did this happen?" Were my first words on seeing Beatris on a litter inside Kaldill's suite. "Why wasn't she brought to me before?" The poison had invaded her brain. If I didn't move quickly, she'd die.

"My mother," Amlis ducked his head, ashamed of the truth.

"I see. I heard what your mother had to say about me." I knelt beside Beatris and drew a deep breath. Amlis' cursing was the last thing I heard before I put my hands on Beatris and began to heal her of the poison sickness.

~

"The ring." Justis set it on the table before taking a seat across from me and accepting a plate of food from a kitchen worker. He and Kaldill had waited until I was awake to have dinner, so we could eat together.

I wanted to hug both of them for it. "When will the people be moved?" I asked.

"Tomorrow morning. It'll be easier to sort out the ones who don't wish to stay at their new location and bring them back, rather than attempt to notify all of them that they're leaving," Reah walked in and sat beside Kaldill. "I think once they see where we're taking them, they'll choose to stay there. We have health workers lined up to give mistjections to those experiencing radiation poisoning—the drug will help them heal from it."

"Good," I sighed. "Justis, what about us?" I asked. I worried about returning to Avii Castle, especially since I wasn't Avii.

"The choice is yours," he shrugged. "I want you there, but you must consider what you may have to deal with when you arrive. I haven't spoken to Jurris, as you know, so I can't say what his reaction will be, either."

"Berel will return to Kondar," I pointed out. I knew I was a citizen and welcome there.

"What do you really want, Quin?" Kaldill asked.

"I want a cure for the poison. I want to know who I am and who my parents are—or were. I want to read the old physician's journal—perhaps he wrote about me and the metal box in it. I want to read the Ordinance, to see what it says."

"Jurris will have to give permission for you to read the Ordinance," Justis said. I watched as he tore a piece of bread and dipped it in the meat broth served with the fowl he ate.

I turned back to my meal of lentil stew and vegetables. "Then Jurris' decision will determine whether I stay at Avii Castle or go to Kondar with Berel," I said. "I want to stay with you, Kaldill and Daragar, but that may not be an option."

"I suggest we serve as Kondar's ambassadors to Avii Castle," Berel walked in as if he'd been called. Perhaps he had; Kaldill's lips curled in a half-smile. "You're a citizen in good standing, and I have no doubt Father will name you ambassador. You've served Kondar well already."

Berel took the chair next to Reah's and smiled at her. Was he only sixteen? He acted so much older—was so mature for his age.

"I will take you both to Kondar tomorrow morning," Kaldill offered. "Daragar will go with Justis to Avii Castle. If Jurris agrees to allow you and Berel as ambassadors in his castle, then I will take you both there, and stay on as your advisor. If Jurris doesn't want you there, then I will do the same in Kondar." Kaldill's smile became a full grin.

"Father will be glad to have your advice," Berel laughed. "He likes you very much."

"Is that to your satisfaction, dearest?" Kaldill asked.

"That sounds wonderful," I agreed.

~

"If Jurris doesn't agree, I ask you to bear a message to your father," Justis informed Berel after the meal was finished and everything cleared away. I walked with both toward Kaldill's suite—Kaldill had stayed behind to speak with Reah.

"What message?" Berel asked, curious.

"I ask to be allowed to visit as time and duty allows," Justis replied. "Wherever Quin goes, I know she will be helping the sick and doing what she can to hold back the spread of poison, but I wish to visit her occasionally."

I was surprised. Yes, he'd become closer, but I worried that if he returned to Avii Castle and I did not, that whatever he felt would die quickly. "What do you think Jurris will say?" I asked.

"I care not what my brother thinks," Justis muttered. "He is King, yes. He cannot control my heart."

"Quinnie," Berel said, his gaze earnest as he took my hands, "I hope we get to stay with the Avii."

Justis laughed.

~

Berel and I stayed up half the night talking and poring over his tab-vid. Kaldill laughed, told us not to stay up too long and went to bed ahead of us. Justis did too, as he had a long flight to Avii Castle in the morning. Berel offered an airchopper ride; Justis refused, saying his wings needed stretching.

"If we are at Avii Castle, perhaps we can convince Kaldill to transport us on Eight-day to Kondar to have a meal with my father and discuss what is happening in both places," Berel suggested.

"I worry that things may deteriorate quickly; the poison is much, much worse," I replied. "I'd look forward to many dinners with your father, if that weren't growing beneath our feet. The people of Kondar are already complaining about food prices and the lack of approved seafood. Everything is being poisoned. Getting the people of Fyris to a safe place is only the beginning. I fear our conversations may not be pleasant ones to recall in the future."

"I know. I just want it to be," Berel shrugged. "I want to see you at dinners with Ampah."

"Ampah?"

"It's slang—colloquial for father. Ampah means father, Gampah means grandfather."

"What about your mother?" I asked.

"She died when I was ten," he said. "An assassination attempt on my father went wrong. They hit her, instead."

"I'm sorry," my wings tightened at the sadness in Berel's story.

"Ampah blames himself. It's one of the reasons he won't consider marrying again."

"That's sad. I hope he isn't lonely."

"You know what that is, don't you?"

"Yes. Even with many around me, I was alone. Does that make sense?"

"Of course. You didn't speak, they all treated you like a slave—I can see that easily."

"Your Ampah carries a heavy burden. He knows what it's like, too."

"If the people of Kondar die as they are dying here, the burden will triple."

"What are we going to do?" I whispered.

"I don't know. I hope the scientists figure this out soon," Berel whispered back.

～

Harifa Edus

"I wanted to bring you first, so you could see where your people will live," Reah said. "There are fields outside New Fyris where the farmers and herders can grow vegetables, grains and livestock. We have people ready to show them how the farming equipment works so they won't have to do so much by hand or with horses or oxen. The sea, as you can hear, lies to the west. New Fyris' fishermen can safely fish these waters, as boats have been supplied for such."

Amlis, Rodrik and Beatris gazed at the castle at the heart of an enormous city. The castle had been constructed (after a fashion) like the one in Lironis, only this one was built of a single color of stone and wasn't crumbling away in places.

"You'll find your suites and such exactly where they were inside your old castle," Reah explained. "We've added modern plumbing, with written instructions. You'll also have comp-vids available to speak with me or Queen Lissa's staff, if you have questions or need help."

"Those people are?" Rodrik nodded toward a crowd of people, all of them dressed in green, who waited in the courtyard.

"The healer's staff. Each person who arrives will be given medicine to combat radiation sickness, and then given the address of their home in the city. Or, if they are a farmer or herder, they will be transported to the farms, dairies and such outside the city. Everything is laid out to be self-sustaining, although there are supplies in each house to keep the inhabitants eating for several weeks."

"Whom do we owe for this miracle?" Amlis breathed. That's what it was—a miracle.

"You owe the Larentii, Queen Lissa, several of her mates and Quin."

"Quin?"

"She made sure you were alive to see this, or do you not recall that, now?"

"I recall," Beatris sighed. "I wouldn't be standing here if she hadn't healed me. Rodrik, shall we visit our new quarters and see the whole of the miracle?"

"I think Quin healed more than poison sickness in Beatris," Reah informed Amlis as Rodrik and Beatris walked toward the castle. "It won't surprise me if Beatris gets the child she wants within a year."

"Then I'm grateful that Quin has a forgiving heart," Amlis said. "Thank you, lady, for this. Thank the Queen I have not met, and express my gratitude to Quin. So much would be different without her."

"If Marid hadn't tapped the core and made things so much worse on Siriaa, she would have continued to protect Lironis. As it is, even she can't hold the growing threat back. I worry for the whole planet." Reah disappeared, leaving Amlis to his thoughts.

He didn't have much time to reflect, however. People from Fyris began appearing by the dozens.

Lironis

Quin

Wolter, Yann, Deeds, Fen and Orik stood outside the door of Kaldill's suite. "We want to stay with you," Wolter announced.

"But," I began, confused. "You'll be so much safer with the others."

"We know. We want to help here," Wolter smiled.

"I barely recall you smiling in the kitchens," I pointed out as I invited them in with a gesture.

"There was little to smile about," Wolter agreed. "Now, I feel as if I'm a free man, making my own choices for the first time. I no longer answer to a despot who thinks himself a king."

"I'm glad Yevil's gone, too," I said. "Have you eaten? Kaldill says he's transporting Berel and me to Kondar first, until we hear from the Avii King as to whether we're welcome there as ambassadors."

"Then, with Kaldill's permission, we'll accompany you and Berel. And we have eaten already," Wolter added.

"Good. Do you have anything you wish to transport? Kaldill says not to worry about packing—somehow, he can will our clothing there."

"Our things are outside," Orik grinned. "Not to worry."

"Fen, are you sure?" I asked him, searching his eyes. They were as dark as his brother Chen's had been. "Yann?" He nodded immediately. "Deeds?" I turned to him. He had a daughter my age—he'd told me that himself.

"Most sure," he agreed. "We talked it out last night. We go with you."

"Gathering guards, dearest?" Kaldill walked in and smiled at the five who'd come.

"I wasn't aware I needed guards," I said. "At least Wolter can cook." Deeds laughed and pounded Wolter on the back.

"I hope to see you soon," Justis said as we stood on the balcony a short time later. He, Ardis, Dena and the four Black Wing guards were preparing to fly from Lironis. Gurnil and Ordin, who'd gathered books and things from the palace, accepted Berel's offer of an airchopper to fly them back to Avii Castle.

The city was already deserted, except for a few who'd chosen to stay behind. "What about Tamblin?" I asked.

"Found dead in his cell this morning—Ordin says the poison sickness took his life. As I could see no marks on the body, I'm inclined to agree with that diagnosis."

"Then Omina won't have to worry that he'll come after her. I hope she realizes she won't live another three days by staying here."

"I saw the fear in her eyes this morning, but she's too stubborn to admit she's wrong."

"Then so be it," I hunched my shoulders.

"Quin, you can't save what doesn't want to be saved. Remember that." With that, Justis leaned in to place a gentle kiss on my mouth. "I promise to see you soon," he said before taking three long strides toward the railing and leaping over it.

I watched his wings spread and beat a steady rhythm as he flew northward. In moments, Dena, Ardis and the others followed his lead.

"Quin, it is time," Kaldill beckoned from the doorway.

I turned once more to gaze upon the abandoned city of Lironis. "I'm ready," I sighed and turned to walk toward him.

"Welcome," the High President greeted us when we arrived at his palace. "Rooms are ready, and these five," he gestured toward my self-appointed guards, "are welcome to stay in the wing that houses my personal guards."

"I figure that will be better than what we're used to," Deeds said. "Thank you, sir."

"You're here with Quin. No thanks are necessary," Edden waved a hand. "Come, let's sit and have tea first, before we turn our attention to the problems of Siriaa."

Le-Ath Veronis

"They're moving the research facility to a point south of Avii Castle," Reah said, sliding onto a cushioned sofa in Lissa's library. Torevik, Garde, Kifirin and Korde had all arrived with her. Lissa asked for a meeting after the last of the people from Fyris were transported to Harifa Edus.

"Do Kaldill and Daragar still have the building shielded against radiation?" Lissa asked.

"They do. I wish I could say the same about the rest of the planet, but it's just not feasible. The poison is bubbling up from the core, so there's not much we can do about it."

"I got the sample of the creatures that create the poison. The ones the Kondari scientists believe are dead."

"What do you mean, believe are dead?"

"They're not dead. They're in hibernation. Whoever created them made them immortal. They don't die. They're so small that were you to blow the planet to bits, they could ride on space dust to other solar systems and infect them, too."

"Even the cold of space wouldn't destroy them?"

"We've tested them. At first, we exposed them to energy, similar to that of a planet's core. They perked right up. We ran more tests—and bent time to do it. They don't die. Remove their food source, they hibernate. Open the core, they yell yippee and go into a feeding frenzy. Siriaa is doomed unless we can find something to stop the cycle. And no, do not even attempt to seal the core, Reah," Lissa held up a hand. "It's too dangerous. Karzac says you don't need them in your system."

"Who made these things?" Reah breathed. "This is horrible."

"I have a feeling that if Liron, whoever he was, were still alive, he might tell us something. As it is, he's dead with the other Hidden and we may never know enough about this stuff to stop it."

"And who knows how many other worlds are infected because Marid was a difik?"

"There's something else," Lissa said. "Karzac checked Morid. He has those creatures in his system. He's been quarantined and we're checking the rest of the family, but so far we've found nothing. Morid helped Marid collect the samples from Fyris. I'm sure that's how he was infected."

"Burning doesn't kill the creatures?"

"They have an outer shell that will withstand anything you can throw at it. This was Acrimus' plan, I think, to destroy everything if he and the other rogues fell."

"You think the spread will be slow on newly-infected worlds because the core is mostly inaccessible?" Reah asked.

"Yes. I'd give anything to know what that Avii Queen did to hold this at bay. Otherwise, Fyris would have died long ago."

"Then perhaps we should visit my Larentii mate, to see whether he has anything in his Archives on the subject."

"I'd like to take Quin, but I don't know whether that can be easily accomplished."

"I like her," Reah sighed. "She's so level-headed. They should have let her run Fyris instead of those difiks who were in charge."

"I like her, too. Kaldill loves her. As does Daragar. That speaks volumes, all on its own."

"I know. Lendill is still in a snit—he thinks Quin will replace his mother's memory in Kaldill's heart."

"That's not true—he should know better," Lissa shook her head. "If he gives Quin any grief, I promise I'll kick his ass."

"I'll help," Reah laughed and lifted her cup of tea.

Avii Castle

"I have the report, my King," Justis handed the tab-vid to Jurris. Jurris handled it carefully—he was used to paper or parchment, instead of mechanical devices. "See, it shows that the remains were indeed Lirin's, and it shows that Lirin was Camryn and Elabeth's daughter."

"At least we know, now," Jurris sighed and handed the tab-vid back to Justis. "Did you thank the Kondari for their services? I can pay, if that's what they want."

"I believe that many things may pass freely between Kondar and Avii Castle, if you allow Berel and Quin to act as Kondari ambassadors. That is what the High President wishes, anyway."

"He does, does he?" Jurris leaned back in his chair and gazed up at his brother. "What if I refuse to allow Quin to be a Kondari ambassador?"

"Then she and Berel will likely stay in Kondar. The High President has named her a citizen of his realm."

"No, you misunderstand me," Jurris said. "Can the Avii not offer citizenship as well?"

"You're willing to allow this?"

"Many things have become clear since I was healed after Halthea's treachery. Wimla may be pregnant, and that could be due to Quin's talents."

"I am surprised by this, brother," Justis said. "Pleased, too, but certainly surprised."

"You think I don't realize what is happening? For too long, I did ignore it," Jurris held up a hand. "I blame Halthea for part of it, but the fault was mine."

"It helps to know that those who killed Camryn and Elabeth are dead, doesn't it?" Justis asked softly.

"Yes. I have been bitter during those years in between. If some way isn't found to combat the poison, those two may have killed us all. It is my hope that Quin will be the answer—or at least part of the answer—to solving this riddle."

"Then I have your permission to extend an invitation to Kondar to send ambassadors?"

"I will send it myself, under the royal seal," Jurris said.

"Do you mean to tell me your brother is making sense?" Gurnil blinked at Justis.

"Yes. I've brought a bottle of wine to celebrate better times," Justis said, holding up the bottle in question.

"Then let us hope that we find a cure for the poison, before we all die or are forced away from Siriaa," Gurnil replied. "Let me find cups and send for Ordin."

"Dena?" Ardis knocked on Dena's door inside the library.

"Ardis?" Dena opened the door.

"I wanted to ask a question," Ardis began. "You know I have no rank, now."

"Everybody knows that. It means nothing to me," Dena said.

"I understand—or at least I hoped you'd say that," Ardis floundered. "What I came here to say is this—will you agree to share my quarters? They're not much at the moment, but if I get my ranking back, you'll be a captain's lady, as you deserve."

"I'd settle for just being Ardis' lady," Dena wiped tears away.

"Thank Liron," Ardis muttered and pulled Dena against him. "I think I love you," he added, making Dena laugh through her tears.

Le-Ath Veronis

"Mom, I found this on a website that Tybus and I keep an eye on in the Campiaan Alliance," Teeg set a comp-vid in front of Lissa.

"What fresh hell is this?" Lissa narrowed her eyes at the offering. "Is this that criminal bulletin board you haven't shut down, yet?"

"We get leads from it, so it doesn't make sense to shut it down. Give me credit for something, okay?"

"Fine. Have a seat. I'll send for drinks. After today, I think I need one. Or several. Do they not know Marid's dead?" she looked up at Teeg.

"Apparently it's not widely known. Those crime bosses who bought that poison are sick, now, and out for Marid's blood for selling it to them."

"Then we need to put out the word that he's dead. It concerns me that they may target his family if they learn he's no longer available to torture."

"There's not a lot of reason or common sense among them if they feel they've been wronged," Teeg agreed. "Do you have any old-Earth Scotch? I wouldn't say no to that."

"I have some. Renée?" Lissa called out. Renée appeared quickly.

"Will you ask Cheedas to bring a bottle of Scotch and two glasses, please?"

"Right away," Renée nodded and hurried out of Lissa's study.

"What else has gone wrong today?" Teeg asked.

"Send for Tybus, he needs to hear it too," Lissa said. "Renée, bring three glasses," Lissa shouted.

"Yes, ma'am," Renée's voice floated back.

Kondar

Quin

"Quin, just smile and say, lovely to meet you," Berel grinned. "Kaldill and I will keep you out of trouble."

"But," I began.

"They'll want to see your wings. They'll be warned that it's impolite to touch," he added.

I had no idea that there was a function, as Berel called it, planned for the evening, and the High President chose to introduce Kaldill and me to the politicians attending. Kaldill had no objections, and I learned that Ildevar Wyyld, his guard and assistant would also attend.

I wanted to smile at the common titles given to Ildevar's companions—one was an elvish seer and the other was the Director of a large and far-reaching security department. The fact that he could become a huge, deadly snake when he felt it necessary only made me want to giggle.

Kooper Griff was quite well-mannered most of the time. Someday, I wanted to see the reptile he could become, but not while he was angry. I was also curious as to what Willem Drifft, the elvish seer, might see in my past. Perhaps he would allow me to ask.

"It's time—we'll stand with Father and meet the guests," Berel beckoned. I followed Berel; Kaldill offered his arm. I took it—I feared I might need his strength to remain standing before we reached our destination.

"Stop worrying, we'll be fine," Kaldill assured me with a smile. "Ildevar and I will make sure of it."

"Something isn't right," I mumbled. "I feel shaky for some reason. Like something bad is about to happen."

"You know I can get you and Berel away with a minimum of effort," he said.

"I know, and I thank you for that."

"Ildevar and Kooper have shields up already, and have included the High President," he added.

"I'm not sure it's that kind of threat—it doesn't feel close," I shivered.

"Quin, we'll get through this," Kaldill soothed. "Come with me and smile."

The Grand Hall was the chosen place to greet arriving guests, and Ildevar and his two companions were already there, speaking with Edden Charkisul as we approached. We never arrived, or so it seemed —Melis Norwal rushed in.

"Sector Two's Vice Presidents have declared war on Sector Three," he announced. "They're saying that you've sold Siriaa into slavery."

CHAPTER 11

*K*ondar
  Quin

"Marid—again. Still meddling from his grave," Ildevar growled.

Edden's guests—at least some of them—were in a meeting with the High President in a room nearby while Kaldill, Berel, Ildevar, Kooper, Willem and I were in a smaller room down the hall.

"Yes—it is easy enough to see that he told those who now are at war with the High President that the Reth Alliance will take everything and force everyone to work under its yoke. It is the same lie told by criminals and politicians elsewhere, when they have no desire to change their despotic behavior."

"I felt nothing of the sort on Le-Ath Veronis," I sighed.

"You can't call back a lie, once it has been told," Ildevar nodded. "Some will choose to believe the lie, no matter how much evidence to the contrary is presented."

"Omina and Rath are dead," I whispered. I'd felt it, even amid the other fears and troubles that crowded into my mind.

"I'll send word to Amlis. I'm sure he suspected as much," Kaldill touched my face gently. "Still, it will be a blow—he loved her very much."

"I know. Why are these people doing this—preparing for a war, when the real war is happening beneath their feet?"

"At times, they are foolish enough to fight something they can see," Ildevar responded. "In order to ignore the greater threat they cannot conquer."

"Funds and resources will be diverted to this endeavor," Kaldill nodded. "The research facility is safe—for now. Sector Two has sent ships to destroy it."

"Our ships are still in the waters surrounding the facility—they arrived there earlier tonight after you moved the building," Berel's eyes widened. "We have to warn them." He rose from his seat and looked about him, as if attempting to determine how to do so.

"Shall we ask for Alliance backup?" Ildevar asked, turning to Kaldill.

"You're the Founder, that is your choice," Kaldill responded. "We can get the airships here, if you want."

"For the greater good?" Ildevar lifted an eyebrow, which confused me completely.

"Most certainly for the greater good," Kaldill said.

"We'll need five at least," Kooper pulled a tab-vid device from a pocket and tapped it with his finger. "Lissa, we need five air destroyers on Siriaa in five."

"Our goal is to protect the research facility only—everything else is off the table for now," Kaldill pulled me against him. "The fate of all worlds rests in what they may discover. It isn't only Siriaa anymore. The fool, Marid of Belancour, and other fools in Sector Two who chose to listen to him, have jeopardized every world."

Le-Ath Veronis

"I'm going to Siriaa, and that's that," Lissa shrugged into a jacket. "I may not be there for long," she added.

"I will come with you," Merrill said.

"Honey, that's sweet, but," Lissa began.

"Come now," Merrill smiled. "You may need help."

"Fine. Come if you want, I can't stop you."

"You could, but you won't." Merrill leaned in to kiss her, before pulling away with a wink. Of all Lissa's mates, only five were vampire. Of those five, two were King Vampires. Merrill was the stronger of the two.

"Then let's go. Ildevar asked for five air destroyers to guard the research facility. He says the idiots in Sector Two believed the lies Marid told about the Alliance, and now they're sending ships to shoot at the research facility. They only moved it into deep waters this morning."

"What can they hope to gain by destroying the facility?" Merrill asked.

"How many politicians do you know who are completely rational?"

"Point taken. Let's go."

❧

Kondar

Sector Five: High President's Palace

Quin

"We're preparing for the ground assault, but as they haven't taken the time to plan this invasion properly, I worry that the population in Sector Three will suffer because of it," the High President said.

"You mean they'll get trigger happy?" Kooper asked.

"We call it short shooting, but yes—I worry that they'll fire on anything in their path. A wiser move would be to send airships, but there aren't any bases there—by their own choice. They chose to house half the navy and a few ground assault facilities. I believe they're regretting their past decisions now."

"Where did the ships come from that are guarding the research facility?" I asked.

"From Sector Three," Edden smiled at my question. "Two and Three have coastlines appropriate to house half the fleet each. I know not to send anything from Sector Two unless I'm desperate."

"Have you spoken to them?" I asked.

"They're refusing my communications," Edden's shoulders sagged. "If they don't stop this madness, lives will be lost."

"We have another communication—from Avii Castle," Melis strode into the room and handed the sealed parchment to Edden. "It was delivered to one of our ships by a winged messenger, and the crew flew it here by airchopper, thinking it could be important."

"Well, let's see what the Avii say, then," Edden cracked the wax seal and opened the message to read. "It's in Gurnil's handwriting," Edden said. "Ah. The Avii King sends his greetings and says that ambassadors from Kondar are welcome anytime."

"Unless Kaldill or Ildevar wish to deliver them, I'd suggest waiting," Kooper advised. He stood, stretching his tall frame and cracking a few vertebrae before continuing. "I hear that Sector Two has sent ships to destroy the research facility. We have five air destroyers on the way, for protection only. I hope you understand that the facility is important to all worlds, and not just this one."

"Defensive only?" Edden narrowed his eyes.

"Yes. We're not authorized to do otherwise," Ildevar said. "I believe Queen Lissa and one of her consorts are on their way."

"You were in a meeting and there wasn't time to make any other decision," Ildevar said calmly to the High President. "Sector Two's ships have already reached the facility, but the air destroyers are merely hovering there, between them and the building."

"Will you take me there? I wish to see this for myself," Edden demanded.

Queen Lissa stood nearby, her arms crossed as she listened to the conversation between Ildevar Wyyld and Edden Charkisul. I understood the High President's fears, but I also understood Ildevar's motives. Both were right, but I worried they wouldn't see it in time.

"It is always thus with politicians," her consort, Merrill Leopard, leaned in to whisper. I blinked at him before nodding at his assessment. He was quite handsome, with black hair and piercing blue eyes, but he didn't care about that. He was special, too. He knew that as well.

"At least they're not threatening each other with weapons," I whispered back. Merrill chuckled.

"I'll take you," Queen Lissa said abruptly. "If you wish to go."

"I do," Edden nodded.

In a blink, we stood on the balcony of the research facility. The five air destroyers hovered around the building, which now stood above the waves on stone-like stilts. Not far away, floating upon those waves, were five large ships from Sector Two.

"Sector Three ships are behind you, on the far side of the facility," Kooper said. Heavy rain fell where we were, and the winds blew rain into our eyes as we studied the military standoff.

"I believe the problem could be eliminated if you gave command of those airships to the High President," I said, pushing sopping hair off my forehead.

"What?" Kooper swiveled his head in my direction.

Lissa, whose hair was just as wet as mine, laughed. "It's not unheard of," she patted Kooper's shoulder. "Troops are on loan all the time to Alliance worlds."

"Well, fuck me and call me a two-headed lizard," Kaldill swore.

"At the same time?" Lissa smiled at him.

"If appropriate," he grinned back.

"Then we have announcements to make to all of Kondar," Edden said. "If you agree to give command of these ships to me."

"All yours, for as long as they're here," Ildevar agreed. "However, we reserve the right to pull them away if we determine that they are not needed or are being used for purposes other than intended."

"What are those unintended purposes?"

"To actually fire to kill," Ildevar shrugged. "We agree to incapacitate ships and equipment, but life-taking is the last resort."

"Then I am in agreement," Edden said, brushing rain off his face. "Shall we go, or are you not wet enough yet?"

Berel, Kaldill, Lissa, Willem, Merrill and I watched the news program, where Ildevar Wyyld, Kooper Griff and Edden Charkisul were answering questions at a news conference.

The conference was hastily put together, but there was a reason for that—Sector Two's war machines had already reached the border between Sectors Two and Three. For now, the only thing holding Sector Three's President back from mobilizing the troops stationed there was the High President's command. The other sectors had already chosen to go to war with Sector Two.

Second and third vid-screens in our meeting room showed journalists reporting on Marid of Belancour, and thanks to Queen Lissa's quick thinking, his image and the bounty on his head for spreading the poison to other worlds was presented to the people of Kondar.

There was no doubt now, where the poison had originated, or that it was set to destroy Siriaa if it wasn't stopped.

Then, images were shown of the warships from Sector Two, which were anchored near the research facility and threatening it. The people of Kondar were getting their first look at the air destroyers the Reth Alliance could provide. The news was widely broadcast that these airships were under the High President's command and that Ildevar said he had *full confidence* in Edden Charkisul.

"Where did the shield that hid this small continent originate?" Sector Four's President demanded at the meeting the following morning. Berel and I were there, as were Queen Lissa and Ildevar Wyyld.

Edden had instructed me to answer any questions I could regarding Fyris and its people. This I knew apart from that. "The wizard—Marid of Belancour—devised that shield long ago," I said. "He knew the poison was there and he could breech the shield easily because he made it. Collecting the poison made him ill, and when his attempt to assassinate the High President failed, he turned his weapon on himself."

I shivered as I stood before the crowd of politicians in the meeting, both from my discomfort at being there and at the memory of Marid's death in Edden's dining hall. I didn't bring up the ring that Justis delivered to Jurris—it was irrelevant, now.

Be brave, dearest. Kaldill's words filtered into my mind.

"Why would he kill the High President? What would he gain?" Sector One's President asked.

"He wanted Siriaa for himself," I replied. "He knew the Reth Alliance was prepared to make an offer to Siriaa for membership. He was already hunted by them, for other crimes. Once he controlled the planet, he could rule as he pleased and keep the Alliance out. Their rule, as I understand it, is that they must have permission from a planet's government to hunt a criminal there, if the planet is non-Alliance."

"So he'd be in charge and certainly not give permission," Sector One tossed up a hand in disgust. "What would he have done with the rest of us?"

"I only saw a little in him, but he was angry, greedy and had no care for others. I suspect he would have invited criminals to set up a base here, as long as they paid him for the privilege."

"He'd have made us slaves, just as he claimed the Reth Alliance would do," Sector Three exclaimed. "I have war machines sitting on my border, idling their engines and waiting for a fool's command to strike," he gestured wildly. "I want them gone."

"We have a message from Yokaru. Their physicians report an increase in the wasting disease," Edden broke in. "Until now, we've held back the news, but it is time they were advised as to what is afflicting Siriaa."

"I vote to authorize our ambassador to release the information," Sector One raised his hand.

Sectors Three and Four also raised their hands. "I agree," Edden lifted his hand. "I'll inform them when this meeting is over. It is time we took steps to safeguard all. Shall we make an attempt to contact Sector Two again?"

Four hands went into the air.

~

"It'll go back and forth—maybe for days," Berel said. He and I sat on the grass in his father's garden, eating a sandwich as our midday meal while the others ate and talked inside.

Ignoring the feel of the poison leaching into the soil beneath the soft, green grass, I nodded at Berel's assessment. "Father will send us to Avii Castle," he added. "You said yourself that the Avii who sickened had eaten fish pulled from the water or somehow got the taint from there. I think the castle is mostly safe for the moment."

"Only the old or very young were affected," I pointed out. "A healthy adult Avii was somewhat immune."

"At least we only had to deal with Presidents and First Advisors earlier," Berel said, changing the subject. "If we'd had Vice Presidents and a full Council, we'd still be there."

"I'm glad we're out here," I said. "Do you mind if I stretch my wings? They feel cramped."

"Not at all," he laughed. "Anytime."

My wings pulled away from my back and extended outward—it felt wonderful to get the kinks out of my muscles. I'd become used to flying short distances every day, and I hadn't gotten that exercise in the last two.

"Perfect," the journalist shouted as he held up a tab-vid.

"You're not allowed here," Berel rose angrily and stalked toward the intruder.

"He was just leaving. Weren't you?" Melis had the journalist by the collar quickly. "I could have you jailed, you know."

Berel and I watched as Melis was joined by two other guards, who took charge of the offender and escorted him toward the palace gate.

"That image will be broadcast in minutes," Melis said as he walked toward us. "I hope you don't mind," he apologized.

"I was seen earlier—in the meeting," I shrugged. Journalists had been there, too.

"But not with your wings extended," Melis said. "They're merely curious. So many of them dream of having wings, young Quin. This will only feed that desire."

"Do you wish for wings?" I turned to Berel, who took his place on the grass again.

"I do," he grinned. "White ones, with gold, silver and copper bands."

"You will go to the Avii tomorrow—with Berel and those four who call themselves your guards," Edden informed me after the meal in his garden was over.

"I will go with you," Kaldill said. "Daragar is already there, combing through the library. I think you should request those books you want from the King's treasury, while he is feeling generous."

"I will," I promised, although the thought of approaching Jurris frightened me. When I'd seen him the first time, he'd ordered my death. Yes, I'd saved his life. I'd have to see the changes in him for myself before I asked for anything.

"Will Sector Two see reason?" I asked.

"That is my hope," Edden replied. "The war machines still sit at Sector Three's border, but they haven't moved forward, yet. We've done our best to ensure that the news-vids reach the citizens of Sector Two, but we can't say for sure."

"Quin," Queen Lissa came forward and smiled at me. "You will always have a place on Le-Ath Veronis if you want it. Send mindspeech—I will hear."

"Thank you," I said, surprise causing my voice to squeak. Her smile widened. "Don't forget—I will always hear you."

"I won't forget."

I barely had time to wave before she was gone.

Le-Ath Veronis

"It won't be long before the scientists at the research facility reach the same conclusions we have," Lissa said as she stalked into her private study. Merrill, who walked behind her, agreed.

"What shall we do when they make that discovery?" he asked.

"Go round up my Inner Circle. We need to discuss this."

Harifa Edus

"It cooks things so quickly—the contraption they call a stove," the master cook complained to Rodrik. "I've burned three batches of bread already."

"The instructions are there—have you bothered to read them? They took the trouble to translate it into our language," Rodrik glared at the cook.

"No. I was never good at reading," the cook hung his head.

"Send for someone who can read and put him or her at the cook's disposal," Rodrik called out. "I curse the day Tamblin decreed that education wasn't necessary. Let me know when you have edible food for the Prince," Rodrik snapped and stalked out of the kitchen.

"We have an illiterate cook," Rodrik flung himself into a chair inside Amlis' suite. "That's why we're getting raw vegetables right now, and no bread."

"I went out yesterday—an older couple invited me to share their midday meal," Beatris smiled. "They could read, and the lady loved the stove—she said it did nearly everything for her."

"Can you convince her to cook for us?" Amlis asked. "We have an abundance provided for us, yet we sit here, hungry."

"I've sent for someone who can read to help the cook," Rodrik grumbled.

"This place is beautiful," Beatris walked to the window and

peered out at the city surrounding the castle. "Fyris hasn't looked like this in sun-turns. Are horses available? Might we ride to the farms outside?"

"Our horses are here, but there are also vehicles we must ask someone else to drive," Amlis pointed out. "The vehicles can take us anywhere we wish to go in very little time. It will take a horse nearly half a day to reach the outskirts of the city."

"The technology here—this is how it should have been, isn't it?" Rodrik asked.

"I think so. So many things held Fyris back, the shield being one of them. We thought only savages lived beyond our borders, when they'd surpassed us long ago. Here we are, attempting to decipher what we should have known already."

"Is there an inn outside the castle? Perhaps we should look," Amlis said. "I want a cup of wine and a different view."

"Prince Amlis?" A health worker knocked softly on the door.

"Yes?" Amlis stood and nodded at his guest.

"I've received word—my condolences, Prince Amlis. Your mother and uncle are dead. They were consumed quickly by the poison in your native lands."

Amlis cursed.

~

Avii Castle

"I think I'd feel better if Quin were here," Gurnil said, stabbing at the potatoes on his plate.

"You've voiced what many feel, I fear," Ordin said. He'd chosen to have dinner with Gurnil in the Library. Even Dena had left, going with Ardis to share his quarters. Ordin suspected it would happen, it merely surprised him that it happened so soon. "Justis wants to snap at everyone, I think."

"What's this about me snapping at everyone?" Justis set his plate on the library table and scooted a chair out to sit.

"We were merely remarking on the weather—and Quin's absence,"

Gurnil said, placing the whole, small potato in his mouth and chewing.

"I flew near the research building earlier," Justis said, cutting into the lamb he'd been served. "The ships from Kondar's Sector Two want to back away from those airships that appeared, but they don't know how without appearing cowardly."

"You didn't get close enough for them to see you?" Ordin asked.

"Probably not. I was just a flying speck to them. I think they're more worried about those huge airships hanging in the air. Jurris received word—Quin will arrive here tomorrow."

"Thank Liron," Gurnil muttered. "Why didn't you say that first?"

"I like to see a Blue Wing break a sweat now and then," Justis grinned.

"Perhaps you find it humorous," Gurnil complained and went back to his plate. "Where is that metal box, now? The one Quin is so worried about?"

"It's in my quarters. I'd like to move it here. If I ask Jurris, it'll disappear inside his treasury and we'll never see it again. I just don't want it to upset Quin more than it has already."

"I'll find a place for it," Gurnil agreed. "I'd like to study it anyway. I believe Daragar would as well."

"That is my desire." Daragar appeared, made himself shorter and joined them at the table. "I will take the information I gather to Nefrigar—perhaps he can help us with the mystery of it."

"Will Kaldill arrive with Quin and Berel?" Ordin asked.

"Most likely. He doesn't like it if he isn't near her," Justis said.

"He showed me a star map, and indicated where his planet is. His people share the same world as the Founder of the Reth Alliance."

"Reth Alliance?" Justis asked.

"The one who approached the High President recently. The same one who likely provided those airships you ogled earlier. Kaldill offered information and images."

"You have been busy," Ordin observed. "And there I imagined you were lounging somewhere, reading a book while Quin and I healed the sick in Fyris."

"While I can't claim to have done anything nearly as important, I did ask many questions. Kaldill was happy to provide information. He even gave me a comp-vid; one similar to Kondari tab-vids, except their reception is better. If I could read Alliance common, I might know even more than I do now."

"Quin can probably read it," Justis bit into a generous chunk of bread.

"That's true—I haven't seen anything she couldn't read or decipher yet," Ordin agreed. "You should see those medical reports she translated from the original Kondari for me. They're wonderful."

"I have a question," Daragar said. "Has anyone seen the Orb in Quin's absence?"

~

Kondar

    Quin

"Are you ready?" Kaldill asked. He, Berel, Wolter, Deeds, Orik, Fen and I stood together in the High President's study. Kaldill had sent our bags ahead already—I wondered what Gurnil would think when all of it landed unannounced in his Library.

"I am," I nodded.

"Ready," Berel said.

Kaldill moved us to Avii Castle in a moment.

~

Avii Castle

"You're to have dinner with the King tonight," Gurnil informed me the moment we landed in his Library. "You, Berel and Kaldill. Justis is expected also."

The widening of my eyes betrayed my dismay—I was hoping to put off that meeting as long as possible. With my wings clamped tightly to my back, I walked past Gurnil and went to sort out my belongings.

"Don't let it unnerve you," Gurnil sighed. "I should have let that wait until later. Justis wants you to join him for the midday meal in the guard's mess," he added.

"What?" Holding my lower lip in my teeth to keep it from trembling, I blinked hopelessly at Gurnil.

"He says it's time to face those who mistreated you."

"I will come," Kaldill's hand dropped on my shoulder.

"As will I," Berel nodded.

I wanted to pitch a tantrum in Gurnil's Library like a small, spoiled child.

I didn't. "Very well," I jerked up the first bag I'd determined was mine. "Where am I to sleep?"

"Quin?" Dena knocked on my bedroom door. At the castle, I was back in Justis' suite while Kaldill and Berel's suites were down the hall. At least they had windows—my small bedroom had nothing of the kind. Justis had the wide windows in his bedroom and sitting room.

"Come," I said. I had to work to keep the anger from my voice. Why was Justis doing this to me? He knew I'd been miserable in the kitchen, serving the Black Wing guards.

"Gurnil says you're upset." Dena opened the door wide enough to enter, then closed it quietly behind her.

"I am," I admitted. Just when the ground beneath my feet felt solid around Justis, he managed to unsettle it again. "Why is he forcing me to have a midday meal in the guard's mess?" I asked.

"I thought he wanted to show you off."

"What?" I jerked my head up at Dena's words. "No. I don't believe that for a moment."

"Then I hope it's not too difficult for you," Dena said. "Tell me what happened in Kondar. I really want to know and Ardis couldn't get anything from Justis."

I spent the next hour explaining the events in Kondar, most of it still unresolved. "I wanted to fly out to see the ships," she said, "but Ardis almost had a fit."

"He's just afraid for you—I can't say whether those people on the Sector Two ships are safe to be around."

"But surely when they hear that the wizard lied to them," Dena scoffed.

"Some people want to believe the lie," I said. "It feeds their beliefs at times, or their desires for a conspiracy, when there isn't one. Either way, it's self-serving of Sector Two's politicians to mislead their people, rather than to focus on the real danger. Fyris did the same, under Tamblin's rule."

"He's dead, isn't he?"

"He is," I nodded. "As is Yevil, if what Justis tells me is true."

"It's true—that's all anyone talks about at mealtimes. Nobody had been sent through the gate since Treven, so I suppose it's fitting that his half-blood son followed in his steps."

"I hope you know not to judge all half-bloods by Yevil's standards," I said. "I'm sure most of them would be just like anyone else, if they'd been given a chance to survive."

"I know." Dena studied her hands for a moment. We'd chosen to sit on my bed to have our conversation; I watched Dena's chest rise and fall with the deep breath she took. "Ardis asked me to share his quarters."

"Do you want that?"

"Yes."

"Then there's no problem. Is there?"

"No. I just hope he doesn't tire of a plain Yellow Wing and look for something better."

"Why would you call yourself a plain Yellow Wing?" I asked. "There is nothing plain about you, and your wings are lovely. Black and Yellow look quite fine together."

"Shall I wear black clothing, then, to say I am his?"

"If you want," I said. "The color you wear should be your choice, don't you think?"

"You make things sound so simple," Dena sighed. "I told my mother about Ardis, and, well."

"She put that notion in your head—that he may look for something else?"

"She can't help it. She has brown wings. My father has yellow."

"Why do people think they're better than anyone else? It makes no sense to me," I flung out a hand. "Your deeds will always speak louder than any wing color you may wear," I said. "Look at Halthea. Most know she acted no different when she wore yellow wings. She was exactly the same—mean, greedy and vicious. It would be the same if she'd worn black or green wings."

"She was favored consort to the King," Dena said.

"He was blinded by her wing color, too, never forget that. I understood what she was the moment I saw her."

"You can't say those things within the King's hearing," Dena whispered.

"I know. Politics and monarchs will always be the same, no matter what. Look, what shall I wear to this midday meal? Bear in mind they'll likely dump the food on my head rather than serve it properly."

"You look nice," Justis said. So far, I hadn't spoken to him. He hadn't asked me about going to the Guard's mess. If he had, I'd have said no. He'd been drilling his guards when I arrived, so I wasn't upset about that. He had work to do, just as most others did.

"Dena dressed me," I mumbled, refusing to look at him.

She had, choosing one of the tunics and matching trouser sets that Queen Lissa had provided. It wasn't overly dressy, but it was raw silk, in a pale blue. For a midday meal, it was suitable—if I were dining with nobles or the High President.

"Is something wrong?" he asked.

"No."

"There is." His hand touched my cheek. I jerked away.

"Quin—I know you're upset—Gurnil told me. I think I know why.

Come with me this once, all right? You don't have to go back again unless you want to."

He lifted my shaking hands to his lips and kissed them. I sniffled once, forced myself straight and nodded.

Moments later, after a short flight over the Castle and then down to the flight balcony outside the Guard's mess, I followed Justis into the castle, entering the same way that guards uncounted had arrived through the years.

Boisterous conversation stopped immediately the moment I arrived and struggled to keep up with Justis' long steps. Just as I feared would happen—all of them stared. Wanting to weep, I kept my eyes on Justis' black wings and looked neither right nor left until we arrived at our table.

CHAPTER 12

J was grateful that Kaldill, Berel, Ardis and Dena were already there and seated. At least I wouldn't have to sit at a table with Black Wings who'd ridiculed me in the past. I had no idea whether I could force food past my lips, I felt so ill.

"Dearest, you look pale," Kaldill said as I sat beside him. Justis, looking somewhat grim, sat across from me. A Black Wing Captain stood at the center of the room and called for everyone's attention.

"Today, I am pleased to announce a promotion," he began. "Ardis, former Captain of the Black Wing Guard, has now been restored to his rank. Welcome to the guard, Captain Ardis."

Ardis stood and beamed as cheers sounded throughout the dining hall. I breathed a sigh. Perhaps this was why Justis asked me to be present—so I could see Dena's joy at Ardis' elevation. Reaching across the table, I took her hand and smiled. Her return smile was tempered with tears of happiness.

When the cheers and shouts abated, I thought the meal would be served when Ardis took his seat. The Captain at the center, however, was still standing. "All the guards know that when the life of a Black Wing is saved, then our highest honor is bestowed upon the one who saved the life," he said.

"I have an Order of the Black Feather with me today." He lifted an object in the air. I blinked—it was made of fragile glass in the form of a large black feather with a gold quill. The skill required to make it must have been wondrous, and I wished I could have observed its making.

"Commander Justis, this is your honor to bestow," the Captain held the glass feather out. Justis rose and walked toward the Captain, accepted the delicate object with a nod and backed away. The Captain took his seat.

"Only a few of these have been given," Justis announced. "I was not among the ones who nominated or voted upon its recipient. Nevertheless, it is with great honor, and my blessing, to present the Order of the Black Feather to Quin, who saved Captain Ardis' life."

The dining hall erupted.

I fainted.

~

"I don't believe any recipient has ever fainted before," Justis' face came into view when I opened my eyes and blinked to clear my vision. At least he was smiling and didn't look embarrassed.

"I'm sorry," my hand went to my head. "It wasn't intentional."

"We know. Sit up and drink this," Justis held out a cup. Kaldill helped me sit up, and then lifted me to my feet, keeping me steady when I wobbled. I took the cup from Justis and drank, discovering the liquid was wine.

With a great deal of embarrassment, I was seated at the table again while a host of Black Wing guards looked on in curiosity. "Um—thank you," I said, as loudly as I could. A few guards laughed. It wasn't a bad sound, and I was grateful. The glass feather was set before me, with room left for a plate of food.

Servers began their routes between tables, setting plates before Black Wings. I was relieved when they turned to their meal and stopped watching me. My dizziness returned when I saw the one who brought our plates on a heavy tray—Jadin.

He served everyone else first. When he set my plate in front of me last, he set another object beside it.

It was a long, wooden spoon. "You have my apologies," he mumbled, his face darkening with embarrassment. "I saw the one who did the murders, when he was forced through the gate. You may hit me with this anytime you wish." He jerked his head at the spoon.

"I don't wish to hit anyone," I said. "But thank you for the spoon. If Justis will cut a notch in it, I can reach the high hangers in my closet."

"That's a wonderful idea," Dena said. "Why didn't I think of that?"

"Is that what you do, Lady? Find the true purpose in everything?" Jadin asked.

"I don't know—it just came to me."

"Back to work," someone called out. Jadin nodded to me and walked away.

"Why did he call me Lady?" I asked the moment he was gone.

"Because you're an ambassador of Kondar, and you have this," Kaldill tapped the glass feather lightly.

"The Black Wings will stand with you always," Justis said. "Because of that glass feather."

"Justis, I'm afraid," I blurted.

"Of what?" I thought he'd come out of his chair when I made my admission. Kaldill gripped my hand under the table.

"I don't know that we can save Siriaa," I said. "While the poison hasn't taken Kondar or Yokaru as it did Fyris as yet, it will. I worry that you'll have to leave your home unless you want to die like Omina and Rath."

"This is a conversation best saved for later, dearest," Kaldill whispered against my hair before dropping a kiss on my temple. "These here believe otherwise at the moment. We should proceed with caution."

"I know."

"We will discuss this later—in the Library after our dinner with the King," Justis nodded. "Try not to worry, although I realize it troubles you. I do see some things, Quin."

"I know that, too."

∾

Kondar

"The news isn't good, Edden." Hadris Jem and Firth Quel, Chiefs of Medical Science and Science, brought a report to the High President. They'd worked with the research facility staff, reviewing records and experiments.

"What is it? What about the standoff with the Sector Two ships?"

"The ships' crews want to leave, but the stubborn Second Vice Presidents refuse to allow it. The crews want nothing to do with those hovering airships above the facility."

"Very well. What's the bad news?"

"We can't kill the creature that produces the poison. If we starve it, it goes dormant. The moment an energy source is provided, it wakes again. When we cut into them with micro-lasers, the creature splits and becomes two or more creatures."

"This is more frightening that I imagined it could be. What do you suggest?"

"The planet will die," Firth shook his head. "It's merely a matter of how long it will take the creatures to kill it."

∾

Le-Ath Veronis

"Morid, if this doesn't work, there's nothing we can do for you except send you to Siriaa," Lissa said. "The poison and the creatures are already there—so you won't harm another world when you die."

Morid, lying in a quarantine unit at a nearby hospital, wheezed and nodded.

"Adjust the oxygen," Karzac suggested to the masked and gowned attending physician. "He's having difficulty breathing. Are you sure you want to try this, Lissa?" Karzac turned to her.

"What else do we have? I hope I can leave the creatures behind when I turn him to mist. Just get that second bed ready for him when I let him go, and be prepared to send this bed to the ocean outside

Fyris. I can't imagine that a hospital bed and a few more creatures will make any difference there in the long run."

"I'm ready," Karzac nodded.

Lissa, one of the few vampires with misting ability, became mist and then pulled Morid into her mist. Karzac, employing only a bit of the vast power he held, sent Morid's bed straight to the bottom of the sea surrounding Fyris, a thousand light-years away.

~

"Did it work?" Renée looked up from her comp-vid when the Queen walked into her office.

"It looks good—Morid is now creature-free, as am I. You understand this is a last resort, though. I had no desire to chase those tiny bastards around Le-Ath Veronis, once Morid was dead."

"I just can't imagine anything that can't be destroyed, somehow," Renée shook her head. "Is it all right if I take a long lunch break today? Montrose asked if he could see me."

"That's wonderful. Tell Monty hi," Lissa smiled. "Have a bottle of blood substitute on me."

Renée was hoping for the bite and not a bottle of blood substitute, but didn't say it. Lissa waved and walked into her private study, closing the door behind her.

~

Avii Castle

I took the old physician's journal to the Library after the midday meal, although Justis wanted me to lie down instead. He'd followed me back to my bedroom after our flight to his suite, and supervised the placing of the glass feather.

I was terrified it would be broken, somehow, and wanted to set it high in a closet. He'd insisted that it go on a table beside a chair instead, so it could be seen by visitors.

I wasn't sure I'd have visitors other than Dena, but I let him make the decision—it seemed important to him. Gurnil wanted to hover, too, when I took a seat on the Library balcony and opened the physician's journal to read.

The physician's name was Ulrin, but the people of Lironis had called him physician or healer so long that few remembered his proper name. His handwriting was tiny, like the tracks a small insect might make should it step in ink and then amble across parchment. At times, I imagined the insect tracks would be easier to read.

Worried that I'd miss something if I left pages unread, I determined to read the entire journal, no matter how difficult. I also resolved to make notes to hand to Amlis, because birth and death records were also recorded in Ulrin's difficult handwriting.

I hadn't gotten far when Dena appeared, letting me know I should dress for dinner with the King. "Berel is wearing the official colors of Sector Five, or that's what he said," she reported. "Kaldill says he's dressing down, so as not to upstage the King."

I wanted to laugh at Kaldill's words, but hid a smile instead. "I will trust your judgment," I said, marking my place in the journal with a scrap of parchment and closing it. "Want to fly or walk to Justis' balcony?"

We walked past Halthea's suite on our way to have dinner with Jurris. The door was closed; I wondered briefly if Jurris wanted to close her door in his mind as well. It made me hope that Gurnil was making a difference—Jurris knew that he'd coupled with his half-sister, who almost killed him at the last. I also wondered at Justis' decision to inform Jurris of the tainted relationship.

The moment I saw Wimla, I knew she was pregnant. She and Vorina stood beside Jurris, welcoming Berel and Kaldill to Jurris' private suite. *Wimla's pregnant*, I informed those with me.

Can you see the baby's sex or wing color? Kaldill asked.

Not yet, it may be too early, I replied.

Are you sure? Justis leaned in to nuzzle my hair. He had mindspeech, he'd merely chosen to use it sparingly.

Yes, I responded. At that moment, I wanted to melt against him as Jurris considered Justis' actions. If he hadn't guessed before, Justis had just announced his feelings for me to his brother.

"Congratulations, brother," Justis stepped forward and slapped Jurris on the back. "Quin tells me that Wimla is with child."

I will never forget the smile on Jurris' face as his and Wimla's hopes were confirmed. It also set the tone for the rest of the evening, which went much better than I'd hoped it would.

"I thought you were—well, I'm sorry for thinking it," Wimla said as we were served small glasses of an after-dinner drink. "I understand who killed Camryn and Elabeth, now."

"It no longer matters," I said. "I was treated better here than I ever was in Fyris. There, under Tamblin's rule and Yevil's influence, everybody was afraid."

"Where are they now—the people of Fyris?" Jurris asked, sipping his wine.

"So far away you can barely see their star in the night sky," Kaldill replied.

"This is so difficult to comprehend," Vorina sighed. "And you—where do you come from?"

"My star is even farther away," Kaldill smiled. "You know of the Larentii. Where did you suppose they came from?"

"I don't know. I'd never seen one—I only heard that Gurnil, Camryn and Elabeth had seen them, until Quin arrived and one began to appear regularly."

"Well," Jurris emptied his small glass, "As the Ordinance no longer holds sway over the Avii since the people of Fyris are safe far away, you may see the book Liron left here tomorrow," he said, turning to me. "Justis will bring you after breakfast and I will open the vault. Just remember that the book may not be removed from my treasury. You will examine it while you're there."

"I thank you," I dipped my head respectfully.

Not long after that, we left Jurris and his mates. I understood they had a private celebration to make—a royal child was on the way.

~

"Does this make you happy? Getting to read the Ordinance?" Justis asked, once we arrived at his suite. I hadn't said much on our flight back to his balcony. It was too late to have our meeting in Gurnil's Library, so we rescheduled it for the following day.

"It does, but something troubles my mind," I said. "I can't say what it is—there's only worry there," I shrugged.

"Jurris has offered a private suite for you," he turned his back to me and relaxed his wings before releasing the hinge and allowing black feathers to drag the floor. They were magnificent—long and blue-black where the light hit them. "I know I'm being selfish when I say I want you to stay here."

"I'm not ready to bed anyone," I began. Dena and Ardis had already coupled, and I was happy for them. I just wasn't prepared for intimacy, yet. There was a fear in me—that I'd lose my independence. That was something I hadn't had long and I savored it.

"I understand that—Kaldill says the same. You're young, but you are so much more than your age, Quin. I can't help but feel the way I do."

"I know. Perhaps I should take another suite, so you won't be tortured by this."

"I'll be tortured more, if I feel you're not safe," he said. "Stay here in your bedroom. I wish I could offer you a window, but that's not to be for an inner room."

"I know. I'll stay here. You won't mind if I visit Berel or Kaldill?"

"Visit anyone you like," Justis turned. "Just don't forget or ignore me."

"How could anyone do that?" I asked. "You're huge. You could probably slap someone across the castle with the ends of your wings."

Justis laughed. Threw back his head and roared. I'd wanted him to smile; instead, I'd achieved the ultimate success and made him laugh.

Then, his wings dragging behind him wonderfully, he came and kissed me, holding my face carefully in his hands while he did so.

"Go to bed, my Quin," he said. "Tomorrow is an early day."

∽

It was an early day—Justis had been up and drilling his troops before breakfast, and returned to his suite to bathe before we ate. We were joining our group in the Library, where the usual table was set up.

"Eggs, fruit and bread," Dena pushed a plate toward me. She was unloading the trays two Yellow Wings brought for us. "Eggs, ham, potatoes and bread," she handed Justis and Ardis their plates next, then went on to serve Kaldill, Ordin, Gurnil and Berel. There was no order to it, merely the way we'd seated ourselves at the table.

Ardis ran a finger down Dena's wing when she sat beside him with her plate of food. She smiled and leaned into him for a moment before lifting her fork to eat.

"I noticed my bed was made and the suite clean when I got back this morning," Justis told me. "You don't have to do that—I can ask the Yellow Wings who clean for Berel and Kaldill to do it."

"It gives me something to do," I said. "I enjoy it—my hands know what to do while my mind wanders. I did put the washing out to be picked up," I added.

"My socks—and other things?" Justis lifted a dark eyebrow and smirked.

"Yes. You'd think I'd never seen underwear before," I said. "I cleaned many a noble's quarters in Lironis, and scrubbed things far worse than your underthings."

Ardis snickered. Dena punched him lightly on the arm for it. Kaldill merely smiled, but his mindspeech surprised me. *I wish to take you for a short visit to Gaelar N'Seith*, he said.

When? I asked.

Soon. I believe Berel wishes to come as well. We won't be gone overly long —less than a day, I think.

I would love to see your home, I told him.

Good. I want you to see it.

Gurnil chose to come with Justis and me when we flew toward Jurris' balcony. He said he hadn't seen the book in nearly a century and wished to do so again. I think he was more than curious to see whether I could read the language that no other could.

I was curious, too—and frightened. The fear I felt I couldn't explain. A part of me worried that I'd learn something about myself, before deciding that was foolish. My other fears were vague and I couldn't determine their cause.

"There you are," Jurris greeted Justis with a hug before smiling at Gurnil and me. "Let us look at this book, then, and learn what we may from it."

Justis' hand went to the back of my neck and massaged it gently as Jurris led us down a hall toward the east end of his suite. A locked door waited there, made of thick metal with iron bands. My trepidation grew as Jurris drew a key from his pocket and inserted it into the lock.

The door creaked, metal on metal hinges, as it opened. Again, we followed Jurris as he walked toward the back of the huge room, packed top to bottom with treasures and important items.

There, on a tall shelf at the very back, lay a large, leather-bound book. I understood what had happened before anyone else.

One of my bloody primary feathers was placed atop the book, with a note beneath it. *You should have taken the key away, so it's your fault,* was scrawled across the note in Halthea's handwriting.

Inside, pages and pages of text had been ripped away. Everything I'd wanted to read was gone—likely burned or torn to pieces and tossed to the winds outside the castle. Jurris—and all the Avii—were paying the final price for Halthea's betrayal.

"I have a copy of the Ordinance, but the other—only the King's book held that information," Gurnil shook his head, his expression heartbreaking. Ordin offered him a glass of wine and he took it. Justis, grim-faced and angry, had escorted us back to the Library before going off to spar with Ardis—he needed to work off his anger somehow.

I grieved for lost writing. Yes, I was afraid of what I might learn, but I needed to learn it.

It was gone, now. Justis had snatched up my feather before storming out of the Library, my hand held tightly in his. We'd left Jurris behind, cursing Halthea's name loudly enough for anyone to hear.

∾

Kondar

"There's been an incident," Melis dropped a tab-vid on Edden's desk. "Some in Sector Three flung rotten fruit and garbage at the idling wartanks at their border. The wartanks' commanders fired back, killing twenty. Sector Three's troops have been mobilized. We are now officially at war with Sector Two," he reported.

∾

Quin

Berel looked pale when he came to find me. I knew just by looking at him what had happened. People had died and more would die as well, because someone had chosen to lie and others chose to believe the lie.

He sat beside me on the bench outside the Library, his shoulder bumped against mine, his tab-vid in his hand. While the screen was now blank, I knew he'd had recent conversations with his father.

Shutting Ulrin's journal and setting it aside, I reached for Berel's hand and laced my fingers in his. Today had been a terrible day for news of any kind. Berel knew what lay between Sector Two's invading

189

forces and answering troops from Sector Three—a city lay between them, filled with people who couldn't escape fast enough. Those who'd managed to get away had few options as to where to run; the nearest cities were filling up quickly with refugees.

"I've asked Father to command one of the Alliance air destroyers—they're coming to pick me up before moving to Sector Two's border," Berel said.

"I'm coming with you," I said.

"But," he began.

"No, we go together, or I swear I'll have Justis drop you in a pig pen."

"Quin, no," he argued.

"I think I have an idea, although it will require Justis' help, permission from the King and equipment from the Alliance. If we have those things, I think we can do this. Together."

"Fine. Lead the way."

"Let me get Ildevar here," Kaldill said the moment I told him what I wanted. If I had the equipment, I hoped to get the right answer from Justis when I took the problem to him.

Worrying that the answers would be no—both from the Founder and from Justis, made my stomach churn. If I'd eaten a midday meal (I hadn't) I would have heaved it up at that point.

"What's this you're asking for? Personal shields?" Ildevar appeared in a brief flash of light and blinked at Kaldill.

"For the Avii guards," I said. "This isn't Kaldill's fault—I'm asking for the shields. The Avii can fly through the rows of wartanks, and with the weapons you have that will render vehicles and equipment useless, I hope we can end this idiotic conflict before more people die."

"So you're hoping to protect the winged guards as they fire on wartanks? These same wartanks that can shoot rounds large enough to knock down entire buildings?" Ildevar's voice—and his words—

were skeptical. I could see he'd studied Kondari weapons during his brief stays—as was proper for any Founder of an Alliance.

"They fly really fast," I said. "The Avii, that is."

"I suggest we get the Commander in here, now," Kaldill said, his voice stern. They were going to override my suggestion, which made me want to weep. There was a way out of this, but we had to act swiftly.

~

"What fool idea is this?" Justis snapped. I wanted to cower—nobody thought it would work.

"Technically, it could work," Daragar appeared and weighed in. "But you must move soon or the plan will fail. The Wise Ones say this."

"What?" Justis whirled to stare at the Larentii.

"I'll explain about the Larentii Wise Ones later," Kaldill raised a hand. "If they say this will work, how much time do we have?"

"Less than two clicks, as the Alliance measures time," Daragar replied.

"This hinges upon you and your guards," Ildevar turned to Justis. "If you say no, then we stand down."

Berel stood with me, looking from one to the other. He was determined to go, no matter what Justis decided. "The answer is no," Justis said, his voice cold. "The King will never agree to this." He turned with a rustle of feathers and stalked away.

My breaths shaky, I turned to Berel. "I'm coming with you," I said. "Justis made his decision, I'm making mine."

"Dearest, are you sure about this?" Kaldill asked. He sounded worried.

"I'm sure." At that moment, I was furious with Justis, but didn't say it. The black glass feather I had meant nothing, after all. The guard—and Justis—were refusing to stand with me as promised.

"How do we get to the airship?" I turned to Berel. "I'll fly if there's no other way."

"An airchopper will be here soon," Berel said with a determined nod. "I sent for it earlier. We have little time, and it will take longer than the time mentioned to arrive at the battle."

"I know." I hung my head, already grieving for those about to die.

The commanders and troops aboard the Alliance airship only spoke Alliance common, so I had to translate their words for Berel to understand. Within minutes, he was determined to learn their language. He communicated with his father often on the trip to the border between Sectors Two and Three; Edden instructed him to make records of what he observed.

Berel and the High President hoped that the mere presence of an alien airship would force both sides to stand down. The ship's commander shook his head when I asked whether he could use the main weapon he had onboard to disable only the wartanks without also disabling other vehicles.

I worried about the ones working to save the lives of the wounded; if they or their vehicles were disabled, then even more people would die.

"It's all or nothing," the Commander shook his head when I asked. "Those ships in the waters would be easy, but when you mix in those bent on saving lives instead of taking them, the onboard weapon will disable all indiscriminately."

"Thank you for you explanation; I'll make sure Berel understands," I told him.

He nodded—he'd seen uprisings before and knew what was coming.

"He says he can't employ the onboard weapon to disable the wartanks without disabling all the vehicles, the airsavers included," I said. "I imagine anything in the air will immediately stop working and fall to the ground."

"This is impossible," Berel shook his head. I could see he was just as concerned as I was.

"I agree. Justis and the Black Wings could have taken the handheld disablers and taken out the wartanks individually. We no longer have that option, and ten times as many will die because of it."

"I don't know what to do at this point—Father has sent for an airchopper squad equipped with anti-wartank missiles," Berel said. "When those are deployed," he shook his head.

I understood, although he didn't say it. There would be no saving of the lives inside the tanks, once those missiles were fired. They were designed to destroy a wartank and anything in or around it.

"Ten clicks away," the Commander called out.

We were nearly there.

I was desperate.

"Is there a way for me to leave the ship easily?" I asked the Commander.

"The same way you came aboard—through the small passenger hatch on the second level."

"Then I want to leave," I said.

"What?" Berel sputtered.

"I have to try to stop this," I said.

"Only one Avii, with one disabler will not make much difference," the Commander snapped.

"I'm not taking a disabler," I snapped back before turning and walking toward the lift that would take me to the second level hatch. "And I'm not Avii."

CHAPTER 13

*W*hat I was about to do was foolish—the most foolish thing I'd ever done or dreamed of doing. Whether I had the strength or capacity to accomplish this task remained to be seen.

Berel was terrified; I hoped he didn't attempt to hold me back—this was my bit of foolishness and if I died, it would be from a decision I'd made for myself.

"Quin, are you sure?" Berel pleaded as the visitor's hatch opened slowly before us. Siriaa's sun gleamed on metal steps as the door yawned wide and I looked at the sky beyond. Airchoppers could be heard in the distance—they and the weapons they carried would be in range of the wartanks very soon.

"The rest of you, clip your safety belts," the Commander ordered, his voice terse, his body tense. I handed Berel's safety belt to him, my fingers brushing his. Giving him a shaky smile, I nodded. He had no idea what I planned, and truthfully, neither did I.

Yes, I had wings and could fly, although that hadn't been for long. Justis and his guards had drilled at tucking in wings and rolling in midair to avoid projectiles. My flight would be awkward at best—I had little experience, no evasive techniques and less guile.

With a trembling breath and shaking limbs, I nodded to Berel and the Commander, took three steps and leapt through the visitor's hatch, snapping out my wings and catching the winds that rushed about the airship.

~

Kondar

Personal Report to the High President

From: Berel Charkisul, Ambassador to the Avii

Father, I wish I could write this report without emotion as I've seen Melis do in the past, but that I cannot do and I am sorry.

My terror increased the moment Quin left the airship behind—the appearance of such a large, alien ship did nothing to stop the battle going on at the border below.

As you know, Sector Three has been an enemy of the Sector Two leadership for some time—their disagreements in Council meetings have often been remarked upon in the newsvids. Therefore, once they were engaged in this battle, neither were willing to back down and call their troops away, although that would have been the prudent thing to do.

The airchoppers were very close and almost within firing range—with the planned attack, all inside the wartanks and any around them would be killed when the weapons deployed.

The worst things, of course, was the number of Sector Three civilians caught in the crossfire—so few of them were able to get safely away before the battle began. I know many hoped it was merely a show of force, but that, as we both know, was foolish.

The airship Commander, once Quin left his ship, had no way of effectively communicating with me and we were reduced to a pantomime of sorts to make ourselves understood.

How I wished for the mind communication that Quin had with others. I know that no Kondari has ever had such, and that left me hopelessly isolated aboard the ship.

Nevertheless, the Commander motioned me toward a nearby monitor, where I could view Quin's progress as she flew just above the wartank projectiles firing between both sides.

What she intended to do I had no idea—until I saw her begin to shine— she projects a golden haze when she heals anyone. Was this an attempt to heal everyone engaged in the battle?

I know not—although after a few moments, the flying projectiles became less, and then less than that as time passed until they'd almost stopped completely. The Commander, who now stood at my shoulder, drew in a breath as Quin, believing the battle over, began to descend.

One last projectile fired, and while it didn't make a direct hit, it burst nearby, hurling Quin far away, like a wild bird struck by an airchopper.

When her body stopped tumbling through the air, it dropped to the ground and lay still in a pile of feathers.

Father, I wept.

~

Kondar

Sector Three

Wartank after wartank opened its hatch and their inhabitants peered out at the ten tall, blue men who gathered about the dead, winged girl. None ever admitted firing the shot that killed her—most of them, feeling peace and contentment like they'd never known, had already stopped firing.

It had only taken one projectile to destroy the beautiful, flying creature. Some men and women wept openly when they exited their wartank, but the appearance of the strange, blue men held them back from approaching the winged creature's body.

When the light began to form about the ten and the soothing hum started, all combatants relaxed with a sigh and waited for an outcome they couldn't comprehend.

~

Avii Castle

"If you'd gone and taken those Black Wing guards with you, this could have been avoided," Kaldill glared at Justis. Justis, angry enough that Quin had taken the situation into her own hands, glared back.

"The Wise Ones have done what they could; she is breathing and her heart beats again, but she won't wake," Daragar sounded frightened. "Berel refuses to leave her side. I know not what to do."

"At least the idiots stopped firing on each other, although I hear nearly two thousand civilians are either dead or wounded," Kaldill snapped. "It is times like these that I curse the non-interference rules. We are allowed to protect our mates, but when they involve themselves directly in a conflict such as this, the mate protection rules become murky."

Kaldill then began to curse in his native language. Justis didn't understand, although his name was mentioned several times. Daragar did understand and nodded upon occasion as Kaldill's rant continued.

∼

Le-Ath Veronis
Queen Lissa's Private Journal

I was and wasn't surprised that Kaldill appeared in my study, and less surprised that he was cursing rapidly when he arrived.

"Kaldill, calm down," I said, rising from my chair and moving cautiously toward him. He wanted to blast something, and I wasn't sure what he might target if he were startled.

Regardless, I kept a very strong shield up as I approached. The moment I put my arms around him, however, he broke down.

∼

"What if she doesn't want to wake? The Wise Ones changed What Was to bring her back, but she's not waking."

"Kaldill, perhaps she is dreamwalking," I suggested. "You know that can happen."

"Reah didn't," he pointed out. "When they made the attempt to wake her, she woke."

"Look at my sister," I countered. "It took days."

"Yes, but that's different," he huffed and turned away.

In all the time I'd known Kaldill, I'd never seen him weep like this —not even after losing three of his four sons. It made me want to weep, too; I felt Quin had a part to play in all that now threatened the worlds, but Kaldill would likely think that just as I did.

"I'm hoping that time will take care of this," I said. "But let me know if you want me to come."

"Yes. I should get back—Berel isn't having an easy time of it, while Gurnil and Ordin are at a loss. I care not what Justis thinks—he could have avoided this altogether if he'd just said yes. Daragar says the Wise Ones saw no loss of life among his guards if he'd agreed to Quin's plan."

"This is what makes me think she is very important to any solution we may find to our poison problem," I sighed. "We need her. All of us do. The Wise Ones believe that, too."

"It would seem that way, and I'm more than grateful. The combatants will never forget their first sight of the Larentii, with all five Wise Ones and their Protectors arriving as they did and performing a miracle, by their standards."

"What idiot fired that last shot?" I asked.

"Somebody who was so entranced by what he saw—Quin flying above him, as she was—that his finger slipped. At least that's the story I hear. All would have gone perfectly had that not happened."

"You can't always predict the human element, even when they're witnessing something amazing," I agreed. "Poor Quin, pouring out her healing ability to keep people from fighting."

"I believe she only recently realized she might do it," Kaldill shook his head. "Desperation drives strange decisions, at times."

"I can attest to that—more than once," I agreed.

"I should get back and see about Berel—poor child, he's caught up in her and will always be. It's unusual—to find the one you want so early in your life." I watched as he folded away with a sad, confused expression on his face. If Quin were destined to wake again, she needed to do it soon. The King of the Elves needed her.

~

Avii Castle

I woke in Ordin's healing suite, three days after the battle. I was surprised to wake at all; the last things I remembered were brief visions as I fell, numb with pain and unable to move wings or limbs. Whatever had been fired toward me had badly battered my body.

"Thank Liron," Ordin breathed. Berel, who sat on a chair beside my bed, shouted with joy when my eyes turned toward him. I could see what he'd known after I'd been injured—that the repercussions of the blast near me had shattered my bones, rendering me helpless.

I'd been dead after I'd fallen to the ground. Now, that was no longer true, thanks to the many Larentii who'd come. I had no recollection as to where I'd been after my life was restored; I only had memories before my injuries until now, when I woke after three days of unconsciousness.

Kaldill and Daragar appeared almost simultaneously, both smiling broadly at me. The missing one?

Justis.

I wasn't sure what to make of that absence. "What," I croaked.

"Water," Ordin handed a glass to me. My hand shook too much for me to take it; Berel helped me, although Kaldill and Daragar moved closer. Berel held the glass, my shaking hand covered his and I drank.

"Father was really worried," Berel said softly, handing the empty glass to Ordin with a nod.

"What about the war?" I asked, my voice as unsteady as my hand.

"Not yet sorted completely, but at least they're not firing at each other after what happened," Kaldill supplied. "The situation with the leaders is still tense, but the troops want no part of further battle. They saw my dearest one fall," he added. "After you gave your healing to them, they were horrified."

"I want to get up," I said.

"Take this slow, Quin," Ordin instructed. "You've been down for three days, and severely injured prior to that. Your suitors may help you stand and walk for a while, but don't tire yourself. You've only just awakened, after all."

"All right, but I want to stand. I feel as if I've slept on my wings the whole time and they're cramping."

Kaldill and Berel pulled me to my feet, where I rocked unsteadily for a moment before gaining my balance. Taking the first few steps was frightening but I did it, then both held my hands as they stood before me so I could stretch my wings.

"Commander Justis, Quin's awake," Dena said, squinting into the early fall sunlight as Justis lifted the heavy, round stone, flipped it over and then bent to lift it again. It was a strengthening exercise, but he'd been doing it constantly for three days.

"I know." The huge stone fell with a ground-shaking thump.

"Aren't you going to see her?"

"Do you think she wants to see me? I almost got her killed."

"You act as if that's the first time it's happened." Dena shaded her eyes with a hand so she could see Justis better. "Jurris told Ardis to kill her when she first arrived. If the Orb hadn't intervened, she'd have died then. Somebody put an arrow through her wing in Fyris," she went on.

"And I still want to kill the one responsible." Justis heaved the stone up, his muscles bulging with the effort as he pushed it over again. Dena almost jumped when the stone hammered the ground near her feet.

"I think you should talk to her. She understands what a difficult thing she was asking—you'd have had to go without the King's permission—everybody knows that."

"Does everybody have such a poor opinion of my brother?" Justis stopped for a moment and studied Dena's face.

"I think they measured him by Halthea's actions," Dena muttered.

Justis cursed softly, flung sweat out of his eyes and nodded. "Yes, I'll see Quin. After dinner."

～

Quin

Justis walked in quietly while I was having dinner with Berel and Kaldill in the healer's suite. He'd recently had a shower—his hair was still damp. That wasn't the only thing I noticed, however.

You look like you've beaten yourself, I sent to him. *Why?*

"Don't you think I deserve it?" he asked aloud, pulling an empty chair closer and nodding to Berel and Kaldill.

"Why? I know it was an unfair and foolish request to ask of you, and even more foolish of me to put all of it on you," I said.

"Ardis and I should have gone with you," he replied. "We could have made that decision for ourselves," he added.

"I don't know that it would have made much difference," I sighed, staring at my plate. They'd provided me with soft foods to eat—mashed carrots, lentils and such. "Have you eaten?" I lifted my eyes to gaze into his. They were dark and troubled—that was easy enough to see.

"I'll get something later," he shrugged.

"I'll go to the kitchens," Kaldill offered. "She forgives you, therefore I will as well." Justis shook his head in confusion as Kaldill disappeared.

"You didn't see her get hit," Berel snapped and stood to leave. "I'll be back, Quin," he flung over a shoulder and walked through the door.

"I have some ground to make up with that one," Justis sighed. "He's right, though. I didn't see it. A part of me is glad. It keeps me from hunting the one responsible and killing him with my bare hands."

"I think it was an accident," I said.

"That's what I heard. Still difficult for me to believe."

"I don't think we can stay here long, Justis," I said.

"Here? In the healer's suite?"

"No. Here—on Siriaa. When I woke—it was as if the poison had

201

multiplied a hundred times since I boarded that ship for Kondar. If the High President doesn't know it yet, he will soon. Relocating Fyris' population was one thing—there weren't many there. Relocating those still here? I don't even know if it's possible."

"Some will refuse to go, I think," Justis looked away. He meant the Avii, as well as Kondari and Yokarun.

"We have to have a place, first," I said. "And then do our best to convince them in a very short amount of time. We may have a moon-turn, Justis."

"The laws in Kondar say it will have to be by a vote of the people," Justis said. "Yokaru has an emperor, so he will have to be convinced. Are you sure about this?"

"As sure as I was the last time."

I watched his face go pale before he nodded. "I believe you," he said finally. "But that doesn't mean the people of Kondar or Yokaru will believe you, and I have no idea what Jurris will say."

I didn't tell him of the growing dread I'd felt since the moment I'd wakened—that I felt as if we stood on a narrow edge of a precipice, where a strong breeze might push us past saving.

Le-Ath Veronis

Queen Lissa's Private Journal

"Kooper, did you release discreet notices that Marid was dead?" I asked. "I still see those bounty offers pop up on occasion."

"I put it out there," he said, "And paid a few informants to spread the news. Even passed along a few images of him after he offed himself."

Kooper had stopped by my private study for a cup of coffee. He sat on the other side of my desk, his long legs pushed out comfortably in front of him as he sipped from the mug of coffee Renée brought. "Still no news of Bree?" he lifted an eyebrow hopefully.

"Nothing," I shook my head. "I've sent out mindspeech several times, but nothing has been sent back."

"It's been two years," he sighed. "I know they don't pay attention to time, but since we have mundane jobs to do, we have to pay attention."

"I hear that," I agreed. "I've been in contact with the worlds where we know Marid dumped that poison. They're noticing a rise in radiation around the burial sites. There's nothing they can do—it's like trying to hold water in a sieve. A few have attempted complete containment of the area—but those creatures, whatever they are, manage to find a way through every material they've tried."

"I can't begin to tell you how fucked up that is," Kooper grumbled.

"We've had reports from three worlds that we didn't know about before, sending information on the rise in radiation on their planets— so we have more coming. If Marid weren't dead already, I'd kill him myself."

"Only if you got to him first." Kooper sipped more coffee. "Did you notice who put up the biggest bounty on Marid?" he asked.

"I only saw two smaller crime thugs," I said.

"Vardil Cayetes offered twenty million," Kooper said. "I still regret that we didn't get him when his brother Hordace died. He stayed inactive just long enough to make us think the Cayetes crime conglomerate was dead, before picking up where his brother left off. I imagine he's been poisoned by what Marid sold."

"You're joking? You think Cayetes is sick, now?"

"I imagine he bought a lot of that filth from Marid, so yes, I think he is. Why else would he offer that much? The second highest bid was for a million credits."

"So Marid built the shield around Fyris to begin with. Why is that? Who hired him? I really need to talk to Bree," I muttered.

"There's a long line for that," Kooper reminded me. "Trajan says everybody on Avendor is getting fidgety because Ashe has been gone so long, too."

"When they get back, we need a conference with all three. There should be a signal or something that they'll pay attention to, no matter where or when they are. I suppose we can put a huge light on top of my palace that'll send a beacon through space and blind all the pilots landing at the space station," I joked.

"That only works for mythical Earth heroes," Kooper pointed out with a grin.

"Hey, I'll have you know I read comic books when I was in high school," I said, pointing a finger at Kooper.

"I studied herpetology," Kooper countered with a grin.

"So, when people called you a snake lover, you took it as a compliment, didn't you?"

"I've never loved a snake in the—what do you call it—the biblical sense?"

"You know, it must have been interesting around your household growing up," I said.

"Mom always made a cake at the full moon, because we were hungry after the change."

"Dessert—after rats and mice?"

"We-ell," he tried to smother a chuckle. "Our neighbors never complained about the lack of vermin."

"Koop, stop making me laugh," I said. "I almost snorted coffee."

～

Avii Castle

Quin

"Quinnie, I hear you have worries." Kaldill handed a plate of food to Justis and took a chair nearby.

"I think Siriaa's end is coming sooner than we think," I said. "I can't say exactly why that is—I only feel it coming."

"Willem sent mindspeech earlier, telling me he feels some sort of shift," Kaldill nodded. "He can't say what it is, either, and that worries both of us. Willem is the best seer among my elves, and when he says something isn't right, then everyone should listen. When my Quinnie says the same thing, then we really ought to pay attention."

"She says we may have a moon-turn," Justis said before biting into a piece of bread he'd coated with butter.

"Willem also says time is short, although he cannot say how long,"

Kaldill sighed. "I fear Kondar will feel it necessary to take a vote, and that will devour time."

"I don't know what to do—where is Berel?" I asked.

"Berel is not happy with me," Justis said.

"Berel is young," Kaldill said. "Although I am still angry, I understand Quin's view on this."

"I'm going to find Berel," I said, pushing my legs toward the side of the bed.

"I'll take you," Kaldill offered. "Stay here and finish your meal, I'll bring her back," Kaldill motioned for Justis to sit after he half-rose to follow us. Placing an arm around my shoulders, Kaldill transported me to the Library.

"Quinn, are you sure you should be out of bed?" Gurnil hovered the moment Kaldill made me comfortable on a chair at our usual table. Berel sat on the opposite side, watching me closely. Until my arrival, he'd been toying with his tab-vid. "What did you learn?" I asked, speaking to Berel instead of acknowledging Gurnil's worry.

"I've connected with the research facility—they say the poison creatures are multiplying at a rate comparable to that of a virus, but by their calculations, we should still have three of your moon-turns before the population is in real danger."

"I worry that we are all in terrible danger," I dropped my eyes. "I can't describe it, Berel, but something gnaws at me."

"Willem feels the same," Kaldill held up a hand to prevent Berel from protesting. "I learned long ago to listen carefully when Willem voices a warning, and when Quin verifies it, then we should all take heed."

"I'll speak with Father," Berel sounded stiff.

"Berel, please," I held out my hand to him. "I care for you. I care for your father. I don't want anything to happen to either of you. Or the people of Kondar and Yokaru."

"I've sent a message to Queen Lissa already, and to the Larentii,"

Kaldill said. "But we can't do anything without the permission of Kondar or Yokaru. I beg you to speak with your father now," Kaldill said. "I promise to do what I can, as long as you and your father promise to do the same."

Berel blinked at me. I held out my hand to him still, but it became shaky as I waited. With a sigh, his fingers gripped mine, keeping them from trembling. "Wait," he said, letting my hand go. I must have made some noise, because he moved around the table quickly, took the empty seat next to me and placed both arms around my shoulders.

"I will talk to my father, but I want you and Kaldill here with me when I do."

~

Le-Ath Veronis

   Queen Lissa's Private Journal

   "Where can we put them?" Ildevar asked.

   "There are two unoccupied continents on Morningsun," I pointed out. "Large ones, although they're connected by a narrow land bridge. Surely the continent of Cloudsong II won't mind—it's an ocean away and they don't have even a fourth of their area occupied."

   "You're talking of bringing in two separate political systems, with new rulers and politicians," Ildevar observed. "Cloudsong II's King will desire a meeting and a compatibility study. Trade will have to be considered—travel, too."

   "According to Kaldill, Willem and Quin, we may not have the luxury of time to work all those things out," I said. "Nobody knows exactly what's going on, but they're worried. I say we make this a temporary move, until the niceties can be arranged."

   "I hate to move a population too many times—it's detrimental to everyone involved," Ildevar mused.

   "I know. We still have to consider the other worlds affected by the poison—they may need a refuge before this is over. You know how I hate Alliance Enclaves, but we may have to call one."

   "You hate them? I detest them," Ildevar grumbled. "At least I can eat regular meals, now, instead of an entire sheep or cow away from prying eyes."

"I've watched you eat," I said. "You have good manners, at least."

"Lissa, don't make me laugh."

$$\sim$$

Vogeffa I

"Lord Cayetes, there's been another delay," Vardil's assistant hesitated and almost ducked as Vardil Cayetes turned toward him.

"What in the name of my brother is it this time?" Vardil hissed.

"The comp-specs aren't right," the assistant mumbled. "You understand why we can't test the equipment first—we only have one shot—at your command."

"Tell them I want this done quickly—we still have to transport it around Alliance patrols and that will take time," Vardil's voice was cold. "If I'm ill enough to die, then I want Marid's accomplices dead, too."

"Of course, Lord Cayetes."

$$\sim$$

Avii Castle

Quin

"A vote can't be called in less than two eight-days, and that's in extreme emergencies," Edden said. "Then we'll have to consider the move itself if that's the vote of the majority—that will involve the decisions of what to take and what to leave behind." I watched his brow furrow—he was quite worried. "Do we have that long?" he asked.

"I don't know." I wanted to weep at my admission—I had no idea why the danger felt as if it were fluctuating from one moment to the next.

"I'm glad you're alive, Quin. I saw the vids," Edden interrupted our conversation to say.

"Thank you. I'm glad, too," I agreed. "Although I have no memory of the time in between."

"I have no memory of when you healed me," Berel said, gripping my fingers tighter. He'd held my hand the whole time we'd spoken with his father. "I regret that," he added.

"I remember it," Edden smiled. "It was a happy day when you came to us, Quin."

"I was happy to heal that day," I said. "It was only right to do it."

"What will you place on the ballot, and how soon will the Kondari know what they're voting on?" Kaldill asked, bringing us back to our original topic.

"We can devise the comp-ballot in two days and submit it to all in a communication," Edden said. "I shall do this, but I warn you, it will meet with much opposition. Most are of the mind that the poison will be brought under control. I have no idea how to present this and expect them to believe it so quickly."

"Has everyone seen the newsvid of Quin at the battle?" Kaldill asked.

I blinked at him—I had no idea why he'd ask such a thing, and it made me embarrassed to think that people had recorded it anyway.

"I believe most have seen it several times," Edden replied, his voice dry. "There are fangroups that have formed, all speculating as to her current condition and every other thing about her."

My breath almost stopped as an idea formed. "High President," I breathed, "May I ask for sympathetic journalists to be contacted? I will grant an interview."

"What?" Kaldill's voice was sharp as he turned to me. After a moment, though, he nodded. "Yes. Call for journalists. Honest ones who are trusted. Quin will grant an interview."

❦

Harifa Edus
Fyris II
"I find myself wishing Quin were here," Rodrik spoke softly to

Beatris. "Amlis has been having fits of melancholy since he learned his mother and my father died so swiftly after we left."

"They were warned," Beatris gripped Rodrik's hand. "I spoke with Reah when she was here. She says that we may have a child within two sun-turns."

"What?" Rodrik's eyes widened in surprise. "Are you sure? That is so soon after your illness, my love."

"I don't know whether I should trust healers when they say this, but Reah's word I believe," Beatris said. "I feel better than I ever have, now. I wish Quin were here; she could say immediately whether that is the case."

"We're back to Quin," Rodrik breathed. "She could help Amlis, I have no doubt. I worry, however, that she has enough to do where she is."

"Will she ever come back to us?"

"My dear, she was never ours to begin with."

Avii Castle

Quin

I had three days to prepare for the interview. Rather than fretting over it, I decided to spend the time recuperating and reading Ulrin's journal. Eventually I reached the pages describing his best years— when he was selected as physician to Prince Tandelis.

He described the wife Tandelis took, who became ill during her first pregnancy and died when the child came too early. Tandelis' grief was described in detail, and Ulrin wrote that he doubted whether Tandelis would ever remarry.

He hadn't, leaving no heir and the way to the throne ripe for Tamblin and Yevil to usurp with a handful of deaths.

I had to get through many years' notes, then, to reach the point where Tandelis was murdered—and it was noted that it angered Ulrin greatly. Had Tamblin known of Ulrin's distaste for him, he'd have had the physician murdered as well.

Disappointment clouded my mind when I found nothing at all about me during that time, as it was then that my appearance was first reported by those in the castle kitchens. I took a moment to curse Halthea and the missing pages in Jurris' book before setting the journal aside—Dena was bringing gossip with my midday meal.

CHAPTER 14

Avii Castle
Quin

"Justis has been with the King and the Council all morning," Dena whispered as I ate. "Berel and Kaldill asked for a meeting, but Ordin said you were still too weak to handle that sort of ordeal, so they didn't call for you to attend."

"It doesn't matter," I shrugged. "You know how most of the Council feels about me anyway. I doubt much has changed."

"They should listen anyway—Berel and Kaldill are telling them what happened to the people in Fyris, and why the ones who didn't die were taken elsewhere."

"You know most of the Avii won't want to go anywhere," I said, spearing a tiny potato with my fork and biting into it.

"I know. My mother is one of them. Change is so hard for most people."

"Change isn't any easier for you or me," I pointed out. "We just recognize the necessity of it."

"Ardis says we're young," Dena frowned. "That we haven't lived long enough."

"I think that's rather prejudicial," I said. "I believe Gurnil and Ordin recognize the danger, as does Kaldill, and I can't guess at Kaldill's age."

"He's really a king?" Dena's voice softened.

"I—yes." I didn't say that Kaldill was more important as a king than Jurris would ever be. Dena counted Jurris as her King, and that was more significant to her.

"Maybe it's because we saw Fyris," Dena said. "If my mother had gone, it may have made a difference to her."

"Nobody should go there now, unless they wish to die," I responded. "That's how dangerous it is."

"Where will we go—if we leave?" Dena asked. A part of her wanted to leave, while another part wanted to stay. For her, much depended on Ardis.

"I will tell you this, as your friend," I said. "This is what I know—none who stay will survive. I want you to live. That's why I went to Kondar—I wanted them to live, too."

"I know."

She did—in some ways. In other ways, she didn't understand at all. Siriaa's days were numbered, and I had no way to impress that fact upon any of its population.

"Ah, she's eating already," Berel and Kaldill arrived, bearing trays of food.

"I haven't finished yet," I said. "Please, sit and eat with me."

Justis walked in just as they were pulling up chairs. Berel didn't speak to Justis, but at least he didn't leave the room. I was surprised, however, when Daragar appeared, fashioned a large chair with the power he held and took a seat behind the others.

I have a terrible fear that many people will die—by their own choice, I sent to him.

I know. The Wise Ones say the same. Do not blame yourself—it is a choice many make, and one we may see as preventable at best and a terrible choice at worst, he returned.

Do you know how those from Fyris are doing? I asked.

Yes—most of them are enjoying their lives for the first time since they can remember. Their animals are thriving and they have enough food to eat.

Amlis, however, is depressed and has been since he learned of his mother's and uncle's deaths so quickly after he left Siriaa.

Their choice, I dropped my eyes to my plate. We were back to that again—choices. Had they known they'd die so swiftly? Was it a mercy that they had, rather than lingering with the poison sickness or the wasting disease? There'd been no healers or relief left for them in Fyris—they were on their own.

Perhaps I will take you to speak with someone who understands these things—that the lives most lead may not be the only lives they've lived or will live.

What if, I began, before hesitating. *What if,* I repeated, *this is the only life I've ever had?* Something in me wanted to say it as fact, but I knew little about myself, after all. I'd stopped reading Ulrin's journal for now—I felt it had gone past the point where any mention of me would be made.

I do not know about that, and what you say may be true, Daragar replied. *Still, one who is wise may convince you, whereas I cannot.*

"Queen Lissa may have found a place for Siriaa's refugees," Kaldill's voice broke into our mental conversation. Somehow, he knew we were talking, and likely guessed at the main subject of our debate. "I've already informed Jurris," Kaldill added.

I wanted to ask if Jurris had made a decision so badly the words trembled on my lips. Holding my question back, I asked another, instead. "Where?" It was simple. Direct.

"There is a world called Morningsun," Kaldill replied. "A beautiful world, actually, deserted long ago by a race who could transport themselves from one place to another. So strong was their wanderlust, they never returned. They found it far easier to prey upon the efforts of other worlds, rather than growing, gathering, making or herding."

"They found no joy in such?" Dena asked. "That sounds strange to me."

"They were a strange people and nearly all of them perished, due to their own foolishness. Only a few survive, now, and they live elsewhere while they attempt to rebuild the race."

"Do they still wander from place to place?" I asked.

"The ability was taken away from most of them," Kaldill shrugged. "By Queen Lissa, who has some of that race in her bloodline."

"I see there's a story in that," I said. "Perhaps you'll tell me, someday."

"I'll let Lissa tell it—she knows it firsthand."

"All right." I set my plate aside and hugged myself—I had no stories to tell. No known bloodline, either. I belonged nowhere. It troubled me.

"Ordin says you may come back to your bedroom tomorrow," Justis said. I watched his hands as he ate—they were strong hands with long, well-shaped fingers. He'd gotten those from his father; Jurris' hands were smaller, the fingers shorter. Did I have a parent who gave me my hands? My hair or my skin? Who'd given me wings?

"Quin, perhaps a visit to the Library?" Kaldill suggested. "I think a glass of wine will not cause undue harm."

"Where is the metal box?" I asked. I struggled to keep the quaver from my voice.

"Gurnil has it in his study," Kaldill answered, although I could see he didn't want to do so.

"Perhaps Berel should do the interview," I said. "He has a true connection to this world."

"What?" Dena sounded shocked.

"Surely you know by now that I have no connections to Siriaa. My DNA—that thing that determines kinship—is like nothing anybody on Siriaa has. Not even those from Fyris or the Avii."

"Quin, I see that this troubles you greatly," Kaldill set his plate aside and stood. "Perhaps we should table this discussion for another time, when you feel better. I know this is rather forward, but one of us should hold you now."

"I will take her," Daragar said immediately. His chair disappeared when he rose. He then lifted me easily off the bed and I was transported elsewhere.

∾

"Where are we?" I asked. Daragar continued to carry me through an immense, brightly lit room, lined with shelves and displays of objects, both strange and familiar.

"The Larentii Archives," Daragar smiled and bent his head to kiss me. He tasted of sunlight and warm days. I huddled against him as he carried me past the first room and into another—and then another.

"Welcome." Nefrigar greeted us with a smile.

I burst into tears.

Avii Castle

"I was forced to place a healing sleep—the distraction failed to work," Daragar settled Quin on her bed in Justis' suite. He felt it would be better for her to wake there than in the healing suite.

"Nefrigar wishes to see the metal box," Daragar continued.

"Will he come here?" Kaldill asked, brushing hair away from Quin's face. She slept peacefully in the healing sleep Daragar had placed, oblivious to the conversation around her.

"He will. Meet us in the Library in a few moments."

"Good. I believe Berel is already there."

"This is a stasis box," Nefrigar examined the metal container carefully. "It was designed around Quin's small body at the time—that much is evident."

"Have you seen such before?" Kaldill asked.

"I have one in the Archives, although it is not as sophisticated as this one."

"How long do you suppose she was in that thing?"

"Difficult to say," Nefrigar replied. "There are no markings anywhere." He'd even removed the padding inside to check the bottom of the container. "The metal is standard titanium, but without further study, it would be impossible to say where it was manufactured."

"It's obvious Marid knew nothing about it," Kaldill pointed out. "He wouldn't have been able to produce such a spell anyway. I feel it took more power than he ever possessed to do this."

"Yes—placing living things in stasis requires a great deal of power and a finesse the Belancours do not have—even the best among them," Nefrigar shook his head. "This is a puzzle I would very much like to solve."

"It's destroying Quin," Berel said.

"You see a great deal," Nefrigar agreed. "It troubles her. She has no past. Nothing to grasp as her heritage. It is causing emotional pain."

"I don't give a flying fornication where she's from," Kaldill grumbled. "She belongs to us, now."

"She's a citizen of Kondar," Berel nodded. "I hoped it would be enough."

"One cannot help but wonder about absent parents, when there is no information to be had," Daragar offered. "I wondered about my mother until I went to find her."

"I'll explain that later," Kaldill whispered to Berel with a half-smile.

~

Harifa Edus
Fyris II

"You can't conduct court hearings and decide on your council if you're drunk," Rodrik snapped. "You need a council, you know—your father's council is either dead or left behind in Fyris to die. The Nobles here at the castle are becoming high-handed again, and that should not be. We need laws and a Prince to enforce them. A council will help."

"I don't need a council." Amlis struggled not to slur his words. He'd had wine with breakfast and had been drinking most of the morning afterward. "This place runs itself."

"It doesn't—and Beatris says that the mayors of all the small towns they left behind are now arguing over who is in charge—none want to give up their authority and step down, although they live in the same city, now. The Prince's intervention is needed." Rodrik shoved Amlis' feet off the table where he'd rested them, rocking Amlis forward in his chair.

"I'll have you sent to the dungeon," Amlis snapped.

"Really? Have you checked, my Prince? You don't have a dungeon, here. One wasn't built. I suggest you consider that when you sober up—you may need a lockup when the mayors flex their authority and order their sheriffs to arrest the mayor who now lives next door."

"But," Amlis sputtered.

"Look," Rodrik hissed, pulling Amlis up by the collar and staring into his bloodshot eyes, "My father died just the same as your mother. By their own choice. I suggest you mourn them in private and do what a Prince should in public. Your people are waiting. They grow restless, waiting for their Prince and his troops to intervene in the power struggle that now threatens our city."

"Tea, Rodrik," Beatris set a tray on the table, which now bore scratches from Amlis' boots. "We need Amlis sober, and we need it fast. A mayor was just murdered not far from here."

Amlis blinked in the weak sunlight filtering through cloud cover overhead. He knew, somewhere in the wine-fogged recesses of his mind, that if he were in full sunlight, the brightness would make his headache a hundred times worse.

Rodrik had saddled Runner for him—he'd fumbled the straps and buckles until Rod pushed him aside and did it instead. *I need Deeds, Wolter and the others*, he thought, before recalling that they'd stayed behind with Quin.

Quin.

He desperately needed her. If nothing else, she could heal his infernal headache. She could tell him how to handle this mess with the mayors, too, who'd suddenly thought it was imperative to stretch their authority in his city.

His city.

"How many troops behind us?" Amlis asked.

"We have twenty," Rodrik replied. "That's the first useful thing you've said in three days," he added.

"Will we face a mob when we arrive?"

"I know not, my Prince."

"Send one back to the castle for additional troops," Amlis said. "Now."

Le-Ath Veronis

Queen Lissa's Private Journal

"There's an uprising already?"

Renée stood before my desk with the comp-vid saying just that. Surely, Amlis and Rodrik were smart enough to know we'd monitor them. The werewolves of Harifa Edus were a continent away, but the peace of their world shouldn't be shattered by the petty squabbles of its newest inhabitants.

"We can go," Drake and Drew appeared in my study, making Renée jump. "Sali says he'll help. Dad and Uncle Crane need some exercise."

"So the Falchani want blade practice?" I lifted an eyebrow at my Falchani twins.

"We won't break heads," Drake promised.

"Fine, just make sure the Prince knows you're on his side, all right?"

"Not a problem," Drew shrugged.

"Take Tory with you," I added.

"Only if he promises not to go Thifilathi."

"Work that out with him. He has experience with these people, you don't."

Harifa Edus

New Fyris

The noise of the crowd reached Amlis' ears before the edges of it came into view. The extra twenty troops who'd arrived would certainly not be enough to quell this uprising.

He should have never taken his hands off the pulse of the people—he understood that, now. Even moving to a new home where there was plenty of room and enough to eat failed to settle everything.

"Amlis, perhaps we should return to the palace and gather the rest of your troops," Rodrik said, pulling Midnight to a stop.

"There's no need."

Tory appeared, with many behind him. Amlis drew in a breath—those with Tory were strange indeed—with long, black hair braided down their backs and inked tattoos showing on arms and chests.

The rest was covered in black leather pants and boots. Each man had two blades strapped to his back, just as Tory did.

"Are these what you are?" Rodrik stuttered the question.

"No—these are Falchani," Tory shook his head. "Trust me, they're all more deadly than I am with their blades."

"You need horses," Amlis said.

"A horse will only hinder me," one of the Falchani stepped forward. "I am Dragon, former Warlord of Falchan. If any wish to impede my progress, they will regret it, I assure you. Queen Lissa says get your house in order or Alliance troops will arrive to do it for you. You are guests here, remember? As yet, you have done little to show appreciation to your hosts."

Amlis swallowed with difficulty before nodding. "Lead the way," he said. "We follow you."

~

Avii Castle

Quin

I woke in my bedroom, after hearing Justis shuffle about in his room preparing to go to work. With an effort, I pushed my wings back, sat up and allowed my feet to slide to the stone floor.

"Justis?" I called out while walking unsteadily toward the door.

"Quin?" He was at my door and holding it open quickly.

"I just wanted to make sure I wasn't dreaming," I held out a hand. "How did I get here?" I added.

"Daragar brought you," Justis said, his eyes going over every inch of me to make sure I was all right.

"I'm fine," I held out a hand and ended up gripping the doorjamb when the brief wave of dizziness hit. Justis reached out to steady me and pull me away from my temporary prop.

"Do you want breakfast?" he asked, folding my body against his. "I was about to fly down to eat with the guard, but I can have it delivered here, instead."

"Can we go to the Library and eat with Gurnil and the others?" I asked peering up at his face.

"Of course." He almost smiled at my request before asking his next question. "Do you want help to dress?"

"Oh. Yes, I suppose." I looked down to see I was dressed in my nightclothes. I couldn't recall this particular set and wondered where they came from. Fingering the fabric, I determined it was silk.

"I believe Daragar thinks you look good in white," Justis did smile this time.

"That makes sense, now," I nodded. "I couldn't remember these nightclothes and I didn't own anything that was white."

"You do, now. He's right, by the way. You look good in white. What would you like to wear to breakfast?"

"Quinnie!" Berel was happy to see me; Justis carried me into the Library after flying to the terrace outside it.

"Berel," I offered him a trembling smile and a nod.

"Please sit—breakfast—and Ordin—will arrive shortly," Gurnil beamed at me. "How do you feel?"

"Shaky," I answered honestly. "But nothing hurts and I feel better today than I did yesterday." I didn't want to explain that I'd been at such an emotional low the day before I wasn't sure I'd climb out of that chasm.

"Father says perhaps we should do the interview together," Berel said, pulling out a chair so I could sit between him and Justis. "He says that we can use the images I recorded in Fyris to help convince the people, as well as pleading with them to choose their lives over a dying planet."

"That would be good. Very good," I agreed, holding out my hand. Berel took it and squeezed lightly. "Where is Kaldill this morning?"

"I just had a conference with Queen Lissa," Kaldill appeared nearby in a flash of light. "She says there was some trouble in New Fyris, but with the assistance of a few troops, the Prince now has the situation in hand."

I could see in Kaldill's face what the trouble was—those used to having authority over a small population thought to expand that authority, regardless of what others might think of it.

I also saw that Amlis had been forced to sober up quickly in order to make an appearance before the people and assert his authority. He'd been wallowing in depression, just as I had. Not for the same reasons, obviously, but wallowing nonetheless.

"Sometimes those things cannot be helped, dearest. We all feel it, from time to time." Kaldill had seen the emotions crossing my face and had read them accurately, just as he always did. "Queen Lissa sends her greetings, and reminds you that you are welcome on Le-Ath Veronis at any time, for as long as you wish."

"I would love to go there again," I agreed. "But we have to see to the people of Siriaa, first."

"I'd like more of those chocolate-covered redberries," Justis agreed.

"We may make a world traveler out of you yet," Kaldill chuckled.

"Berel, I suppose we should work on what we want to say in the interview," I said, changing the subject.

"I'll bring my tab-vid; you can sit on the terrace and we'll work on it, with help from Father and his staff."

221

~

Harifa Edus
   New Fyris

"I wish I'd had some warning that he could actually become a dragon," Amlis brushed a hand over his face. He wanted a drink but didn't think it was appropriate, considering the circumstances.

He and Rodrik now had more than a hundred mayors in the council chamber, waiting for Amlis, Rodrik and their guards to appear. Many of them had been prepared to fight the Prince.

One of the strange men accompanying Amlis had become a huge, red dragon and roared at the seething crowd, his breath fiery and fierce when he bellowed. Most of the mob had screamed and scattered, their plans of a coup forgotten immediately.

Then the job at hand became rounding up the mayors—Tory and those who came with him had no trouble sorting them from the crowd, although many thought to hide themselves from the Prince.

Tory, the one called Salidar and one set of twin Falchani—Drake and Drew—stayed, to make sure that the council meeting remained peaceful and ensure that any of the guilty were punished. Dragon and his brother, Crane, left after the crowd was subdued.

"I don't know what you were expecting—we've both seen what Tory becomes."

"I thought that was the most frightening thing I'd ever seen," Amlis shook his head. "Until today."

"This Queen Lissa must be powerful indeed to have such at her command," Rodrik pointed out. "I feel it would be most unwise to challenge her in any way."

"I had no such thoughts," Amlis replied. "And even less, now. Shall we go and sort through what we have? I think we should elevate those who disagreed with the rebels, making them council members, then work out a proper punishment for the murderer and those who supported him."

"I support that decision," Rodrik agreed. "Shall we, my Prince? Your people await the authority of their monarch."

~

Avii Castle

  Quin

"These are the ulcerations, before you healed them," Berel showed me an image of a young woman who'd had sores covering much of her body. She'd bathed in a stream near her home before falling ill. Berel's image only showed arms and legs—I knew the rest of her body was covered with the weeping abscesses, too, as I'd healed all of them.

"Yes," I nodded. He added that image to the collection to be shown on the newsvids. Fyris had been a microcosm of all the diseases and ailments that would visit those who elected to stay on Siriaa, rather than moving to a safer planet.

"We have to save as many as we can," Berel sighed. "If we must shock them into making the right decision, then so be it."

"I worry that Sector Two will say it's all a lie again," I said.

"They say that about everything," Berel shook his head while continuing his search for appropriate images. "The other Sectors expect it."

"Are there none who live there that will be convinced?"

"Of course, but they are in a minority, you understand."

"Berel, how many do you think we can save?" I asked. "Your best guess."

"That depends on whether Yokaru's Emperor decides to leave or not. His people will go or stay, depending upon his decision. That's nearly one hundred million people. As for Kondar, it's down to a vote. If the majority votes to leave, then all should leave. If the majority votes no, it's the same. Everything hinges on those things."

I watched Berel—his jaw worked as he considered whether Siriaa would live or die. I understood that no matter what Kondar decided, Edden Charkisul expected Berel to leave Siriaa with me.

I worried that we'd have to plead with the peoples of Siriaa in order to convince them of their imminent danger, so they'd leave their dying world behind. "Father is sending three journalists—ones who have already delved into the mystery of the poison and reported what they knew to the public. These are reliable professionals who don't report what they can't substantiate. We need that unbiased reputation so we can present the strongest case possible."

"Perhaps I can convince Kaldill to record images of New Fyris, where Amlis is," I said. "Or of the place where Queen Lissa suggests that the people of Kondar and Yokaru will go. That may help to convince them."

"Again, we'll have to deal with the mentality of Sector Two, who will refuse to believe it or say that this is merely image tampering."

"I never thought of that," I shook my head. "Do people do that?"

"All the time. We'll have to do our best to prove the images we have are untouched and real."

"This is impossible," I mumbled, my frustration rising.

"It is healthy to question—most of the time," Berel pointed out. "Except in this case, where we don't have time for a debate. Father told me this morning that the Alliance scientists at the research facility are backing up their records and preparing to leave with the five air destroyers. He says Ildevar Wyyld has called them away—they're not needed for a dying world."

"What is happening?" I whispered. Once, I'd held hope that Siriaa could be saved. That was no longer true. Now, I could only hope to save those who lived there, and if they chose otherwise, even that would prove impossible.

"Father says he'll stay if the people of Kondar vote to do so," Berel hung his head.

My breath stopped. Edden intended to die with his people, if that was their decision. "What are we going to do?" Berel lifted his eyes to mine. They were bright with unshed tears. The High President was the only parent Berel had left, and I understood all too well what it meant to be an orphan.

"We have to convince them," I said. "We have to."

CHAPTER 15

orningsun
Queen Lissa's Private Journal

"This is fine—the Southern Continent is suitable for the Kondari—the one farther north will do for the Yokaru." I waded through tall grass on the plains of the Southern Continent—the soil would grow grain enough to feed Kondar and Yokaru together.

"I'm sure Kondar will go right back to their five-Sector plan," Merrill said. He and Gavin escorted me as I examined the continents before visiting the continent of Cloudsong II. "They can import fruit and nuts from Cloudsong II that won't be easily grown here," I added. "I think all three economies can coexist. There's just one problem."

"What's that?" Gavin asked.

"The Avii. The waters surrounding this continent are too warm, while those around the Northern Continent are too rough. Neither place is good for the Avii. There's something more suitable around Cloudsong II, but that's probably not an option, either."

"I have a suggestion," Gavin said. Merrill and I both stopped in our tracks—Gavin seldom took the lead on things such as this.

"What's that?" I asked.

"You know where the Tooth used to stand—among the tall, rocky spikes and spires far to the west of Sun City?" He'd named one of Le-Ath Veronis' natural treasures—before its destruction on the sunny half of Le-Ath Veronis.

"The rock spires that Gren, Zellar and Tandias destroyed?" I asked. It still made me angry—the earthquake generated that day had killed thousands, in addition to destroying a natural landmark.

"Yes. I believe those waters would be suitable for Avii Castle."

"What? Bring the whole thing? I thought we'd just make a new one."

"No, I think this one is important," Gavin said. "I can't say why. You said yourself that it was fired upon and didn't show a crack or chip afterward."

"So we move the whole, damn thing," I shook my head. "Yeah. You're right. That's a good location for it, too. The waters are deep enough and the proper temperature."

"It will place Quin close—I know you like her," Gavin's arms went about me. "They'll make dark curtains," he added. "To block the constant sunlight."

"Everybody has a problem," I shrugged and tilted my head up for a kiss.

~

Avii Castle

Quin

Ordin arrived at midday to call a halt to our planning session. Berel had two screens filled with small images that we'd selected—he intended to send the lists to his father for final approval before handing them to the journalists. We'd written the best descriptions we could for each image, so they'd be readily understood.

We'd sat on the grass eventually to be comfortable while we worked, and that's where Ordin found us. "You should rest this afternoon," he said as Berel helped me up, then took my arm to escort me to the Library and the meal waiting there.

"I will." *We'll work again after dinner*, I informed Berel silently. I caught the barest of nods and a curving of his mouth.

~

Morningsun

Queen Lissa's Private Journal

Brandelin II welcomed me as was proper. His grandfather had ruled Cloudsong II when it was first founded, and I'd worked with him, his son Jenderlin I and now his grandson, Brandelin II.

"It may be several more generations before the damage Zellar did to my grandfather's world is completely gone from our race and our bloodline," Cloudsong II's king nodded as we walked through his private garden. At least his world was a member of the Reth Alliance in good standing. His great-great-grandfather had allowed a rogue warlock to destroy Cloudsong I, even as he attempted to join the Alliance. Ildevar, wise Founder that he was, refused the application.

"If you bring a population here that is fighting many of the things Cloudsong I did in the past, who am I to say no? You brought my grandfather and my great-uncle here in the beginning, to get them away from Zellar's poison," the King sighed.

"Your grandfather and great-uncle were good men," I shrugged. "It was the least I could do."

"Do you have information—on the ones coming?" he asked.

"I do. One continent—the Southern one—will hold a technically advanced race, with equipment and discoveries only slightly less than what is accepted in the Alliance. The other is behind them, somewhat. The first has five Sectors, each with a president and several vice presidents, plus one high president who rules over all five Sectors. The other is a monarchy, with an Emperor. He is benign and fair for the most part, has seventy wives and the stamina of a warship, if I understand correctly."

"I imagine he'd need it," Brandelin chuckled.

"The Alliance will be watching closely—they will be allowed to live here as long as the general laws are observed and peace is maintained,"

I continued. "If that changes, then they may find themselves outside the Alliance without friends."

"When will they arrive?" Brandelin asked.

"Well, that's still up in the air," I said. "There's no doubt their world is dying, but everything hinges on a vote of the people in Kondar and the decision of the Emperor in Yokaru. I'm sure that's what their continents will be named, should they accept Morningsun as their new home."

"Then I will study the information you've brought most diligently. I hope these rulers will accept an invitation to dinner?"

"I'll look into it," I said with a nod. "Is Willow here at the palace?"

"He is at his farm outside the city—he doesn't come often, unless he's needed," Brandelin shrugged.

"Then I'll visit him," I said.

"I heard." Willow, if anything, was a Green Fae of few words. I'd found him in his barn, kneeling to tend a new calf and her mother.

"Corent sends his regards," I said.

"I return mine," Willow grunted as he stood and stretched. "You worry that nobody may show up, don't you?" He offered his full attention, then.

"Yes. They'd be fools not to leave, but yes."

"Why do you need me?"

"Because you're Green Fae, and in your lifetime, you've moved many times. Granted, your race was persecuted by superstitious humans and that resulted in the moves, but these people will be terrified of the unknown. You know this world. I'm asking you to be an ambassador."

"Think they'll listen to me?" Willow walked out of the stall, closed the gate behind him and nodded toward the barn's wide opening and sunlight beyond that.

"I'd be willing to do hand puppets if I thought they'd pay attention," I muttered, walking beside him.

"Sounds demeaning," Willow shrugged. "For a Queen, anyway."

"Are you teasing me?" I lifted an eyebrow.

"I suspect you'd be the best judge of that." I caught the hint of a smile, however, so my question was answered. "What do you want me to say?" he asked. "To these people?"

"Tell them that Morningsun is waiting. That it will have everything they need. Anything else you can think of," I said.

"I'll think on it, then. When do you want me to go?"

"Tomorrow?"

"I'll be ready."

~

Avii Castle

Quin

"Dearest?" Kaldill found me, sitting with Berel on his bed after dinner. I had a stack of parchment before me, where words had been written and then marked through many times. I'd never had trouble writing my thoughts before, but then the fate of Siriaa's inhabitants had never rested on them, either.

The soft mattress gave under Kaldill's weight as he settled on the edge, watching as I wrote Berel's and my latest attempt at catching the interest of newsvid viewers. "Kaldill?" I lifted my head after writing the last word. Already it felt useless and inappropriate.

"Queen Lissa is sending someone tomorrow, who lives on Morningsun. He will answer questions about the world chosen for Siriaa's people. She also has information as to where Avii Castle will be placed—the intention is to take the entire thing and set it in the waters outside Sun City on Le-Ath Veronis."

"I thought it was dark there. All the time," I responded.

"The planet rotates on its side. Half is in constant darkness, half is in constant light. Sun City is on the border of both, and due to a wobble in the planet's rotation, the light dims at times but never completely goes away. They're considering dark curtains or heavy shutters, so the castle's inhabitants can sleep."

"What about the castle's bowl—and the animals there?" I asked. "They need sleep, too."

"Sheds and additional trees?" Kaldill smiled. "Better than death, don't you think? Lissa chose that particular spot because of the depth of water, water temperature and the sea itself—it closely matches what Avii Castle has now."

"Yes," I lowered my eyes. We had to convince everyone to move, first, and that looked to be daunting enough. Sleeping animals could be dealt with later.

"Our visitor's name is Willow, and he will arrive before midday tomorrow. You may ask any questions you wish—Willow knows much about Morningsun, its animals and people. He is advisor to the current King, and to his father and grandfather when they were kings."

"How old is he?" I asked.

"Willow keeps his age to himself, but I believe he is quite old, indeed. No one knows more about animals and growing things than he does. Like you, he eats no meat, although he raises cows for milk and cheese."

"What about the others—do they consume meat?" Berel asked.

"Oh, yes. The King has extended an invitation for your father and the Emperor of Yokaru to join him for dinner, but perhaps that should be put off for a bit, until a decision is made."

"Does the King not want us to come?" Berel asked. "And I don't like the idea of Quin being on another world."

"Ah—I knew you'd say that," Kaldill laughed. "There is no worry—I or one of mine can transport you anytime, and I expect your father wishes you to retain your ambassador status to the Avii."

"Good—ah—thank you," Berel dipped his head respectfully before grasping my fingers in his.

"Now, should you not consider resting?" Kaldill turned his focus on me. "I understand that this troubles you, but sleep can often bring fresh ideas. Shall I escort you to Commander Justis' suite, or would you prefer that Berel take you?"

"I'll come with you—Berel needs rest just as much as I do."

"Quinnie, I'll see you at breakfast," Berel nodded to me before letting my fingers go.

"All right." Kaldill took my arm and led me from Berel's suite.

∼

"There are days—most of them, in fact—when my body wishes you were older," Kaldill smiled as we stopped right outside my bedroom door. "Nevertheless, I will be patient." He leaned in to place a swift kiss on my mouth.

He was right—I was so much younger than he and inexperienced. Berel, like me, was young and we would fumble. Kaldill, Justis and likely Daragar, would know exactly what was to come.

"I will get there," I said before opening my bedroom door. "I promise."

∼

"This," Kaldill set the bottle before Justis, "is one-thousand-year-old brandy, made by those of my people most talented for such. Would you have a glass with me?"

He'd found Justis on a terrace facing the bowl of Avii Castle. It was a bar, tended by Yellow Wings and reserved for the Black Wing guards.

"Is it better than this ale?" Justis lifted his cup, his dark eyes focused on Kaldill.

"Most assuredly," Kaldill replied before holding out his hand. Justis watched as two small glasses appeared there. Each was delicate, cut crystal such as the elves could make. "One glass of this," Kaldill said as he poured, "would cost three thousand Alliance credits."

"Is that a lot?"

"The ale you're drinking would cost one credit. Something similar is served in most bars across the Reth Alliance. The shelf life and preservation of it is of little concern, as it is so common."

"It achieves its purpose," Justis rustled his feathers.

"Ah, but that is before you try this," Kaldill handed a glass of brandy to Justis. "Don't worry, I'll help you back to your suite if necessary."

"Are you saying I can't hold my alcohol?"

"I'm saying you may not where this is concerned. Come now, share a drink with me." Kaldill lifted his glass. "To Quin. May the next three years pass rapidly."

"Three years?" Justis sounded confused.

"It may take that long before she is ready for us."

Justis cursed before tipping the glass to his lips and swallowing his portion of elvish brandy in one swallow.

Quin

"Elf, I know not what was in that brandy, but I'll consider taking longer to drink it next time," Justis told Kaldill at breakfast the following morning.

"Was it not effective?" Kaldill lifted an eyebrow, although his eyes twinkled with mischief.

"Most effective. So effective the castle about me could have melted and I would have slept through it."

"Then the goal was achieved," Kaldill laughed.

"What are they talking about?" Berel whispered next to my ear.

"Drinking, I assume," I replied. "Although they smell better than most who've spent a night in their cups," I added.

"And how would you know?" Justis turned to me.

"Because she saw more than her share of Fyris' nobles, intoxicated and unconscious, when she cleaned their fireplaces every morning." Wolter arrived, followed by Fen, Yann, Orik and Deeds. "Thought we'd check in and have breakfast with you, this morning," Wolter grinned.

"I like it when you smile," I said. I knew, just by looking at him and the others, that they'd been honing their blade skills with Justis' guard.

I imagined that the Black Wings were teaching them things they never thought to learn.

"You won't be cleaning fireplaces again," Justis growled and turned back to his food.

"Don't concern yourself—back then, she kept herself dirty so as not to draw attention," Wolter said, taking a seat at the table. "She was only Finder, the mute kitchen girl," he continued. "None thought to look past that, or considered dallying with her."

"Because Wolter would have hit them with a wooden spoon," I said.

"I wanted to throttle the Prince when he came for you," Wolter told me.

"I know."

"Commander Justis?" a Black Wing captain stepped up to our table.

"Yes?" Justis said.

"The King wishes to see you."

"I'm on my way." Justis scooted his chair back and stood.

"I'll take no chances with my child," Jurris paced while Justis watched. "Our tenure as guardians for Fyris is long over—they're gone and those responsible for Elabeth, Camryn and Lirin's deaths are now dead. We leave when we have transport. While I regret leaving the castle, I want my child to live and be healthy."

"Kaldill says that the ones providing transport can move the castle to suitable waters elsewhere," Justis broke in.

"What?" Jurris stopped in mid-step to stare at his black-winged brother.

"That's what I understand—that there'll be no need to pack anything—the entire castle and its inhabitants will be moved as one."

"How can that be?" Jurris shook his head. "It confounds my senses."

"I think we can petition to have the Avii as a separate land, apart from the host planet. While we will be subjects of the Alliance, it is my understanding that we will not be unduly burdened by it."

"I recall Kaldill saying as much. It is Wimla's wish that she be attended by Master Ordin and Quin during her pregnancy," Jurris went on. "To ensure the health of our child."

"I think both will be pleased to do so," Justis agreed. "When do you intend to make the announcement to the others?"

"Soon. Perhaps in an eight-day. Until then, the information stays with us."

"Of course, my King."

~

Quin

Justis was frowning when he walked into the Library after landing on the terrace outside. Berel and I were already working on our interview, but I looked up to watch Justis walk toward us.

What I saw sent frozen fear through my heart. "Quin, I wish to speak with you. Alone," Justis snapped.

"All right." I struggled to keep my voice even. The place for that, it appeared, was my old bedroom down the hall. I hadn't been inside it for a long time—since before I'd traveled to Fyris, in fact.

Justis shut the door behind us before turning on me. "What in the name of Liron did you do to my brother?" he hissed.

"What?"

"When you healed him," Justis went on. Every muscle in his body was tense while anger washed across his features. "My brother is gone —replaced by—by—I have no idea who that is I just spoke with."

I didn't want to say that Jurris was rational. Reasonable. That would only anger Justis more. "The only thing I did was save his life," I said, crossing arms defensively over my chest to keep my hands from trembling.

"You did something," Justis accused. "He hasn't been the same since that night."

What good would it have done to point out that Jurris no longer had Halthea pouring poison in his ear?

"I saved him for you," I quavered. "Because you love him. That's all I did—I healed his injuries. That's all. I swear."

It didn't help that the Orb chose that moment to appear, when it had been absent for days. It floated above my head, its light bright and pulsing, forcing Justis to back away. "What power do you have over that Liron-forsaken thing?" Justis demanded, shielding his eyes with a hand.

"I have no power over it," I unfolded my arms and brushed tears away with trembling fingers. "I have no idea why it does as it will."

Justis cursed, then, before flinging the door open and stalking away. I knew the moment he reached the Library terrace, he would take flight.

Like words that couldn't be called back, once they were spoken, Justis was just as irretrievable.

∾

"I'm sorry Quin isn't here to greet you," Kaldill apologized to Willow. "There was an unfortunate incident earlier and she's, well, she's not herself."

"What happened?" Willow set two covered cages on the Library floor.

"Quin is an extraordinary healer," Kaldill sighed. "She recently healed the King. Before that, I'd have said that the Avii King was somewhat affected, shall we say, by his parentage. His father was what I'd term a sociopath."

"You believe Quin healed that in him, too? That would be incredible," Willow shook his head.

"It's possible. Now Justis, the King's half-brother and Commander of the black-wing guard, is accusing Quin of tampering with his brother. Can it be tampering if you heal a genetic aberration?"

"An unusual question," Willow nodded. "Not so easily answered. Do you believe lives may have been saved?"

"At least one," Kaldill said. "Perhaps the entire Avii population as well."

"Then why quibble?"

"I'm not the one quibbling."

~

Quin

If Daragar and Berel sat any closer, I'd be squeezed between them. Writing an interview now was out of the question—I was too upset by Justis' accusations. We were inside Berel's suite—I had no desire to go back to the bedroom in Justis' suite.

Ever.

A small part of my mind worried, though—had I affected Jurris' actions and decisions? I couldn't see that anyone was harmed by it if I had. In fact, lives had probably been saved, Ardis' first among them.

Omina, on the other hand; when I healed her, she hadn't been affected in that way. She'd retained her prejudices. She'd died for them, too.

A part of me blamed myself. Another part of me blamed Justis, for being unreasonable.

"People change for all sorts of reasons," Berel huffed. "If I read this correctly, this is a change for the better and not for the worse. Why is he complaining?"

"It doesn't matter," I shut my eyes and leaned my head against Berel's headboard. "I'm moving out of his suite."

"I will move your things to Kaldill's suite, if that is your wish," Daragar said softly.

"It is my wish," I said, keeping my eyes closed. What I feared most, I think, was that Justis, who told his brother everything, would tell him that he'd been tampered with, when that had been neither my intention nor my purpose. I'd only wanted to heal Jurris because Justis cared for him.

He'd told him about Halthea. About Treven and Yevil, too. For the first time, Jurris would be a father. Why was it so impossible for Justis to imagine that his brother might be changed by that?

"Berel, we have to write the interview," I sighed and opened my eyes. "No matter how upset I am, that's more important."

"Want to stay here or go to the Library?" Berel asked.

"I suppose the Library. Kaldill said Queen Lissa was sending somebody to help. He's probably already here."

"Are you hungry?" Berel asked. "It's midday. We can eat and write." His stomach growled, telling me how hungry he was.

"Yes. We'll eat and work." I held his hand as we slid off the bed.

"Would you prefer to walk?" Daragar asked.

I looked up at him—at the earnestness in his beautiful, blue face. "Yes. Perhaps I can stop shaking if my legs have a purpose."

"Very well. Send mindspeech if you need me." He disappeared.

"Someday, I want to do that," Berel breathed.

"Yes. Someday." We walked out of Berel's suite together.

"This is Willow." Kaldill introduced the tall man sent by Queen Lissa. His hair was a pale, flaxen color and he had bright-green eyes.

He was also old. Perhaps not as old as Kaldill, but old nonetheless. Still, he looked young, as most immortals do. He studied me before smiling, the corners of his eyes crinkling nicely as he did so.

"Your wings are magnificent," he said. "I have never seen such in all my life."

"Thank you," I said, the words automatic.

"I brought these," Willow pointed to two covered cages. "From Morningsun. Come."

Long legs carried Willow to the cages; he gripped both covers and pulled them away, revealing birds and an animal I'd never seen before. Did he know, somehow, that animals were precious to me? That any would come to my hand if I asked?

"These are fruitbirds," Willow pointed to the brightly-feathered birds hopping from perch to perch inside the cage, their tiny feet clicking happily as they settled on one post then another. Their feathers were yellow, blue and green and I thought them beautiful. Kneeling beside the cage, I had their attention immediately.

"May I open the door?" I asked.

"You may—they come to me willingly," Father Willow said. "If I offer seed." He pulled a pouch from a pocket and held it up.

"Oh, come," I opened the cage door. All six birds flew out, circled my head and then perched on the tops of my wings, chirping happily.

That's where Berel ended up feeding them—his hand held out as they sat on my feathers having their meal. Willow and Kaldill watched in fascination—Willow said that fruitbirds were difficult to tame. These he'd raised as hatchlings after animals killed their parents.

"Birds and other animals always trust me," I said, trying not to move too quickly; I had no desire to dislodge my feathered guests. "I never told anyone in Fyris about this, because I was worried they'd order me to lure the animals they hunted so they could kill them."

"What a horrific thought," Willow sounded outraged.

"I think so, too," I agreed.

"What about Pink Paws—he looks lonely," Willow smiled again.

"Will he eat birds?"

"No. He likes mice."

"Ah."

I studied the cat-like creature in the second cage—he watched me patiently, as if waiting his turn.

"Open the cage, please," I said.

Willow opened the door and Pink Paws slipped out. First, he wound his way sinuously around Willow's legs before hopping on the table and coming to my hand. Like a cat, he could purr, although he looked more like one of the weasel family to me.

"Animals develop differently to suit their environments," Willow said as Pink Paws walked beneath my outstretched hand before turning and going the opposite way, each time begging for a scratch. I obliged.

"Willow has been on too many worlds to count," Kaldill explained while fruitbirds chirped happily from my wings and Pink Paws purred affectionately. "He likely knows more about the plants and animals on those worlds than most scientists. If anyone from Kondar or Yokaru wish to know anything about Morningsun, Willow can supply that information."

"Will the same crops thrive there?" Berel asked. "After all, Kondar is quite fond of the vegetables available here."

"I've looked into that—I saw nothing that would not be suitable as far as food crops go," Willow replied. "There are a few other plants and such that might not work, but only because they would overpower what already grows on Morningsun."

"What are those?" Berel asked.

"Goldleaf Ivy," Willow said. "First and foremost. Kondar's soil is more acidic, keeping its vines small and containable. Morningsun's soil will allow it to grow rampant and cause problems for farmers."

"I think we can live without goldleaf ivy," Berel laughed. "The farmers here hate the stuff."

"There are only a few other things of the same nature—you call them weeds," Willow said. "Morningsun will be better off without those things."

"What about the animals?" I asked.

"I saw nothing that wouldn't thrive on Morningsun, including the tiny leafmunk," Willow said. "All serve a purpose, and if taking those things will make the people of Kondar and Yokaru more comfortable in their new surroundings, then there is no need to leave them behind."

"First we have to convince the people, and that means Berel and I have to write the best interview we can," I pulled my hands away from Pink Paws. He grumbled about it, so Willow lifted him and returned him to the cage.

The birds, too, weren't pleased to be removed from my wings, but Willow eventually convinced them. With the cages sitting at one end of the table so the creatures could watch me as much as they liked, our midday meal was brought and Berel and I began the task of writing our interview.

Again.

CHAPTER 16

*K*ondar
High President's Palace

Quin

"These are the topics Willow would like to cover," Berel handed a tab-vid to his father. "These," he handed a second tab-vid over, "are the ones Quin and I want to talk about."

"I'll look them over with my vid-experts this afternoon," Edden nodded to Berel and me. "Quin, do you have something suitable—and comfortable enough—to wear for this?"

"I do. Queen Lissa sent some things."

"She has a blue silk tunic and trousers, Father. She looks wonderful in them."

"My team wants the interview to take place where you had lunch that day—in the garden," Edden said. "The image taken by the journalist who sneaked in that day has been shown everywhere, including the newsvids, alongside images of Quin at the border war."

"I'd prefer not to discuss that," I shuddered.

"I know." For the first time, Edden pulled me against him and kissed the top of my head. "I've already warned them that this troubles you—Berel says so."

"How soon do you think a vote can be taken?" I asked.

"That is a more serious subject," Edden pulled away and shook his head. "It must be debated in Council before the Presidents present it to the people. I hope this interview eases the way through these arguments. My scientists say there's not much time and deaths among the very young and the elderly are already rising rapidly."

"So we have the scientific vote already?" Berel grinned.

"Nearly all of them are on the side of evacuation. Much of what we'll face is fear of the unknown," Edden agreed.

"I hope Willow can convince them, then," I sighed. "I have no idea whether I can."

Avii Castle

"What did you expect would happen?" Dena took a seat next to Justis. He sat on his terrace, head in hands, the midday meal Dena brought untouched.

"I suppose I wasn't expecting that," Justis let his hands drop before leaning back with a sigh. "I suppose I just wanted her to say that she'd had something to do with Jurris' change of heart. I've never seen him so—so," Justis fumbled for words.

"You mean you've never seen Jurris so reasonable?" Dena asked.

"Yes. That's as good as anything I can come up with."

"Look, I overheard Kaldill and Willow talking. They said something about DNA—I know that much, although I still don't know exactly what that means. They talked about evil being passed from parent to child. I can see that it happened in Yevil and Halthea's cases. Treven was terrible." Dena shivered. "At least that's what my mother and father say."

"Did they say that Quin may have had something to do with—well, you know?"

"I heard Kaldill say that if she did, she likely didn't know it—that her intent was to heal him. You have to understand though, that she can only heal what's wrong with the body. Remember that Omina's prejudices remained intact after Quin healed her."

"I recall. Now. Why didn't you say that before I ruined my relationship with Quin? Everything in her bedroom is gone—it's moved into Kaldill's suite. He isn't speaking to me either, as you know."

"You didn't ask me," Dena snorted. "You just flew right off that terrace without spreading your wings, first. Now, Quin's hurt. You're upset. Over what? That Jurris is suddenly making better decisions?"

"You make me sound like an idiot. Yes," Justis held up a hand. "I've already thought it myself. I don't know how to fix this, though."

"I don't either." Dena stood and stretched. "I have to dust Library shelves this afternoon. See that you stay out of trouble." Dena spread her wings and flew toward the Library terrace.

"Easier said than accomplished," Justis muttered as he watched her go.

~

Le-Ath Veronis
Queen Lissa's Private Journal

"Look at this," Kooper tossed a comp-vid on my desk.

"I already know," I said, looking at him rather than the tablet now lying in front of me. "Trik and Nissa sent mindspeech."

"How the hell did Cayetes manage to kill three Belancour wizards so easily?"

"You know there are still warlocks and witches for hire. Rylend has a list longer than your lion snake, filled with names of Karathian rogues."

"He's targeting the entire family, isn't he?"

"I think so," I said. "I just hope he doesn't target Trik, although Trik can take care of himself. I just hate the fact that someone has the idea to come after him."

"The records of your adoption are public, Lissa," Kooper reminded me. "He's married to your daughter. You may ask him to stay on Grey

Planet until this blows over. I have as many people as I can spare on Cayetes' trail, but I wish the fucker would just go ahead and die, already. Maybe that will eliminate this spate of revenge killings."

"I'm concerned about what he might do to stay alive," I said, tapping my temple.

"You don't think," Kooper immediately looked worried.

"Yeah. He has enough money and that is a powerful tool to convince someone to perform illegal surgery."

"How long do you think it would take for the new body to sicken?"

"No idea—it may depend on whether the mind is already affected. If not, then we could be looking at another full lifetime of Vardil Cayetes' criminal behavior."

"I'll see if I can pull more agents off other projects," Kooper rumbled, raking long fingers through his hair in frustration. "Who the hell would do this kind of shit?"

"Ask Reah—she dealt with the last known incidents," I said.

"I'll do that," Kooper said and turned to leave. "Any word on the Siriaan vote?" He swung back for a moment.

"They haven't even started the debates. You know how politics go —nobody's in a hurry until it's too late, and then it's all finger-pointing and blame."

"You'd know better than I would," Kooper agreed. "Keep me posted. Something about all this bothers me, but I can't say what it is."

"Me, too," I muttered. "Me, too."

～

Kondar

High President's Palace

Quin

Queen Lissa knew precisely the right person to send. Willow, with the aid of a special comp-vid, had three-dimensional images presented to the vid-journalists, who recorded everything shown and said by Morningsun's representative.

Berel and I were seeing Morningsun for the first time—the shape of its continents, which ones were reserved for Kondar and Yokaru, and Willow provided information on the already-inhabited continent of Cloudsong II.

Willow provided a short, concise lesson in geography, politics, zoology and botany. Soil quality was discussed, as well as climatology and geology. The continents were much larger than those currently occupied by Kondar and Yokaru, with samples of how to split the Kondari area into Five Sectors.

Willow had done so much with very little time. I worried that Berel and I hadn't done a tenth that well. Our interview was scheduled next, and my hands betrayed how unsteady I felt.

~

Vogeffa I

"Lord Cayetes, I have good news," his assistant beamed.

"What good news? I feel like excrement," Vardil complained.

"We've started a list of surgeons and wizards, we only have to choose one and convince him," the assistant announced first. "Second, three of the Belancour wizards are dead and third—the weapon is ready to fire."

"Why didn't you tell me the last item first?" Vardil growled. "Has it been loaded onto the ship? Are we ready to go?"

"The moment you give the word," the assistant smiled.

"The word is given."

~

Kondar

The High President's Palace

Quin

"The people of Fyris watched their children die—if they weren't stillborn," I said. "Crops withered or were stunted at first. At the last, nothing grew that could be consumed." Berel tapped his tab-vid, matching appropriate images with what I said.

"You already know the fish pulled from the seas are contaminated. It will only grow worse. Your scientists have already warned you that there is no cure for this poison—it will only continue to spread."

"What about the gods?" One journalist interrupted my speech.

"What if this is their way of providing help?" I answered. "To take all of you to a safe place? Is there a set of rules that your gods must abide by—a single, specific way spelled out to save the people?"

"Well, no, I suppose not," the journalist—a young man—replied.

"This is the best solution to the problem so far. If there is a cure found someday, I'm sure you'll be welcome to return to Siriaa— nobody else wants to come near it."

"What would you do—if you could?" another journalist—the only woman—asked.

"I wanted to heal Siriaa, but that is not my ability," I said. "Therefore, I want to save its people by any means possible. Now. Before the poison worsens and more people die."

"Do you feel confident that we'll be safe on this other world— Morningsun?" the third journalist asked. He was older and carefully considered his questions before he spoke.

"Yes. Willow has lived there for more than one hundred sun-turns. You see he is healthy enough. The people on the third large continent—Cloudsong II—are still recovering from the effects of the poisoning of their world two generations back, as Willow explained," I said. "They understand what it is to be displaced and will be most sympathetic, I believe, to the plights of Kondar and Yokaru."

"Where are the people of Fyris, now?" the woman asked.

"They are on another world called Harifa Edus," I said. "Their health and well-being improved immediately, now that they have enough food and access to medical care." I didn't want to explain about the attempted coup—that would dismay many. Kaldill's last word on the subject was that Amlis was now firmly in control—with a bit of help from Torevik Rath and a few others.

"What would you say to the Council if you could?" the young man asked.

"That there is little time. Differences must be set aside in order to protect the people of Kondar."

"All Sectors of it? Remember that someone from Sector Two nearly killed you," the woman said.

"All Sectors. I have no blame to levy and no grudge is held," I shrugged.

"Who were those blue men?" the older man asked. "The ones who helped you after you were injured in the border war?"

"I understand they are called the Larentii Wise Ones. There are no other races like theirs—they are unique. I am fortunate they chose to help me."

"I'd never have believed that such powerful beings actually existed, without such overwhelming proof," the older journalist said.

"The Larentii have visited the Avii for generations," I shrugged. "Master Gurnil, the Librarian for the Avii, has seen Larentii many times."

"They've been coming here all along?" the young man asked.

"You'd have to ask Master Gurnil—or a Larentii, to get the best answer," I replied. "They only come to study Siriaa—and until recently, when they helped me—have never interfered in any way with it. That is not their purpose. Mainly, they are curious, and with the power they have to visit worlds, it is understandable that they would do so."

My interview went on for two more hours, until I was nearly hoarse and barely able to speak. Edden and Melis, at Berel's urging, ended it, saying the journalists had more than enough material.

At the end, though, I was asked to speak directly to the people of Kondar.

I did.

Perhaps it was because I was so weary by that time, but I wept as I begged them to save their lives and the lives of their children. I pleaded with them to set aside their fears of the unknown—because what awaited them when the poison consumed Siriaa would be so much worse. Their lives would end in pain and suffering, and I begged them not to let that happen.

I knew about that pain—had healed many from it including Yissy, the youngest survivor from Fyris.

Berel dropped to the grass beside me at the last, while the recorders were still going, and pulled me against him. Clutching at his shirt and burying my head against his shoulder, I sobbed.

~

"Berel is with her—I've sent food and drink for both," Melis informed Edden. "I couldn't have predicted what happened at the last, but if anyone in Kondar remains unmoved by that plea, then they have hearts of stone."

"You know someone will find fault or say it's a lie," Edden sighed as he sat behind his desk and leaned back. The chair creaked as the cushion curved about his body, providing comfort. "I don't want Quin exposed to their vitriol. I want to send her and Berel back to Avii Castle while the debates are ongoing," he continued.

"I can send for an airchopper," Melis nodded.

"Ask them to come tomorrow morning—after breakfast."

"As you say," Melis replied. "By all the gods, I hope this is enough to convince the people."

"I hope it's as she says—that this is their way of protecting us," Edden agreed.

~

Quin

If the journalists knew that Daragar appeared in my bedroom the moment Berel and I were alone, they'd have run back to speak with him.

I doubted he'd answer any of their questions. He was only interested in making the tears stop and between his and Berel's efforts, they eventually did. Afterward, he sat cross-legged on the floor with Berel opposite, while I was held comfortably on Daragar's lap.

That's where I ate my meal—with Daragar's arms wrapped about me and Berel doing his best to make me smile.

~

Le-Ath Veronis

Queen Lissa's Private Journal

"This is all you found? A note?" I held the note in question in my fingers and waved it in front of Trajan.

"He does that sometimes. Usually he leaves notes for his past self, but this, well, it's written to you and me."

"*I needed Terrett?* What the hell is that supposed to mean? Now there's a Sirenali out there—where we have no idea—because Ashe said he needed him?"

"I'm guessing it's a good thing he's not here right now," Trajan ducked his head to hide a smile. Too late—I'd already seen it.

"Look, I realize Quin thought Terrett was all right, but what if he falls into the hands of another criminal—or another idiot, like Marid? He was only at SouthStar for three days," I wailed.

"Let's hope Ashe knows what he's doing," Trajan shrugged. He was still grinning, too.

The schmuck.

~

Kondar

Quin

I sent mindspeech to Kaldill, telling him that Daragar would transport Berel and me to Avii Castle, but Daragar had already told him. Melis Norwal offered an airchopper, but Daragar had things well in hand.

Melis couldn't help staring at the tall, blue Larentii as he escorted Berel and me to breakfast, then sat there, smiling and answering a minimum of questions for the High President.

"The Larentii never reveal the location of our homeworld,"

Daragar's voice was solemn as he nodded at Edden's question. "That has always been the way of things. There was a race, once, who found their way and attempted a takeover. They learned how powerful the Larentii were—and how resistant we were to their powers of suggestion."

"Were you there? When that happened?" Melis asked.

"No. That was long before I was born. Thousands of your years, actually."

"How old are you? If it's not rude to ask."

"Larentii value age and wisdom," Daragar replied. "I am young, according to my race. I am barely one thousand years old."

"One thousand years? That's incredible," Edden breathed.

"Yes. Kaldill has been King of the Elves far longer than that. Many older Larentii recall conversations with Kaldill, far in the past."

While Melis might have wished for a lengthy conversation as to whether immortality was a blessing or curse, Daragar whisked Berel and me away the moment our meals were finished, depositing us in Gurnil's Library and causing Dena to laugh in delight.

She stood with a bird-feather duster in her hand, smiling widely when the three of us appeared not far away. "Have you eaten?" she asked, first thing.

"Yes, thank you," Berel smiled at her. "We just had breakfast."

"Quin, you look tired," she said.

"Quin had a trying day, yesterday," Berel said.

"I am tired. I'm thinking of reading more in Ulrin's journal, and perhaps making a few notes for Gurnil—I haven't done that as yet."

"I'll bring a midday meal when it's time," Dena promised. "Are you reading in the Library or in your bedroom? It's raining outside, or I'd say the terrace."

"I'll read in my bedroom," I said. There was a chance Justis might appear somewhere in public, but he wouldn't walk into Kaldill's suite without an invitation.

"There's my dearest," Kaldill appeared with a smile. He pulled me into a hug before letting me go with a nod. "By all means, read in your bedroom until midday. Sleep if you want. Daragar tells me you're exhausted after yesterday's ordeal."

I did feel exhausted but was too worried about the debates, which were just beginning in Kondar. No word had come from the Yokarun Emperor, but perhaps he waited to see what Kondar's decision would be. After all, Yokaru now depended heavily upon trade with Kondar, and that would disappear along with the people of Kondar if their decision were to leave Siriaa behind.

"I see many things trouble you," Kaldill smiled. "Read the physician's journal and take your mind away from these things."

Dena brought me a cup of tea while I settled on the bed and pulled Ulrin's journal into my hand. "Let me know if you need anything else," she said. "I believe Justis would like to grovel, but whether you let him or not is your decision."

"I don't know what to do about that," I hunched my shoulders uncomfortably. "Perhaps soon, but not now. His words hurt too much."

"The people you love can hurt the most, can't they?" Dena said softly. I knew she was thinking about her mother, who'd belittled her many times for having yellow wings.

"Yes," I agreed. "Sometimes I think they fail to realize how much harm they've done."

"Ardis says hello," she said.

"How is he? Doing well?"

"He appreciates being Captain Ardis again," she smiled. "He and Justis are drilling the Black Wings this morning."

The thought of it made me sigh. Justis—drilling his troops for a war that might never come. I'd offered him the opportunity to make a difference in the border war. He'd refused.

"I'll just get to this, then," I held up the journal. "Gurnil may be quite bored when he reads the report, but the births, deaths and lineage records may be of interest to Amlis. I'll make separate reports for him."

"I'd rather dust the entire Library at once than do that," Dena frowned. "I'll see you at midday."

She closed my bedroom door behind her, tucking her wings closer so they wouldn't catch between door and jamb. Shoving away thoughts of Justis, which still pervaded my mind, I opened the journal where I'd left it last and began to read.

~

Avendor
   EastStar
"There are two ways to shift into another body," Reah handed a cup of coffee to Kooper, then sat at the kitchen island across from the tall, lion snake shapeshifter. Both Farzi and Nenzi, Reah's lion snake shifter mates, had come to see Kooper, whom they admired.

"You've seen both, or so I've heard," Kooper sipped his coffee. "This is excellent—what did you put in it?"

"Vanilla, milk, cinnamon and sugar," Reah smiled. "And I frothed the milk."

"You think grz-gitch Vardil Cayetes do this?" Farzi asked. "Steal bodies?" He and his brothers eliminated unnecessary words when they spoke—a habit they'd acquired early in their lives.

"Vardil has enough money to convince a surgeon to do the work. I understand if a warlock is involved, the stolen body begins to die quickly so a continuous supply of fresh bodies has to be found."

"Either way," Reah shrugged. "As a criminal, if he got a warlock involved, it would be impossible for the ASD to track him, because the image could change every few days."

"Vardil is wealthy enough—and nasty enough—to do either," Kooper shook his head. "Even Karzac can't predict what could happen if Vardil's brain is affected already with the poison, and then is transferred to another body."

"Have you kept an eye on the black market employment listings? Anybody looking to hire a powerful warlock?"

"Nothing so far. Look, what do you think would happen if the brain transfer was performed first, before he went looking for a warlock?"

"No idea. I've never heard of anybody stupid enough to try that. After all, you have to keep the warlock with you at all times once the first transfer is done, just to make sure he's available when the new body fails. It makes an unholy alliance, and somebody is going to tire quickly of their partner, I think."

"Unless the money is really, really good," Kooper observed. "In Vardil's case, that's exactly how it'll be."

"If this happens, you'll have to look for worlds where significant numbers of people disappear, then reappear not long after, their bodies dumped and not only dead but looking ravaged for no apparent reason. Soul shifting isn't easy on either party."

"You know there are plenty of non-Alliance worlds where we can't get good information," Kooper said. "We have spies on many, but not all."

"Does Lissa have any updates on Siriaa?" Reah asked.

"Not yet—they've just started the council debates."

"I heard from Tory—after the brief uprising in New Fyris, things have smoothed out. Amlis is learning what it means to be Prince."

"That means being a diplomat, instead of the murderer his father was."

"There's always an adjustment to be made," Reah smiled.

"I should get back to Le-Ath Veronis—I have to release a bulletin on what the agents should look for," Kooper stood and stretched.

"You need help, Kooper, we go anytime," Farzi offered. Nenzi, seated beside Farzi, nodded his agreement with enthusiasm.

"I may take you up on that," Kooper grinned at both.

~

Avii Castle

Quin

My eyes are going dark, the journal read. *Therefore, it is time I made my confession, in case Liron returns to Fyris one day.*

I'd almost nodded off before I came to that section of the journal.

Ulrin's words, however, made me push myself straighter on the bed and pull the journal closer.

"Liron went to Fyris?" I breathed, running a finger down the page. Clearly, Ulrin's eyesight was failing him—the words were larger and fewer on the page. Hastily I turned the page and gasped—the writing was like none I'd ever seen before.

It was upside down and backward, at the same time.

I will write in this manner, as neither Yevil nor the King are adept at reading and this will likely confound them, Ulrin noted. *It is no wonder they burned the books in Tandelis' study, and removed pages from many others—they failed to understand their importance.*

I discovered I'd been holding my breath, so I released it with a sigh before continuing.

Liron appeared to me one night, only a few moon-turns before Elabeth would arrive to perform the Saving. Yes, I knew what it was, although I'd never witnessed it and have no idea how it was accomplished.

Nevertheless, Liron came to me and laid the metal box at the foot of my bed. To say I was frightened would not be an accurate description—my fear was far beyond that of anything I'd ever experienced.

My voice trembled when I asked him why he'd come to me.

"You are in a position to help save Fyris and the lands outside Fyris," he said. I was much surprised at the softness of his voice, as if he were speaking to a friend, rather than as a god to an underling.

"How can I do this?" I questioned him. "I am only a physician."

"Your comings and goings throughout the castle are not questioned," Liron informed me. He was correct—the guards all knew me and allowed me through, whereas anyone else could be stopped at any time, by Tandelis' orders. After all, I was physician to everyone in the castle, not just the Prince.

"Your task is simple," Liron explained. "All you have to do is release the child inside this box. She is connected to the Orb that guards Avii Castle. Together, they will prevent a terrible injustice from happening, which will spell doom for all on this world."

"What must I do after the child is released?" I asked him. I admit that I was trembling by that time—Liron was predicting the end of everything if I

failed to comply, and the idea of a girl in the metal box he'd brought? That was terrifying. How could a girl be kept in a box for moon-turns?

"See?" he lifted the lid and I stared—not just at the light coming from inside the box, but at the beautiful child that lay within. "When you lift the lid, she will breathe and wake. You must take her to the throne room, where Tandelis will greet Elabeth and her Avii companions. The girl is connected to the Orb. If Tamblin or any of his raise their hands against Elabeth, then the Orb will see and arrive to protect. Thus, you will have a hand in saving Fyris, just as Elabeth will."

Of course, I was prepared to do Liron's bidding.

Then.

After Liron left, I hid the box beneath my bed and resolved to keep anyone from dusting beneath it until I removed it. It is with great sorrow that I must report what came about after.

Everyone, with the exception of Tandelis, I believe, knew of the disappearances and secret murders performed or commanded by Tamblin and Yevil during that time. Nobody was safe—even the servants were too afraid to gossip concerning the evil taking place. If it were learned that they had, they also disappeared and many bodies were never found. Liron had known this was coming, but trusted me to do as he'd asked.

During that time, I continued to do my work, but my head was lowered around Tamblin or Yevil inside the castle and I scurried away the moment my work was done.

On the day that Elabeth and Camryn appeared, carrying their tiny child with them, I was too frightened of Tamblin and Yevil to do as I was bid. Shivering in my quarters, I informed servants that I was ill and remained there, the box still hidden beneath my bed.

Afterward, Lady Rinda's severely wounded child was brought to me by a servant, who asked that I keep her survival secret. He feared that Tamblin, who'd murdered Tandelis and the Avii Queen and King, would also kill the last survivor of the throne room massacre. The poor girl died before I could do anything to help her.

I pretended this was not so and several days later, I released the girl from the metal box. Just as Liron said, she breathed and woke. For a day I dithered, feeding her and asking her questions.

She was curiously silent, and that I could not explain. Perhaps that was the way she was meant to be, connected to the Orb at Avii Castle as she was.

Regardless, eventually I cut away her hair, called the servant and placed the child in his arms, asking him to hand her to someone willing to take her.

He carried her to the kitchens and that is where she stayed, working as a drudge from a very early age.

After sun-turns had passed, I learned from Wolter, the chief cook, that something was wrong with Finder's back.

Yes, they called the girl Finder, because that was her talent. I looked at her back and knew exactly what I was seeing—the girl was growing wings.

I knew Tamblin would kill her immediately if he learned what the nubs actually were, so I did the only thing I could and asked the stablemaster to cut them away with hoof nippers.

Every sun-turn afterward, I ordered him to do the same. The girl suffered great pain because of it, but it was the only way to keep her alive. I hoped, even when Fyris began to die about us, that somehow, she and the Orb could still find a way to save all of us.

I worry, however, that due to my cowardice, I'd killed Fyris just as effectively as Tamblin and Yevil did.

Liron, I am sorry I failed you.

Your humble servant,

Ulrin.

CHAPTER 17

vii Castle
   Quin

Sheep and goats bleated far below as I sat on the edge of a terrace facing the bowl of Avii Castle. The owner of the attached suite was working elsewhere—she was one of the glassworkers and a part of me wondered if she'd had a hand in forming my glass feather.

It didn't matter. Liron had placed his faith in a humble physician, who'd failed to keep his promise. Somehow, had Ulrin performed his duty, my connection to the Orb would inform it that Elabeth was in danger.

I imagined that it would appear in the throne room of Tandelis' castle, saving those there much as it had appeared and saved me when I was dumped at Avii Castle.

The images of such played through my mind. Had those things occurred, then Siriaa would be healthy instead of facing evacuation to save its people. The people of Fyris, whom Liron had been most anxious to protect, were already gone.

Was that my purpose, now? It did seem that I was driven to save Siriaa. Had Liron given me instructions, just as he had Ulrin?

If he had, I didn't recall them.

Ulrin's journal still hadn't explained my origin—where I'd come from before Liron chose me as his instrument. Perhaps he believed that a child would be less of a target for Tamblin and Yevil, or easily overlooked.

The Orb would have blasted those two back, I know that much—it had rendered Ardis unconscious with its force. I hugged myself. So much had depended upon a simple action, yet that action had not been performed.

It left all of us where we were—with a fate we'd never imagined. I couldn't curse or blame Ulrin—he had no idea what his inaction would eventually cost Siriaa. He'd been too afraid of the evil that was Tamblin and Yevil.

Spreading my wings, I allowed myself to drop off the railing and glide toward the animals below. This time, when I landed, the shepherd boy offered a curt nod and no insults. Lambs and ewes alike bumped and jostled as they came forward for a touch of my hands. I offered them as much of my attention as I could, preoccupied as I was with Ulrin's words.

That's where Justis found me.

"Quin," he began while tucking in his wings and attempting to wade through the entire flock surrounding me. By the time he reached my side, I was already weeping. Without a word, I was pulled to him and comforted while I sobbed against his chest.

"It was written upside down and backward." I slid the journal toward Daragar. He'd arrived as I wearily attempted to explain my findings to Justis, Gurnil, Ordin, Berel and Kaldill.

That's when Daragar added to the mystery. "Nefrigar tells me that when things are connected as I suspect you and the Orb are, that both have to be constructed at the same time."

My breath stopped again. The Orb was ancient—Gurnil said so. He said there were records of its appearance when Avii Castle was created by Liron far in the past.

"The Orb could only appear in one place in Fyris," Justis said. "The site of the Saving. Elabeth told me long ago—that the Orb was prevented somehow from going anywhere else on that continent. I suppose this was Liron's way of getting around that. I'm sure Yevil knew it, too—through Treven. That's likely why he and Tamblin chose the throne room to do their murders."

"Why didn't Ulrin open the box when he was supposed to?" I wiped more tears away—my vision was blurred as I blinked at Justis. "How old am I?" I wept.

"Dearest, you mustn't allow this to upset you. Time began for you when Ulrin finally opened that box," Kaldill said. "Nefrigar calls it a stasis box. You were kept from growing or aging as long as you were inside it."

"But where did I come from?" Brushing yet another tear away, I chewed my lip and struggled to clear my watery eyes.

"Dearest, perhaps only Liron had that answer," Kaldill replied.

I understood, just by looking at Kaldill, that Liron was dead. He was considered a rogue god, capable of terrible things. Was I also capable of such?

"Never think that," Daragar said softly. "Liron did what he could to save the people of this world. What better person to choose than the best you can find to perform that deed? Never place yourself among the ranks of the Hidden rogue gods. You do not belong there."

"We only have reports that he was capable, never that he acted in any way against the laws set out to watch and protect," Kaldill said. "It may be that he was coerced in some way to join the Hidden."

"This is too complicated for me to consider right now," I brushed more moisture away. "Berel, have you heard anything about the debates?"

"I've been watching live vids," he said, tapping his tab-vid. "It's the usual back-and-forth, now. I can see which ones already have their minds made up, and which are still unsure of their decision."

"They'll die if they stay—it's as simple as that."

"Today has been a trying one for you," Justis ran a hand down my feathers. "As was yesterday. Shall we have a quiet dinner and then rest?"

"I'm not very hungry," I mumbled, allowing my head to droop against Justis' shoulder.

"You should eat anyway—as much as you can," Ordin scolded gently. "Dena has Yellow Wings bringing a meal soon, and she and Ardis will join us."

"What will they think of all this? What about your brother?" I leaned away from Justis to ask. His dark eyes studied mine for a moment before he answered.

"When my brother learns you were brought here by Liron, he may curse himself," Justis sighed. "As should every Avii who has raised voice or hand against you."

"I hope the others never find out," I let my head fall against his shoulder again. "Tell Jurris if you like, but I don't want the rest to stare or ask questions I can't answer."

"There will be time to worry about these things later. Meal first, then rest," Ordin said.

He made it sound so simple.

There was nothing simple about any of this.

Something about Daragar's words concerned me, too.

He'd said that when things are connected, as the Orb and I were, that they had to be constructed at the same time.

Constructed.

I was a golem.

I'd never had parents. Ulrin had noted that I was curiously silent when he opened the box. Perhaps Liron intended that I never speak. I could carry no tales, that way. Why I did find my voice eventually, I couldn't fathom. Had Liron carefully plotted my life, or had he devised me for one thing and one thing only, with everything afterward an accident of sorts?

I felt like a fraud. A machine. Would anyone listen to me if they learned what I really was?

It made me wish to hide and weep from the sorrow and frustration I felt.

There was no time for self-pity. Siriaa's fate was uncertain because a poor decision had made it so.

"I'll eat," I mumbled.

"Good." One of Justis' wings lifted and covered me, pulling me tighter against him.

~

Vogeffa I

"How long will it take for the ship to arrive at the designated location?" Vardil asked.

"Two days at their best speed, provided there are no detours due to ASD entanglements," his assistant replied. "The ship left earlier this morning."

"Have any other Belancours met an untimely end?" Vardil asked.

"None yet, but we have several leads. One is hidden on Grey Planet, and another is still imprisoned on Le-Ath Veronis, as you know."

"Can one of ours bribe or infiltrate?"

"I will look into that immediately," the assistant replied. "Meanwhile, we have interviews with surgeons and warlocks to consider."

"I'll assess the lists very soon. Notify me when Siriaa is destroyed."

"I will, Lord Cayetes."

~

Kondar

"How in the names of all the gods did they get distracted over what parcels of land they wanted on Morningsun, rather than deciding whether they would go there in the first place?" Edden thumped the mug of tea on his desk.

"You know how easily some are lured away from the topic at hand," Melis shifted in his seat. "This is the usual delaying tactic, designed to divert attention and bring the vote closer, so that few know what they're doing when the vote is cast. If some think they won't get the best deal or exactly what they want, they'll vote against leaving."

"What can they hope to achieve by that?" Edden growled. "Time grows short. Who cares who gets a shoreline we don't even have, yet?"

"I realize that those who've offered the land did their best to match what the Sectors already have, and that was a noble thing to do. Who knew that it would become a petty squabble over who has the best parts of it? They haven't even set foot on it yet, and already it's a point of contention."

"It's times like this that I wished we could be a monarchy for just a few moments. I'd approve the exodus, everybody would be moved and then we'd go back to the way things were."

"Yokaru is prepared to follow Kondar's lead," Melis agreed. "Their Emperor has already informed our ambassadors of such."

"Why is it written into the law that we can only call a vote at the earliest in two eight-days?" Edden massaged his forehead.

"Headache?"

"A rather large one. It's called my Council."

Larentii Archives

"A verified reproduction of the original," Daragar handed a copy of Ulrin's journal to Nefrigar. "I've not encountered many who've employed this form of mirror writing. That means little, as I am merely one thousand years old."

"It's still quite uncommon," Nefrigar opened the journal to the proper pages to study them briefly. "I believe Quin's ability to read any language enabled her to decipher this easily, whereas it may have confounded many others."

"I may have made a mistake, repeating your words, Archivist," Daragar hung his head. "She now believes she is nothing more than an automaton, created by Liron."

"Perhaps care must be taken to remove that belief—the gods made all races in the beginning, or at least the building blocks of all races. Having parents does not make one legitimate as the gods measure things. Not having parents—especially in Quin's case—does not diminish the capacity to love. That is what makes us real," Nefrigar smiled as he placed a hand upon Daragar's shoulder. "Tell her that she is more real than many we have met, and more loved than most."

"I wish I could reveal what Lissa really is—that should convince Quin faster than anything else," Daragar lifted his head and gazed into Nefrigar's bright-blue eyes.

"We have promises to keep and identities to hide," Nefrigar inclined his head. "Nevertheless, if Lissa considered Quin as anything other than real, she would have said it already. She cares for the girl."

"Then I have damage to repair," Daragar said. "I shall ponder the best way to do so."

～

Harifa Edus
New Fyris

"Here are images of the werewolf cities on the other continent," Tory handed the comp-vid to Amlis. "You see they were provided much the same as you. Many chose not to live in the two major cities, preferring a wilder, more rustic existence outside."

"Because of what they are?" Amlis, sitting behind the desk in his study, looked up at Tory.

"Partly, but also because of where they came from before they were moved here. They were persecuted on other worlds; most of those worlds had the same sort of rustic societies. To keep them alive, my mother brought them here. This was the werewolf planet eons ago, so they were returning home after a very long absence."

"Fascinating," Amlis pulled a finger across the screen to examine more images. "Do you think we might trade with them eventually?"

"That is our hope," Tory replied. "If you can increase your herds and flocks, that would be a very good export, as well as grains—their continent isn't the best for growing such. Some have turned to manufacturing glass and metals, so there is certainly the possibility of a thriving trade."

"I have none who understand glassmaking, and few prepared to produce metal in any quantity," Amlis agreed. "Trade for those things would be most welcome. My question is this—will they welcome us? You say they are shape changers. Are they dangerous?"

"That's a question for Sali—Salidar," Tory grinned. "He's werewolf."

"The blademaster?"

"Yes. Dragon, Crane and Dragon's sons are only marginally better. Sali is quite talented. I learned bladework from him and the one who taught him."

"I didn't realize he was anything except what I am," Amlis shook his head in wonder.

"That's the way they prefer it, keeping their other sides hidden, just as I do," Tory said. "You shouldn't worry about your safety. They are just as concerned for their children as the people of New Fyris will be about theirs."

"I understand," Amlis sighed. "We will begin with trade and perhaps friendship will follow."

"Exactly what my mother wants to hear," Tory grinned.

∼

Avii Castle

Quin

"You were created by a god," Daragar said, lifting my face so his eyes would meet mine. "That makes you more special than those about you, and also makes you no less worthy than any other sentient being."

"But," I said, attempting to pull away. He'd found me, moping on the Library terrace the following morning.

"No. Do not say that word," Daragar instructed, holding onto my chin with careful fingers. "Where you are concerned, that word does not exist. You love and are loved. To those who created all races, that is what matters most."

"I still can't help feeling that I'm only here to serve someone else's purpose."

"Quin—at least you have a purpose, and I believe your choices are yours and no others. Besides, many have been chosen instruments of the gods in the past, and those are still talked of and admired by many. They merely came into their lives in a more mundane manner."

"You have other Larentii to point to," I said, blinking at him. "There are no others like me. Nefrigar says so."

"Had Liron not died, perhaps you would have been the first of many," he smiled. "Nefrigar and I have calculated the timeline. Liron's death occurred shortly after he left the stasis box in Ulrin's hands."

"Do you think he knew?" I asked. "That his death was coming?"

"Perhaps. I have also given it some thought, but as we have insufficient information, we can only make logical guesses. I ask that you do not allow this to upset you in any way."

"I understand you speak the truth, but I can't help the way I feel," I said. "I'll deal with it—I've dealt with everything else so far."

"I know, but that doesn't make it any less painful to me to know that you suffer."

I understood his meaning all too well. I was able to heal anyone else—just not myself. If Liron still lived, I had a long list of questions and complaints for him. Perhaps it was just as well that he'd died—he would grow tired of me in very little time.

"Justis asked me to move back into his suite," I said, rustling my feathers and changing the subject.

"Did you give him an answer?"

"I said I'd think about it."

"What do you really think?" Daragar smiled.

"I think I like seeing his wings every morning and night," I said. "He lets them down and I see him when he is relaxed. Once he walks out the door, he is Commander Justis, who is stern and uncompromising."

"See, we all have our assignments," Daragar said, reaching out to ruffle my hair. "Whether they are assignments from a king or a god, it matters not."

"It depends on the king—and the god," I retorted, causing Daragar to laugh. "I want to check with Berel on the debates. Want to come?" I slid off the bench and stood.

"I have an assignment with Nefrigar," he said. "I go, and so shall you."

I watched him disappear before turning away to find Berel, who was likely in his bedroom watching the debates carefully and communicating with his father.

~

Larentii Archives

"You were wise to ask for a reproduction of the Avii Queen's book before Elabeth died," Daragar said.

Nefrigar nodded in agreement before handing the large, leather-bound book to Daragar. "As was noted before, some of it is in a language I have not seen and likely written by Liron himself. It is my guess that only Quin might decipher it, and as she is in such a fragile state, I will not hand it to her yet."

"You worry that she may find other things to trouble her," Daragar sighed. "That is also my fear. She knows not that this copy exists."

"It is my wish that you and I sit with her when she reads it," Nefrigar said. "That way we can provide support if it is needed."

"I agree," Daragar replied.

~

Avii Castle

Quin

The rest of my day was spent with Berel, while scant time was taken away for meals and such. We watched the debates flounder—each side passionate about their stance but neither able to convince the other.

"Is this how it always is?" I asked Berel as we shared a cup of tea while sitting at a Library table between midday and the evening meal.

His tab-vid was set on the table so both of us could watch the feed easily.

"Much of the time," he nodded.

"I feel uncomfortable about this—that they're wasting time we do not have," I said.

"I think so, too, but this is the law in action," Berel responded.

"I feel the urgency in my feathers," I sighed. "Every part of me feels afraid for the people of Kondar and Yokaru."

"You have a unique perspective on the situation. These," he gestured toward the images of the debate, "only have what they've been told and what evidence we can produce. Many things can be manipulated, including the truth. Some enjoy making lies of the truth, no matter how persuasive the facts are."

"Because they have their own agenda and the truth interferes with it?" I suggested.

"In some cases. You cannot judge all by the same measure," Berel said. "Each has his own experiences and acts accordingly. Yes, some are self-serving. I cannot say that about all—each, in their own way, makes an attempt to serve the people of their Sector first and Kondar second."

"You're right," I inclined my head. "You have more experience at this than I."

"Your experience is tempered by the service of a very bad monarch, who named himself King after he murdered his brother."

"True. I will try to be less cynical in the future." My words made Berel laugh.

"How go the debates?" Kaldill asked when he arrived in the Library for dinner. He'd been absent most of the day, making a trip to Wyyld II for a conversation with Ildevar.

"Much the same as the day before," Berel smiled as he answered Kaldill's question. "Quin, however, has adopted a more tolerant attitude toward politicians."

"Don't tell Queen Lissa that," Kaldill laughed. "She grumbles before every Council meeting on Le-Ath Veronis."

"How is she? Queen Lissa, I mean?" I asked.

"Fine," Kaldill said. "You could send mindspeech and ask her yourself, you know. She would love to hear from you."

"Perhaps I will," I said, accepting a plate of food from a Yellow Wing. Dena, Ardis and Justis walked in together—Dena's feathers were ruffled and damp, letting me know that she and Ardis had romped and bathed before coming to the Library to eat.

I didn't begrudge her that happiness; Ardis made her quite happy indeed.

"Did you sort out Kondar today?" Justis teased as he took the chair opposite Berel.

"I wish we could," Berel responded. "Quin is getting jumpy over the debates. She keeps saying they're taking too long."

I didn't say anything; I was happy to see that Justis and Berel had arrived at an amicable truce and were talking to one another.

"Difficult to get anything done quickly with that many people—Jurris has enough trouble with the handful of Avii on his Council."

"I beg your pardon. Two of those Avii are at the table," Gurnil pointed out with a grin. "Three if you count yourself."

"Hardly a quorum," Justis bit back a laugh.

"You're in a good mood," I said.

"Oh, it's nothing. Except that I heard you like my wings." I watched his mouth curve into a wonderful smile. Somehow, he'd discovered what I'd shared with Daragar earlier in the day. Dena had the grace to turn pink and look guilty.

"I would have told you so myself," I said with feigned haughtiness. "If you'd asked."

If I could, I'd pull you onto my lap and share my food with you, he sent. I'll admit, the mental image was a tempting one.

Someday, I replied.

Good enough.

∾

That evening, I sat with Berel on his bed, watching the last of the debates before they ended for the evening in Kondar. Absently he stroked my primary feathers, smoothing them and tracing the patterns of gold, silver and copper.

I understood that his body was waking as he became an adult, but I think we both knew our time wasn't yet. It was enough to know that we cared for each other.

"Another day gone," he sighed, taking his hand away from my feathers and turning his tab-vid off. "We can pick this up again tomorrow, after breakfast."

"All right," I agreed and slid off his bed.

"Quin?" Berel said as I reached the door.

"What is it?" I turned toward him.

"You don't think less of me because I'm young, do you?"

"I'm young, too, according to Kaldill," I offered a shaky smile. "Age matters not to me."

"Good. I hope—well, we can discuss that later," he ducked his head and nodded.

"Good-night," I said and walked out the door, closing it softly behind me.

～

Called to a meeting on Le-Ath Veronis, Kaldill's note read. He'd left it on my bed so I'd be sure to see it. *Don't wait up—K.*

His initial was written in a beautiful, formal script, which transformed itself from one shape to another while I watched. Sometimes it was decorated with leaves, other times with flowers or birds. I'd never seen such, realizing quickly that Kaldill employed a bit of his extensive power merely to entertain me.

Carefully placing the note next to my black feather on the nightstand, I went about readying myself for bed.

No, the uneasy feeling hadn't gone away, but I'd resigned myself to the fact that I had no power to change anything past what I'd already done. Siriaa's fate was out of my hands, now, although I was prepared to do my best to protect what I could.

~

Vogeffa I

"Lord Cayetes, the ship will be in range early tomorrow. Would you like a vid-feed so you may see the destruction?" Vardil's assistant puttered about the bedroom, straightening things and preparing the bed for his ailing master.

"Yes. Have the kitchens prepare my breakfast to coincide with the event," Vardil heaved himself onto the bed and allowed his assistant to cover him with soft blankets.

"I will see it done, my Lord."

~

Avii Castle

Quin

Kaldill hadn't returned when I woke early after a restless night. Knowing that an attempt to go back to sleep would be useless, I rose, bathed and dressed before taking flight to the Library terrace.

No others had arrived yet, so I took my favorite bench and watched the sea as the sun broke through clouds and gleamed across the water's surface. Somewhere, on Fyris' western edge, I imagined that the view might be the same from the spires.

That's when the Orb appeared.

Come, it commanded. I hesitated while questions ran through my brain.

Hurry, it said. Standing, I began to walk as it floated away. By the time I reached the Library's interior, I was nearly at a run.

Dena, who'd just appeared, wore an expression of surprise as I passed her swiftly, following the path the Orb chose. When I reached the steps leading downward into the belly of the castle, I could hear Dena's steps hurrying behind us. The Orb quickened its pace, as did I.

Behind me, I could hear Dena's footsteps become a run as she followed. A growing sensation of dread enveloped me the farther down into the castle we went—I followed the Orb, Dena followed me.

Precious time passed as I raced after the glowing ball, while terror squeezed my heart, making it difficult to breathe. By the time we reached the lower levels, I could hear a roaring in my ears.

Perhaps it was foresight—I do not know. Regardless, the Orb led me onward, and I would have followed it except for Dena's shriek.

"No, Quin! That's the gate!"

The fear in her voice forced me to slide to a stop and turn toward her. "What?" The air around us felt thick, making it difficult for my voice to travel the short distance to my friend.

"The gate," her voice sounded slow. Labored.

That's when time stopped—for the briefest of moments. Suddenly, with a clarity that I'd never experienced, I understood exactly what was happening. That when time resumed, Siriaa and all its people would be blasted into the atoms Berel sometimes mentioned.

There was no time to formulate a plan. No time to determine what would be the best decision. *Queen Lissa*, I mentally shouted her name. *They're firing at Siriaa.* I sent the image my mind had produced bare moments earlier.

Time resumed.

Siriaa disintegrated.

Dena screamed as the Orb flashed its light and blew me through the gate.

CHAPTER 18

*L*e-Ath Veronis
Queen Lissa's Private Journal

Five years have passed since Siriaa's destruction. Without Quin's warning, its people would have died.

I'd already held meetings with those prepared to help before that unexpected event, should Kondar and Yokaru decide to leave their world behind.

As it was, that decision was taken out of their hands by a vindictive criminal bent on the worst sort of revenge. Today, he still manages to elude even the best Kooper has to track him. Five years ago, it took all our power—Kaldill, Ildevar, Trajan, Kooper and I—to remove the population from Siriaa before it was destroyed.

The worlds Marid poisoned are growing worse, while the rest of us sit and wait as infected dust left from Siriaa's destruction travels through space toward unsuspecting worlds. If this were one of Acrimus' carefully laid plans before his death, it was perhaps his masterpiece. Even now, no solution can be found to combat the creatures creating the poison. I worry that eventually, when all is dead within this bubble of universes, that those of us powerful enough will be forced to leave, closing the door to it firmly behind us.

Quin is dead. Dena, the poor woman, wept painfully as she described Quin's last moments before the Orb took matters in hand and destroyed them both by forcing Quin through the gate.

Perhaps that had been Liron's plan all along. Quin had been placed upon Siriaa, perhaps, to act as its temporary keeper in order to save the people. She'd done everything she could to make that happen. Then, her final task accomplished, the Orb had forced her through the gate and then followed.

Today, on the anniversary of Quin's death and the founding of Siriaa's population upon other worlds, Kaldill holds a memorial for his lost love.

He, like the others, mourns her.

Justis, who acts as Jurris' ambassador to Le-Ath Veronis, attends Council meetings with Berel, who holds the position of New Kondar's ambassador to both Le-Ath Veronis and Wyyld II. Outside those duties, he attends University here on Le-Ath Veronis. Aryn calls Berel his best student.

Still, it is painful for either Berel or Justis to speak of Quin.

Avii Castle stands where Gavin suggested it should, in the sea far to the west of Sun City. In a few moments, I will join Dena, Kaldill, Daragar, Justis and Berel outside the entrance to the gate near the castle dungeon. There, where Quin was last seen alive, we will lay a blanket of flowers. Kaldill will place a spell so the blooms will last until the next anniversary.

I imagine he will do this as long as Avii Castle stands.

EPILOGUE

My scream at landing in the dark upon something hard and wet was cut off when a large hand clamped over my mouth. "Shh," he hissed in my ear. "Cayetes is hunting bodies again."

The End

www.ingramcontent.com/pod-product-compliance
Lightning Source LLC
Chambersburg PA
CBHW060250100726
47907CB00003B/826